"Would it make a difference if I told you I've wondered what it would be like to kiss you from the first time you poured my coffee?"

She almost choked. "Coffee is a thing with you."

"Not before meeting you."

"I think you mentioned a kiss?" She tried to swallow but found that didn't work either. Her entire body and most of her brain had abandoned her.

"That's the G-rated version of what I want." He touched her then. Dragged the back of his fingers over her cheek in a gentle caress.

"Is there an R-rated version?" Because she really wanted to jump ahead to that one.

He slipped his thumb over her bottom lip. Back and forth. "Oh, yeah."

She was never going to survive this. "Let's start with G and see how it goes."

One second she saw the room behind him and the light above. The next he leaned in, blocking her view of everything, and his mouth covered hers.

By HelenKay Dimon

THE ENFORCER
THE FIXER
UNDER THE WIRE
FACING FIRE
FALLING HARD
PLAYING DIRTY
RUNNING HOT (novella)

the Enforcer

Games People Play

HELENKAY DIMON

AVONBOOKS

An Imprint of HarperCollinsPublishers

HarperCollins PUBLISHERS
Since 1817

Excerpt from *The Fixer* copyright © 2017 by HelenKay Dimon.

First Avon Books mass market printing: May 2017

ISBN 978-0-06-244133-1

17 18 19 20 21 QGM 10 9 8 7 6 5 4 3 2 1

For every reader who loves strong, imperfect heroines.

the
Enforcer

CHAPTER 1

Upstate New York

The shower burned hot enough to scald her skin. She didn't care. After two hours of running and months of training for the half marathon, her muscles rejoiced at the healing heat.

She rested her hand against the white subway tile and let the water rush over her neck, through her tangled hair and down the sides of her face. Just a few more minutes and a good dose of bath gel and she'd be human again. Or as close as she got to that these days.

The dull ache in her knee kicked up to a steady thump, but she couldn't take the time to baby it with a foam roller and more stretching. Minutes were all she could spare because she had dinner plans with her roommates. Not that she wanted to go, but she'd promised. They were waiting downstairs for her now. Would probably bang on the door any second. Sometimes they acted more like circus animals at feeding time than college students. Though, in reality, many days there weren't many differences between the two groups when it came to two of her roommates, Nick and Steve.

As soon as she thought about being interrupted, she heard a loud slam. "Oh, come on," she mumbled in the stall, letting the water run into her mouth.

A second thud interrupted her building frustration. It sounded like they were playing basketball inside the house instead of in the driveway . . . again. Well, they could all exercise a little patience while she found underwear and a brush.

"I need two minutes," she called out to anyone who might be hovering nearby ready to bug her with an unending stream of whining.

Somewhere in the house glass shattered.

"What the hell?" She reached out and turned off the spray, letting the rings rattle against the metal bar as she pulled the curtain back.

Straining to listen for the inevitable screaming match that usually came with broken dishes, she waited. She expected to hear her name or for someone to call for her to hurry up. Quiet thundered around her. Missing were the expected creaks of the two-story house and punch of the air conditioner as the ancient, rarely used device kicked on.

The total absence of sound was so odd, so unlike every other day in the house, that it chilled her. Cold radiated through her and her teeth started to click together despite the humidity hanging over the room.

Wrapping a thick towel around her body, she climbed out of the chipped tub. With the cotton edges knotted in her fist between her breasts, she opened the door and peeked into the hallway. The slap of her bare feet against the floor echoed around her as she stepped out of the sticky warm bathroom.

"Hello?" When no one bothered to answer, a strange whirling took off in her chest. "This isn't funny, you know."

A click broke the silence. The front door. She'd know that sound anywhere. She'd slipped in often enough to identify a covert return. After all the nagging about her being late and holding up the food, maybe they took off. Figured.

Leaning over the banister and peering down the steps, she could see the overhead family room light was on. Darkness fell over the rest of the floor. Since she had the keys and the car, the idea of them leaving didn't make much sense. If this was their way of getting her downstairs . . . well, it was about to work. But she'd had it with the passive-aggressive crap. She could tiptoe in and scare them first. That would teach her so-called friends to play stupid games.

She edged around the one spot on the hardwood floor guaranteed to produce a loud squeak. Sneaking was not easy in this place. Getting down the steps without clueing them all in on her approach would be harder. She tried to balance her weight because almost every one of those stairs made a sound. Hell, she could play a tune without even trying, so she barely let the balls of her feet touch while shifting from one step to another. Slow and careful.

Getting down took forever. She could swear she felt

the minutes tick by through the thick silence. No one on the first floor made a sound. She had no idea when they'd picked up those skills.

With one hand on the railing and the other in a death grip on the towel, she rounded the bottom of the staircase and stepped into the main room prepared to make some noise of her own. She'd see how much they liked the interruptions.

Words caught in her throat as red flashed in front of her. Streaks of bright crimson slashing across beige paint and linen lampshades. Splashed on the walls. Sprayed across the drawn curtains. Forming a puddle on the area in front of the couch.

What the hell was she looking at? Her brain refused to function. It sputtered as the images ran in fast-forward in front of her. Her heart raced until it pounded in her ears. Her heavy breathing filled the room as she struggled to take it all in.

No chatter or laughter. No television or music. One body on the couch. Another on the floor reaching up to the cushions. Eyes open and deep gashes across their throats. Two bodies in the family room. Her friends and no signs of life.

Blood stained everything, seeping and growing, leaving a sea of red running through the family room. She inhaled a faint mix of metal and men's cologne as she tried to shake the numbing darkness before it settled in her brain.

Nothing made sense. They should be joking and drinking beers. Sitting around complaining about how long it took her to shower.

She tried to gulp in air but her lungs refused to work. Had to grab on to the towel around her, digging her fingernails into the material until she heard a ripping sound.

After a minute, reality crashed through her brain. They were dead. Her best friends. Massacred.

Panic exploded all around her. It filled every cell until it nearly choked her. Every muscle tightened as the room's stale air smacked into her face. Her feet tangled with something beneath her as she stumbled back. Losing her balance, she grabbed for the entry table but missed. The lamp bobbled and then tipped. Her keys jangled as they fell.

In a whoosh, she went down, landing hard on her side and hip. Throwing out her hand, she barely missed cracking her head against the floor as her towel fell open and slipped off. Even without moving, the air refused to return to her lungs. Bile rushed up her throat as the blurriness left her vision. It took several gasps before she could inhale without gagging and lift her upper body.

She closed her eyes and tried to count down from ten. Around three her brain blinked out again. Her eyes popped open and she looked around, hoping the horror movie scene had vanished. But this wasn't a dream and it was worse than any nightmare. Blood and death thumped off every wall. Blinding fear screamed through the room and skated down her spine.

When she tried to sit up her foot knocked against something hard. Her gaze swept down her legs. The sight that greeted her had her jerking, pressing her back hard against the wall. Another body with lifeless eyes frozen in a look of pure terror. Hand outstretched with scratches against the wood floor. Her friend had fought and clawed . . . and died.

Nick . . .

A crush of pain rolled over her. Trembling started in her muscles then rocked hard enough to send her entire body into a shaking frenzy. She whimpered and fought for the fine edge of sanity as the full shock of her surroundings finally registered in her brain.

While she stretched and cooled down listening to music, while she showered, someone had broken into the house. She'd been locked away upstairs from her friends for ten minutes, maybe fifteen, and this.

The why and how swirled around her, making her dizzy, until a new bolt of fear shot through her. *He could still be there.* The attacker . . . him . . . her.

She had to move. Run.

Panic washed away the shock as her heartbeat hammered in her ears. She listened for footsteps but couldn't hear anything over the wheezing pull of breath into her lungs.

Without moving her legs or stopping her constant scan of the room, she reached behind her and tugged on the phone cord. The receiver shook on the stand before tumbling. She grabbed for it as it knocked against her bare shoulder, fumbling before it fell to the floor. She pushed random buttons without looking and hung up then tried again. *9-1-1.*

A man answered on the second ring. She heard the

deep voice, felt the cool plastic under her fingers, as the words clogged her throat. "I . . . I need . . ."

"Ma'am?"

She closed her eyes, trying to block out everything in front of her. She had to concentrate. Had to move before an unseen knife sliced through her.

"They're all dead." The harsh whisper had her glancing around until she realized it had come from her dry throat.

The operator hesitated. "What?"

"They're gone."

"Who?"

Naked and shaking, she dropped her forehead to her knees and started rocking. "Help me."

"Ma'am? I can barely hear—"

"Hurry."

CHAPTER 2

Washington, DC
Seven years later

Matthias Clarke started this meeting like he did
every other one that happened outside of his
secure office space. By walking around the room,
checking for hidden entrances and exits. Looking for
the easiest way out if someone stormed through the
only recognizable door. Figuring out where he would
hide a weapon if he owned the place.

Not that he didn't trust the men in the room with
him, because he did. They were actually two of the
handful of people he could turn his back on. Not that
he ever did that sort of thing for long. His was a small
circle, tight and efficient.

He never believed in the *keep your friends close but
your enemies closer* adage. To him it made more sense
to limit his friends to only a vetted few and keep a gun
aimed at his enemies. He'd made it through thirty-four
years of hard living with that mantra and he wasn't
about to abandon it now.

Matthias stopped across the table from the most

solid guy he'd ever met. He went by a pseudonym as part of his near pathological need to hide his true identity, but Matthias was one of the few people who knew his real name—Levi Wren. Ever since they were thrown together in training more than a decade ago at the private security company Matthias now owned and ran, Wren had been Wren, and even that was only between close friends. Wren had another name he used in public. It all struck Matthias as convoluted and annoying, but it wasn't his life.

Wren could shoot like a pro but he preferred to spend his time behind the desk. Strategizing. Being Washington DC's biggest hidden secret, a powerful and influential fixer. A man who made problems disappear. Matthias could attest to Wren's ability to maneuver and plot, since his own company—Quint Enterprises—was the one Wren called on when he needed muscle. Wren was the idea man. Matthias provided the actual bodies and put the complex plans into action.

The business arrangement benefitted them both. Made them very rich men in a town full of very rich people. But they maintained their privacy. Neither sought the limelight or congratulations. While Matthias didn't go to the same lengths to avoid being known in public, he did avoid people. Whenever possible.

But today he needed Wren and his assistant, Garrett McGrath, on a project. A very personal project. And that's what had Matthias even more on edge than usual.

Wren flipped his pen end over end through his fingers, stopping each time to thump the point or cap on the conference room table. "It's not like you to demand a meeting."

Wren usually picked his words precisely. Matthias didn't like that one. "I *asked*."

"Funny how everything you say sounds like an order." Wren put the pen down and leaned back in his chair, tipping until the front legs left the floor. "What's going on?"

"I need you to do something for me." It almost killed Matthias to say that. He never asked anything of anyone. Not ever. Not the social worker who tracked him as a kid or the adults in the series of foster homes he'd grown up in. Not a teacher. Not even Wren. Until now.

Wren nodded. "Done."

Matthias almost smiled at the near-automatic reaction. "You should know this one is personal."

"Same answer."

Yeah, Matthias gave in to the smile that time. He never offered advice or assistance. Not until he knew every detail and studied the ways the operation could go wrong. Lucky for him, Wren did not suffer from the same need for outright control of everything. "I like that about you, Wren."

"You're one of the few people who actually knows who I am. That means you've earned a favor." Wren's shoulders relaxed as he balanced his elbows against the side of the chair. "What is it?"

"I need to borrow your girlfriend."

Thwap. The front legs of Wren's chair hit the floor as he sat up straight again. "Excuse me?"

"Oh, man." Garrett laughed as he pushed away from

the wall just inside the door and took a seat on Wren's side of the table. "I'm so happy I skipped lunch and stuck around for this."

Okay, admittedly that might not have sounded right. Matthias wasn't exactly in the weighing-words business. "Not her. Her brain."

Garrett kept on smiling. "Do you think that's a better answer?"

"She finds people, right? The blank look on Wren's face. The stupid amusement on Garrett's. Matthias decided they were making this hard on purpose. "I need to find a woman."

Garrett switched back to laughing. He even made an annoying snorting sound. "She's not a dating service."

"Matthias." Wren dropped the side of his hand against the table with a soft thump. "Explain."

"Can't I give you a name and then you go and tell your woman to hunt this person down?" Seemed simple enough to Matthias.

Wren's eyes bulged. "Only if you want to make sure I never have sex again."

"Why would I care about your sex life?"

Garrett shook his head. "That's cold, man."

"I don't get it. Just tell her. What's the big deal?" Wren had been all but stapled to Emery Finn's side since they met. The whole thing was weird, but Matthias figured while she was right there, she might be able to help.

"It's amazing you're single." Garrett whistled. "I mean, damn."

For just a second Matthias thought about whipping

out his gun. Amazing how that quieted down a room and got everyone to focus. Instead, he pointed a finger at Garrett and turned to Wren. "Tell me why you keep him around."

That seemed to wake Wren up. "You've tried to steal him away not once but twice to be your right-hand man at Quint, so you know very well why Garrett is here."

Matthias's gaze switched to Garrett. "You told him about that?"

"I use your offer as blackmail to get my way in this office all the time," Garrett said. "Which reminds me, I'm thinking another raise is in order."

Wren never broke eye contact with Matthias. "Let's stay on topic. Tell me about the woman."

"She knows something about a murder." They just stared at him, a fact that might have made Matthias shift around in his seat if he hadn't been trained to maintain his position no matter what. "What? That's my answer."

Wren made a humming sound. "Not a very helpful one."

"You could try using full sentences," Garrett added.

They were messing with him. There was no way they insisted clients spill every fact. Matthias didn't intend to either. "She—this woman—was in the house when a guy I know was murdered."

The "guy" was more than a guy, but there was no need to get super personal here. A murder. A woman. Seemed simple enough to him. He also noticed neither of them blinked at the mention of a killing. They might sit in a room and design strategy, but death didn't scare them. They dealt in tragedy and life-ending consequences all the time, which was part of the reason Matthias had started his search here. Give him a target and a mission and he was good. Research, talking to people, interviewing—no fucking way.

"You're describing him only as 'a guy'?" Wren asked.

Matthias wasn't really one for repetition, but he engaged in it this one time. "Yes."

"You need to give me a bit more than that." Wren sighed when Matthias stayed quiet. "Why do we care about this *guy*?"

"Is that relevant?"

Wren sighed louder this time. "Let's pretend it is."

The conversation really was starting to annoy Matthias. "He's my brother."

There. Enough said. They could all get to work now.

Instead, Wren frowned. "Since when do you have a brother?"

"Technically? All but the first eight years of my life." He'd only known about Nick for the last seven months, but that really wasn't the issue for Matthias. Blood was blood even if up until a short time ago he hadn't known he had any. Now that he knew, he needed answers. Might even have to avenge the kid.

Wren picked up his pen again. "I'm debating your sudden claim of a sibling."

The steady tap of the pen hitting the table started all over again. *Thud. Thud.*

It took all of the control Matthias possessed not to reach over and snap the thing in two. "I have no idea what you're saying. That sentence was a complete clusterfuck."

"It's so obvious you two spent a lot of time together. You know, back during your formative ass-kicking years." Garrett shook his head. "It almost scares me how alike you are."

"We're nothing alike." Other than the fact they both had dark hair and ran successful companies, Matthias didn't see it. Of course, they'd also shared a mentor and an apartment for years . . . so there was that. "He deals in information. I prefer a much more pragmatic approach."

"Shooting things." Wren sounded amused at the idea.

Matthias wasn't sure why. That was a valid skill and only one of many in his range. "Sometimes I use explosives."

"Which makes it even better you two don't go to cocktail parties together," Garrett said.

"We're getting offtrack." Wren's fingers tightened around the pen. "Back to the woman."

"It's a long story." And that should be enough. Matthias really didn't feel like coughing up the why and why-now angles. Just coming here, skulking around with his hand out for a favor, made him twitchy.

"And you're not in the mood to tell it."

Wren finally seemed to get it, which was a relief to Matthias. Took the guy long enough to come around. "Exactly."

"I'll make a deal with you."

Not Matthias's favorite thing. "I thought you were doing me a favor."

Wren shrugged. "I'll find the woman."

"You? But Emery is—"

"She finds missing people by matching records and information in databases. She searches Jane and John Doe records. But what you want? This sounds more like what I do." Wren flipped a page on his lined yellow notepad and started writing.

Matthias had no clue what he could be scribbling down. But even with his questionable people skills, Matthias guessed something else was happening here. "You still afraid to have your woman meet us? Us, your supposed oldest friends in the world?"

"Actually, you're one of his only friends," Garrett said. "Except for me."

Wren didn't look up as he wrote lines that filled the page. "I'd have no control over what you'd say to her. You—all of you guys from the original Quint crowd— are unknown variables in this type of situation. You know, with other humans."

Matthias was pretty sure Wren was actively trying to piss him off. "What does that mean in English?"

Wren glanced up then. "You all have to be on your best behavior and there will be rules. I might make you all sign agreements."

"You know that's ridiculous, right?" Garrett asked. "For my own sanity I need to know that *you* know that."

Matthias didn't wait for the answer. "We're talking about meeting your woman."

"I would really like it if she didn't leave me, so yes.

The introductions can wait. But when they do happen, please refer to her by her name—Emery—not as *my woman*, because she will kick you."

"You've gotten soft." Matthias would laugh if the idea weren't so absurd. But they were all talking about it, the group of five of them. They'd met in their twenties, taken in by a man named Quint who stopped them from wandering down their respective destructive paths and insisted they accomplish more. They'd added Garrett to their small group later.

Ruthless men. Tough men. Very private and incredibly capable. Some more dangerous than others, but all of them bonded to each other and walking as close to a legitimate path as possible. They'd been boys back then. Now they were men. Successful men, and they still relied on each other.

Garrett smiled. "He's in love."

"That's fucked up." And Matthias thought that was an understatement.

The idea of Wren being spun around by sex . . . or whatever . . . yeah, didn't make sense. Not for Wren, the one who back then had been so wrapped around with hate and screwed up that he was determined to kill his own father. That guy, the same one politicians and heads of countries and billion-dollar businesses now came to for top secret help, had fallen in love. He was downright stupid with it.

Matthias had never seen anything like it and certainly didn't want any part of it, but the whole group wanted to meet her. To spend an hour talking with the one woman allowed to call their friend Levi. Garrett promised they would all like her.

Wren cleared his throat. "Back to *your* woman."

Maybe with his newfound understanding of women Wren was *the* guy for this task. Matthias still wondered if Emery might handle the situation better, but he'd go with this. "Okay, Mr. Fixer. You can give it a shot."

"That's nice of you."

"For free." This was supposed to be a favor, after all.

"Right. That seems fair to me." Wren rolled his eyes. "I'll need a name and some general information, like locations and dates, but we'll handle it. And by *we* I mostly mean Garrett."

"Lucky me," Garrett said as he took a small notebook out of his jacket pocket.

Looked like these two were ready to go. That worked for Matthias. "I don't know her name now, but I know what it was seven years ago."

"When your brother—the same one I've never heard of before despite knowing you for more than ten years—died."

Man, he was just not going to let that go. Never mind that Matthias didn't know about the brother back then either. "It was so much worse than that."

Wren's eyes narrowed. "How so?"

"It's more like while someone managed to take out an entire household of college kids, including two members of the lacrosse team, she—this woman—walked away without a scratch."

Garrett winced. "Sounds like she's a suspect."

Damn fucking straight. "And that's exactly how I'll treat her when I meet her."

"You plan on shooting her?" Wren asked.

"We'll see." And by that Matthias meant if she turned out to be the killer—then definitely.

CHAPTER 3

Matthias liked to eat as much as the next guy, but it was two in the afternoon and he couldn't figure out what meal this was supposed to be. Also didn't understand why he was at a dive café outside of Annapolis, Maryland, on a random Tuesday.

He looked around at the mostly empty tables. All twelve of them. Here, tucked into a row of shops at a marina, was this little restaurant. Lucky's, though he somehow guessed the place didn't live up to its name.

It was clean enough. The red fake leather booths bore the cracks from the passing years and too many sneakers and jeans roughing over them. A thick strip of tape held the cushion under him together. Every time he shifted his leg the wrong way he heard a slight tearing sound.

The best thing about the café, as far as he could tell, was the waitress. Tall with a big smile and the highest, tightest ass he'd ever seen. Like, *holy shit* fine.

She had her reddish brown hair pulled back. Not that he was looking at her head all that much. Which likely made him an asshole, but he tried to be subtle about it as she moved around with ease, serving the four old guys sitting in the corner booth and the two ladies huddled in a conversation about something over by the counter.

All that walking gave him a front-row seat to her legs. Damn impressive. Long and lean. Tan and muscled. She wore a waitress uniform that hugged every curve, and she had more than a few of those. The sneakers made him smile. They looked battered and well used. This was a woman on the move.

Garrett banged his spoon against the side of his coffee cup.

Oh, right. Him . . . "What are we doing here? Talk." Matthias pulled his gaze away from the only interesting part of the room and scowled at Garrett.

Garrett's eyes narrowed as he studied the dessert menu the pretty waitress had dropped off. "The pie looks good."

Matthias smacked his hand against the paper and slammed it against the wobbly table. "I have a gun."

"That's charming."

Being dragged out of his office and forced to drive through DC traffic made Matthias even less patient than usual. And that was saying something. The construction zone that decreased the average highway speed to a negative number didn't help. "You should know I have more than one kind of weapon on me. And I lied—I actually have two guns."

"Is Maryland even an open-carry state?"

As if he cared. "Answer my question, Garrett. There are cafés in Georgetown. Why am I down here?"

Garrett put a folder on the edge of the table. "As Wren promised, we found her."

He meant *the* her. Damn, Wren worked fast.

"Already? It's only been four days." But Matthias noticed Garrett wasn't exactly handing the information over.

"Don't act so surprised. This is the kind of thing we do." Garrett stopped to take a long sip of coffee. "You know, for a living."

The waitress appeared at Matthias's side. She smelled good. Like a mix of baked goods and flowers. Not his usual thing, but it was hard to resist a woman who reminded him of doughnuts.

"More?" She held up the coffeepot.

He didn't want anything except intel, but since she asked. He nodded as he slid the cup closer to her. "Yes, ma'am."

Her smile lit up her face. Actually turned her cheeks a soft pink. How fucking hot was that?

Once she left, Garrett rattled his cup again. "Aren't you polite?"

"Seems to me getting people their food would be a shitty job. Imagine the complaining she must hear." He'd never taken a lunch order in his life, but spending long hours on his feet then fighting with idiots who wanted to skimp on tips struck him as thankless work, which was why he overtipped. Always.

"You could let her have one of your guns," Garrett said.

"I might." Tempting as that might be, he was here

about a different woman. He nodded toward the folder. "Is that for me?"

"It has information on your woman."

That sounded like an answer Wren might give. One with a bunch of words that didn't say much. "I prefer to think of her as 'the woman' for now. She might become a target as I find out more."

Garrett smiled over the top of his cup. "Oh, she's definitely the woman."

He sounded far too impressed with himself. Matthias didn't like that tone at all. "What are you saying?"

"*The* woman."

The waitress came back. She glanced around the tabletop. "Anything else?"

Before Garrett could order half the menu, Matthias stepped in. He handed it back to her. "We're good. Thanks."

She slipped away a second time. Matthias let his mind wander, just for a second, to the swing of her hips. The steady back and forth. This woman made rushing around look calm and even. Even at an increased speed, she seemed to be in full control.

He watched his team on maneuvers all the time. Put them through drills. Had them run in almost unconscionable conditions. He was accustomed to seeing people snap to attention, scurry and race. Her cool manner, the ability to buzz around without looking harried, impressed him.

He could feel Garrett's gaze and thought about ignoring it. But when the waitress also caught him looking and shot him a smile, Matthias knew it was time to get his head back in the game.

He looked at Garrett. "You have five seconds to tell me what I need to know."

"You were staring." And Garrett was smiling. Practically laughing.

"That ass is worth a second look."

Garrett snuck a quick look. "No arguments here."

Yeah, that was enough of that. The woman deserved better than to be drooled over by two idiots in a ripped-up booth. Matthias stared at the folder. "Give it to me."

"Your woman dropped out of Syracuse University after the killings." Garrett's voice dropped to a whisper and stayed there. "She traveled around, changed her name three times and has run through a series of jobs."

Racing, staying one step ahead of the people who might stop her and ask questions. He knew the type. Hated the type. "Sounds suspicious."

"Or she's running from something out of necessity."

Sounded like the same thing to Matthias. "The police."

Garrett shook his head. "Doubtful, since she's not a suspect."

"How can that be? She was the sole survivor. She gave excuses about strange noises and a fuzzy memory. Reality is, she walked away from a bloodbath and no one can explain that." There was no innocent reason Matthias could come up with for someone to kill the others and leave her alive. Add that to the whispers about a lover's triangle and jealousy and the answer seemed clear to Matthias.

"The police and private investigators on this over the years never believed she could overpower a female friend and two male college athletes, or kill them all without trouble."

Many men in law enforcement underestimated women. They saw them one way. Matthias didn't make that mistake. He had women on his team. Strong and smart. "This woman could be pretty tough."

Garrett glanced at the waitress and smiled when she made eye contact. His gaze shifted back to the table. "Oh, I think your woman is definitely that."

"*The* woman. Not my woman." Matthias wanted that point to be very clear.

"She'd have to be to survive, don't you think?"

The walking away condemned her in his eyes. "Is she a survivor or the killer? That's the question."

"Agreed, but my job was to hunt her down and get a location, not dissect her motives." Garrett held the folder. Waved it around. "Unless you want me to tell Wren we should keep going."

Matthias thought about reaching for the file but stopped himself. He was not the type to lunge and make a scene in public. "I can take it from here."

"You sure?"

"Are you going to give me the damn file or no?" When the older men looked over, Matthias knew he'd yelled that last part. He waved a hand to try to calm any concern.

"Well." The waitress appeared out of nowhere this

time. She stood there with a frown on her face. "You two okay?"

Matthias wiped a hand through his hair. "Except for how annoying my friend here is, yes."

"I'm afraid I can't do much about that." She winked at Matthias. "I'll just leave the check, but let me know if you need anything else."

She dropped the paper on the table in front of him. One of the older gentlemen derailed her walk back into the kitchen, and Matthias watched every second of it.

Garrett snapped his fingers in front of Matthias's face. "You're still staring."

"It's still a mighty fine ass."

"It is." Garrett slid the folder across the table. "And it happens to belong to Kayla Roy."

"What?" Matthias's mind blanked out. For a second he sat there, trying to match the ass-watching to whatever the hell Garrett was babbling about.

Garrett snuck a peek at the waitress again before his voice dropped even lower. "If you'd prefer to use one of her former names you could try Samantha Weldon."

Matthias reached for the folder but his arms seemed to be moving in slow motion. "What are you trying to tell me?"

"Or you could go with the name you gave us to investigate—Carrie Gleason." Garrett leaned in closer. "Though I doubt you could use it without her taking off again." Garrett nodded toward the waitress. "She looks fast."

Reality crashed through Matthias like a body blow. "Wait, you're saying she's—"

"*The* woman." Garrett glanced in the waitress's direction again then back to Matthias. "Right here in Annapolis. So close to your home turf."

"Son of a bitch."

Garrett nodded. "You're welcome."

THEY'D FOUND HER.

Private investigators or law enforcement of some kind. Kayla recognized the type. The suits, the way they held themselves. The constant scanning of the room and dropping of conversation whenever she came by the table.

She'd never seen these two men before but she'd spent what felt like her entire adulthood being hunted and questioned by ones just like them. It could be innocent, but this place served locals and boating types. They might actually be businessmen who decided they'd skip work in the middle of the afternoon in favor of cheap coffee and homemade pie and traveled way offtrack to get it, but she doubted it.

Her brain kicked into action. She performed the assessment she'd done so many times before—the pros and cons of stay or flee. Could she handle the renewed scrutiny and inevitable threats and hate-filled stares that came with a new round of questions? At first that pattern had won out. These days she ran.

She had to sneak out of here first.

With a fake smile plastered on her face, she refilled the cups of her regular customers then slipped past the counter. Her heartbeat hammered so hard she was surprised the men couldn't hear it. But she did. She felt every nerve ending jump to life.

Her hand shook and the pot rattled as she set it down next to a tray of muffins. One turn and she disappeared into the kitchen. The cook glanced up, shooting her his usual how-dare-you-be-in-here glare. Fine with her since she intended to keep moving. She'd been doing that for seven years—what was one more time?

As soon as she let her mind wander about ripping up roots again, a sharp pain slashed across her chest. She pressed the heel of her hand against the ache. Stepped into the hall that led to the employee bathroom and the small office in the back. From there it was just a few steps to the alley and freedom.

Not that she considered anything about her life to be free, but she'd finally found a tentative peace here. She'd moved into that small studio above the boat rental place. Adopted a new name, settled into a new life. Even started taking classes at nearby St. John's College.

But that was over now. She'd move on again.

She twisted the dial on her locker. Passed the first number by a mile and had to start again. She shook her hands and flexed her fingers to calm down. Leaning in, she pressed her forehead against the cool metal and tried to block the moment when that customer's expression had changed.

She'd watched the switch. It would have been tough to miss; she'd been stealing peeks since the bell above the door chimed and the guy came in. His head almost grazed the top of the doorframe. He was wild tall, like maybe six-four.

He carried that body with an air of strength and confidence. The dark suit didn't do anything to hide the broad shoulders and trim waist. And the fact he'd skipped a tie and kept the top few buttons of his pristine white shirt open said something about him. She wasn't sure what, but that deep voice had echoed through her with every word he uttered, and there had only been a few.

His presence drew her in. Made her look twice . . . three times, even. The dark hair and brown eyes. The faint shadow of scruff around his chin. He was good-looking in a knew-how-to-please-a-woman sort of way. Not pretty. Not the type who would spend more time in the bathroom than she did in the morning. A guy who didn't care about the brand of his shampoo or tag on his shirts.

Strong hands, long fingers. All of it came with a very real sense that the fancy clothes didn't fit the man underneath. That something hot and maybe a little dirty lurked there.

He and his friend had started arguing. They'd passed a file back and forth and lowered their discussion to a whisper. The shorter one shot her more than one odd glance.

Like that, the energy pinging through the room had morphed into a pounding tension. She knew the anxiety came from inside of her and colored everything around her. A strange darkness descended around her, choking her. When the tall one had looked over at her the last time, her mind filled in the blanks and panic moved through her.

Her past had taught her to be careful and wary. She could read the signs and sensed when a man's interest turned and he started to question her. When his mood flicked from attracted to distrust. When flirty glances shifted to glaring.

None of that happened with the tall one in the suit. He remained calm and detached. Kept watching her. Except for a brief narrowing of his eyes, which he quickly schooled, nothing in his demeanor changed. Still, she felt the seismic shift. Deep in her gut she sensed he was here for her, not coffee. If past experience was any guide, that meant one thing. He knew. Somehow he knew.

Now the threats would start. The prickly sensation of being followed would swallow up every hour. Her control would slip away until the revving need to run flooded through her. She could confront him, but she'd lose that battle. He was bigger. And whatever questions he thought he had would go unanswered. She'd never be able to fill the hole inside either of them.

So, she'd go. Now, before the notes appeared under her door.

She spun the dial again and this time hit close enough to the right numbers to get the lock open. She could hear the cook calling for her as the locker banged open. She ignored it all, from the screech of metal against metal to the soft mumble of sounds from the other side of the diner.

She stared down at the small black bag tucked into the bottom. Her alternate to-go bag. The one with limited extra provisions. That's all she'd have now. After two tugs, she had it out and balanced the strap over her shoulder.

Careful not to make too much noise, she tiptoed to the emergency door on the other side of the room. Stopped and took one last look around. Ignored the clogging sensation in her throat and the dragging feeling of loss. In time the sadness would fade, but right now it pummeled her. Nearly drove her to her knees.

She bit it back, pushed it down and typed in the code. The lock beeped and she opened the door. Sunlight streamed in from the side alley, but before she could take another step a shadow moved in front of her. She tried to say something—anything—but words piled up in her throat.

The guy from inside. Those dark eyes didn't show one ounce of emotion. Didn't flicker with any sign of life as they narrowed.

"Going somewhere?" he asked.

That deep voice. She could only shake her head.

He slipped his hands out of his pants pockets. "Good."

She couldn't stop staring. Couldn't get her legs to move either. Somehow she choked out two words. "Is it?"

"I need more coffee."

CHAPTER 4

He followed her past the kitchen and back into the heart of the café. A cook called out, but Matthias ignored it. His attention centered on one woman, and this time not on her fine ass. He couldn't see much of anything through the angry haze clouding his vision. He'd temporarily been reeled in. He wondered if that's what had happened to Nick.

Matthias waited until she picked up the coffeepot to pivot around her and retake his seat. If she ran now, he'd catch her. Even though he no longer worked in the field, he kept in shape.

But right now he went with sitting. He slid back into the booth.

"I'm afraid to ask what just happened," Garrett mumbled under his breath as he looked around the room.

"I asked for more coffee." Matthias made a show of holding up his mug as he glanced at the woman he now thought of as Kayla.

It took longer than it should have to grab her attention. When he did, she nodded but didn't exactly come running. She sauntered around, carrying the pot and checking on every table. Even stopped at one without any people in it and straightened the napkins and forks sitting there.

She stayed cool and detached. Seemed unemotional. In any other situation he would have been impressed. He was too busy assessing and staring to be that right now.

"You went outside and around the back of the building to ask for more coffee. Isn't that the hard way to do it?" Garrett kept a hand he must have grabbed back.

Matthias wasn't in the mood for arm wrestling for it right now, he moved on. "I needed to stretch my legs."

The corner of Garrett's mouth lifted into a smile. "Sure. Makes perfect sense."

"I didn't touch my gun."

Garrett clapped without making any real sound. "Well, look at you exhibiting all that self-control."

The smartass thing was enough to get Matthias fully focused on Garrett instead of the waitress. "I could pull it out now."

"I see it's your common sense I still need to be concerned about."

"How does Wren get through the day without firing you?" Matthias appreciated Garrett's skills but not the sarcasm or the constant back talk. When he gave an order, he expected it to be followed without question.

People talked about how nothing was black or white, and how you had to deal with gray areas. Bullshit. People mucked everything up with feelings and rethinking and failing to act. Right and wrong shouldn't be open to interpretation.

Seemed obvious enough to him.

"What makes you think Wren doesn't?" Garrett scoffed. "I get fired and rehired multiple times per day."

That made sense, but still. "Most employees would learn a lesson."

"That Wren has no intention of actually getting rid of me? Yeah, I figured that out long ago." Garrett drained the rest of his coffee from the mug. "And, like you, he needs someone to keep him in line. Make sure he doesn't go too far and get arrested."

Matthias wasn't sure how to respond to that. He'd never needed a babysitter in his life. "It's hard to imagine Wren being that stupid."

"You'd be amazed."

"Tell me what I need to know about her until I can read the report." The "her" in question hovered behind the cash register. She didn't make a move to come over or bring him more coffee. But she wasn't running either, and that worked for him. For now.

He could wait her out for a month, if needed. She might be operating in panic mode, but he'd been trained. That gave him the advantage.

When Garrett didn't say anything, Matthias looked over at him. He couldn't believe he had to tell the man to start talking a second time. What kind of operation was Wren running? Matthias planned to talk to his friend about control and how to command a situation. Right now, he settled for glaring.

Garrett shrugged. "I already told you what I know."

"I refuse to believe that's all the intel you picked up about her."

"I gave you a name and you scared the hell out of

her and sent her bolting and then . . . well, I don't know what happened in the back. So this"—Garrett spun his finger around in a circle in midair—"whatever this is and what's happening now and her looking ready to jump through a wall, is on you."

"Like I told you, I asked her for more coffee." Seemed innocent enough to Matthias. He'd wanted to sit her down and start an interrogation but he suspected that sort of thing might piss off Garrett and get some of the locals to call 9-1-1 on him. So, he waited.

"Is that code for something?"

Matthias wanted to concentrate on the woman, but Garrett just never shut up. "What the hell are you talking about now?"

"That's really it? You're saying she looks hunted because you told her you wanted more coffee."

"I don't like to repeat myself." Matthias had no idea how Garrett failed to pick up on that fact.

"You're a joy to work with."

Matthias reached out and slammed his palm against the file. The thwap had the woman jumping and provided enough subterfuge for him to grab the file back. "For."

Garrett shook his head, something he seemed to do a lot. "Yeah, keep thinking that."

"Speaking of which, you can go. You provided what few details you have, so Wren's favor is complete and . . . why are you still shaking your head?" The gesture was starting to piss Matthias off.

"Wren told me not to leave your side until this— whatever 'this' is—is over." Garrett leaned back in the booth. "Consider me your temporary assistant."

What the fuck? "Do I look like I need help?"

"Should I really answer that?"

"Even if I did, I have an entire staff I could call in." Just as Matthias started to say more, the woman moved. She inched closer to the kitchen and Matthias felt every cell inside him switch to high alert.

"You get me," Garrett said.

But Matthias was barely listening now. He was too busy assessing the room—the people, what furniture might be blocking his path, any collateral damage—to care about Garrett. "Why?"

"That's a broad question." Garrett glanced around the restaurant. "I think your woman is trying to bolt, which is weird since the way you demanded more coffee was so charming."

"She can't scare me away or lose me."

"Lucky her." Garrett's eyebrow lifted. "Oh, wait. We have movement other than running for her life in the other direction. Interesting."

After some hesitation, she headed straight for them. Didn't stop until she hovered by the edge of the table on Garrett's side, staring and generally doing nothing to hide her wish to be almost anywhere else.

"Are you ready to pay the bill?" Her voice was flat, all signs of flirting gone.

Shoulders back. Making eye contact. Matthias couldn't help but take notice. He wasn't sure if she stood there, so sure and confident, because she lacked any human emotion or because she was tough as hell. He kind of hoped it was the latter. "I asked for more coffee."

"Right."

"Thank you, Kayla." Her eyes widened. Just for a second, and since he didn't want to spook her, he nodded in the direction of her chest. "It's on your tag."

"Oh." Her hand went to the small plastic square. Fumbled with it. "I'll get that for you right now."

She scrambled away from the table. It was the only sign of what was going on in her head. Even then she quickly adjusted. Within a few steps she was back to rushing around without breaking a sweat.

He admired the coolness, that ass and the way she moved. Except for brief moments, reading her proved tough. That meant one thing—he was going to be stuck in Annapolis for a few days.

AN HOUR LATER Matthias stood on the sidewalk outside the café with Garrett. Matthias half expected her to rush over and lock the door behind them. She didn't, but that didn't mean it couldn't happen.

This was not a woman he could shake easily. She held her outward calm. She didn't appear to be intimidated, which was a damn shame. That was his go-to move. It was amazing how often that resulted in him getting his way.

Instead of staying inside and pushing—the solution that screamed through him, begging to happen—he'd lingered over that second cup of coffee, assessing her. He debated hanging around but decided giving her a little space, but not much, was the right answer. This way he could study the file and watch her from a distance.

But he didn't venture far. He stopped on the board-walk a few feet away from the café's front door and only steps from the marina. He was willing to have only so much space between him and Kayla. That woman was a runner and he didn't feel like tracking her or calling another favor from Wren. Hell, he couldn't get rid of the leftover part of that favor—Garrett.

"Tell me again what you said to her in the back," Garrett asked as he pivoted around a trashcan.

Matthias stopped walking, which forced Garrett to do the same. "For the third time, I asked for more coffee. That's it."

"Then we need to work on your creepiness factor."

That was exactly the wrong answer. "It's not a bad thing for her to be wary. She might mess up. Make it easier to figure out what she's hiding and what really happened in that house years ago."

"Do you also want her to be armed? Because she looked ready to hit you with the coffeepot."

Matthias appreciated a good fight-or-flight instinct. He also understood how people acted when trapped. Some made mistakes. Some got scary. He wasn't sure where she would fall on the scale. Not yet. "I need her to be a little less sure of herself."

Garrett stepped forward so an older couple walking by could pass, and waited until they moved out of easy hearing range. "You're not great at dealing with humans, are you?"

"Not especially." Matthias didn't see that as a par-ticularly helpful skill anyway. Strategy and fighting would be much easier to implement without the human factor, but he tended not to mention that because it freaked people out.

"How do you expect to get answers if you terrify her?"

Matthias didn't understand the question. "She'll tell me what I need to know."

"Or . . ." Garrett held up a finger. "If she's as smart as I think she is, she'll run like hell."

"Then I'll follow." So far Matthias hadn't heard anything to cause concern.

"That comment does not make you sound less creepy."

Again with the *creepy* thing. "I'll work on that this week."

Garrett groaned. "I hate to ask what that means."

The next few days called for subtlety. Admittedly, not one of his strengths. He preferred the barking-at-people-until-they-broke method.

"A vacation seems in order and this marina might not be a bad place to take it." He had no idea about vacations. He hadn't taken one since . . . had he ever taken one? He'd tried Las Vegas years ago but quickly flew home again after seeing people throw money away for no good reason. "You're still free to leave now that you told me where she is."

Garrett rolled his eyes. "As if I'd miss this."

CHAPTER 5

Kayla tried not to flinch when Mr. Suit walked in again the next day. This time he was alone. He actually gave her a little wave as he slipped inside the café around ten in the morning and sat down.

She reached under the counter and touched the gun she kept there. He might be fine and not really a danger, but she was not taking any chances.

She had other customers and had sent off coolers packed with food and snacks for pleasure cruises. The morning had been busy but nothing unusual. Enough that she was looking forward to a short break.

She'd settled in to enjoy a post–breakfast crowd cup of coffee when he picked up a menu. The temptation to ignore him kicked strong. She was torn between encouraging repeat business and fighting off the strange mix of wariness and interest that hit her when she looked at him.

When he put down the menu, she reluctantly set down her coffee mug. Thought about chasing him out using that gun and decided that might be too dramatic. But she'd keep an eye on him. She'd taken those personal safety classes for a reason and knew how to shoot, run and scream. Boy, could she scream.

Time to get up and get back to work, but she needed to be smarter today. Maybe amp down on the friendliness factor and skip the flirting. No tip was worth potentially having to fight this guy off for getting the wrong idea.

He watched as she drew closer. Didn't pretend not to. He didn't smile. She wasn't convinced that was his style, but something about the way he stared—all intense and moody—had her involuntarily swallowing.

She stopped across the table from him. "You're back."

"Couldn't stay away."

That almost sounded like flirting. "You had one cup of coffee and we hooked you."

"Three."

"Excuse me?"

"Three cups." He tapped the menu and slid it toward her. "And I'll take another."

Okay, nothing weird about that. People drank coffee. Hell, she drank coffee. But she didn't get all dressed up and drive out of her way to get it. "Be right back."

A half hour later he put down his mug and got up and walked toward the window. The sight of him pulling back the dainty white curtain made her smile. A look—from his black watch to the sprinkling of dark hair on his bare arm to the rolled-up sleeve of his white dress shirt—had her strangely breathless. He'd abandoned the jacket almost immediately but there was nothing casual about him. Even without the tie he looked in command . . . almost predatory.

She inched a bit closer to that gun.

"Do you get out on the water often?" His voice boomed through the café.

Since he'd waited to get up until the last two tables left and she was the only other person in there, she assumed he was talking to her. That this was his form of small talk. Little did he know he'd found the one subject sure to make her twitchy. "Never."

He glanced at her over his shoulder. "You never venture out there?"

"Technically you're looking into the parking lot right now. I go there every day. But the water? No thank you."

"Really?"

When he continued to look at her with that half-amused expression, her defenses rose a bit. "Don't judge."

"It's just odd you'd pick a job here when you don't like the water."

Now he sounded like a lawyer or an investigator—her two least favorite things. "I tend to pick my work more on who will actually pay me than location."

"Smart." He walked toward her, every step determined and not too fast or too slow.

Something about him struck her as practiced and deliberate, which made his presence here for the second day in a row all the weirder. "How long are you in town?"

"A few days, maybe more."

Good Lord. He needed to find another café. He set her on edge. Had her peeking over her mug at him like a silly teen and checking her windows at night for trouble.

"For work?" she asked.

"I have a project I'm working on."

The answer sounded fine at first. Then she turned the words over in her head and realized he hadn't actually said anything. "Are you a lawyer?"

He slid onto the barstool across from her. "Hell, no."

Okay, she understood that reaction. "Yeah, I'm not a fan either." She poured herself another cup of coffee and got him a new mug for more, too.

"Businessman."

"Banking?"

He drank a sip of coffee. "I think your radar is off."

This guy was all about mystery. She asked a straightforward question and he responded with half sentences. She picked up on it because she used that skill often. Look at him walking all over her turf.

"You're a hard man to pin down."

"Do you want to pin me down, Kayla?"

His deep voice brushed against her. Drew her in. She ignored it, stuck to mindless chatter. "I'm thinking no to fishing or sailing."

That seemed as good a way to avoid the question as any other. And that's what she had to do because when he asked, her stomach bounced a little. She wanted to write the sensation off as indigestion, but she feared it was really excitement.

Not going to happen.

"Correct. I develop long-term projects. Move people in to implement work that needs to be done."

Uh, okay. "That barely sounds like a thing."

"You aren't the first to say that. Think of me as the person who supplies the manpower to make other people's visions a reality."

Still sounded made-up to her. "For the record, that description is not any clearer."

"It's not very sexy."

She ignored the word and his face and almost everything about him and focused on the wariness bubbling inside her. "And that's why you're in town?"

"Yes. I have to finish up an old issue that should have been resolved a long time ago." He winced. "It's not my usual project. I'm alone in an office, hence the coffee breaks."

He'd said a lot of words without actually giving much away. She appreciated that skill, since she'd lived her entire adult life that way so far.

He studied her. Whatever he saw had him talking again. "Basically, I sit at a desk, read reports."

Before she could think twice, her gaze traveled all over him, or at least the part she could see over the counter. The impressive part that included broad shoulders and that strong chin. "You look like you spend most of the day in the gym."

He glanced down. "You can see that through my clothes?"

Yes. The dress shirt fit snug enough to highlight bulges and she couldn't spy one. "Of course not."

"Do you ever eat dinner?"

She froze with her mug halfway to her mouth. It took her another minute to slowly lower it to the counter. "That's an odd question."

"I was asking you on a date."

His gaze flicked from her hands, which had a death grip on the mug, to her mouth, which she guessed was hanging open. He was a customer, and a confusing one at that.

She winced. "Are you sure?"

"That bad, huh?"

"The delivery was a bit . . . off." She hissed to make sure he got the point.

"We could go to dinner and talk about it."

Well, she had to give him points for tenacity. But that was it. Dating was out in general and this guy . . . there was something she still couldn't get a handle on. Something that had her teetering from savoring his company to waiting for the building's roof to fall on her head. She didn't enjoy the out-of-control sensation at all.

"I don't think so." That was the safe answer, the smart one, so she invoked it.

"Boyfriend?"

"No."

"Ah." He started drinking his coffee again. Even eyed up the apple pie in the container next to him.

He seemed to take the refusal in stride. Didn't storm out or even go back to his table. Just sat there. Once again he had this zigging response that intrigued her even more. "I'm not sure what to say to that."

He shrugged. "When a guy realizes the problem is him and not some outside factor, that's really the only response he can give."

Not in her experience. She'd had more than one pleasure-boat dude come on to her, and when she politely refused whatever he proposed, he'd fall back on calling her names under his breath. "Some act like complete jackasses."

His eyebrow lifted. "Then it's good you turn those men down."

For some reason she found the conversation weirdly charming. "Problem is you don't always know the jerks right at the beginning. Unfortunately, they don't wear a sign."

"They give the jerkiness away eventually, right?"

She thought back to another time, to a boy who turned out to be much worse than a jerk. "You'd be surprised what good actors some of them are."

"Dating sucks."

"Amen to that." She lifted her mug in a toast. "So, do you have a name?"

He smiled. "Matthias."

That wasn't at all what she expected. She'd thought John or Tom . . . solid and short. "Really?"

"You think I'd make that up?"

She thought about the question for an oddly long period of time before choking out an answer. "It's a good name. Solid."

"It got my ass kicked in junior high."

Now, that she understood. "Breathing got my ass kicked in junior high. Teen girls are rough."

He put out his hand. "Nice to officially meet you, Kayla."

She should pull away and not care. Instead she held out her hand. "Nice to meet you."

The touch scorched her. She'd expected smooth, flawless hands. She got the firm grip of a workingman.

He held on to her hand for an extra beat. "Would it sound too stalkerish if I told you I intend to keep coming back here until you change your mind about dinner?"

It should. Any other time alarm bells would be chiming in her head. "Absolutely, yes."

"Then forget I said that."

"Done."

CHAPTER 6

By his third day of café sitting and coffee drinking without Garrett, Matthias was having a hard time pegging Kayla as a murderer. While some hid their nature well, he didn't get any sort of "off" vibe from her. None.

He'd studied the files Garrett had provided and retraced every piece of information he'd found on every name she'd used. Nothing about her present fit with her supposed past.

The idea of her going wild one day, killing men who outweighed her by fifty or sixty pounds just because and then slaughtering her female friend didn't fit with her past or her psychological profile. God knew he looked for signs, for inconsistencies in her behavior and patterns in her background.

Nothing popped. Literally nothing.

He was beginning to understand why the police dropped their pursuit of her. The pieces didn't fit. She'd survived, but that seemed to be the biggest strike against her. There were rumors about love triangles and fights but she'd managed to get through the rest of her life without killing anyone else. Those urges generally didn't just disappear in a person without something else happening.

She had secrets. She was on the run and changing her name for a reason. He guessed she knew more than she said, and that's where he would make his move. If he then figured out that his instincts blinked out when it came to her and she was some sort of death mistress, he'd take care of her.

Once he mentally put her in the probably-a-witness category rather than killer category, his priorities shifted. Her not being the killer didn't answer who *did* kill Nick, but she might be able to give him a clue.

Every day he'd come in and order. They'd talk. She'd smile. He'd ask her out and she'd say no. He was starting to think he lacked game.

"Food or just coffee?" she asked as she whizzed by his table on the way to another.

"We'll start with caffeine then go from there."

She nodded and was off. Taking an order from this group. Delivering soup to that guy. In between she smiled at everyone and talked about the weather. He liked to think she saved more interesting topics for him, but truth was this woman knew how to have a conversation without really saying a thing. She poked around by asking questions. He poked back. Neither of them learned a thing.

It was a weird sort of dating; at least that's how he thought of it in his head. Impersonal and without sex. He half wondered how the human race survived if men and women had to navigate this nonsense just to have dinner together. He'd stick to his solitary life, thank you.

Without stopping she swung around to him again. Dropped off coffee and a piece of what looked like some sort of custard pie. He caught her arm just as she moved away. "I didn't order pie."

"It's on me." She winked and left again.

He wondered if she'd be half as friendly if she knew he'd been following her. He spent as much of the day in the café as he thought he could get away with before people might start asking difficult questions. The rest of the time he listened in from the small microphone he'd tucked up under the table where he usually sat, or watched from across the parking lot through his high-powered lens. Pushing that curtain back had made that easier. At night he sat in his car outside her studio, followed her around, though the only places she had gone so far were home, work and the grocery store.

In just a few short days he had become a stalker, but a purposeful one. He needed intel. Needed to understand who she was so he could figure out how to ask her questions without sending her into a dead run in the opposite direction.

He picked up his fork, prepared to stab into that piecrust, when the bell above the door dinged. He glanced up, expecting to see one of the regulars. He now knew who they were and had run facial recognition on all of them.

Garrett stood there.

"Son of a bitch."

"Imagine how I feel," he said as he slipped into the booth across from Matthias.

He slowly lowered the fork back to the table. "Why are you here?"

"I missed you."

The last thing he needed was a chaperone. "Never forget that I can shoot you and not have an ounce of remorse."

"Nice." Garrett reached across the table and picked off a piece of crust then popped it in his mouth. "Wren made me come back."

"Your boss is a pain in the ass."

"You say that like it's a surprising fact." Garrett slid a folder across the table. "This is for you."

"What is it?"

Garrett snuck a glance in Kayla's direction. Waved to her when she caught him staring. "More on the other players. He thought it might help you."

"To do what?"

"Finish your business here then get back home." This time Garrett moved the plate closer to him and picked up the fork. "I think he's convinced you're going to get arrested."

"That's probably not an unreasonable assumption." Matthias figured he'd lost any chance of eating that pie. "We could get you a piece of your own."

"No, I'm good." He scooped up a generous bite and ate it.

"You came all this way to deliver this message?"

Garrett took his time chewing and swallowing. "I have one more."

When he started eating again, Matthias grabbed the fork. "Tell me or I reach for a weapon."

"This time I'm really not allowed to leave unless you come back with me." Garrett frowned. "And can we talk about what a shitty assignment this is for me? You're not exactly my idea of a good time. So, feel free to wrap this up quickly."

He didn't shut up. Garrett had managed to say more in five minutes than Matthias had said in three days. "What are you talking about?"

"There are rumors you've lost perspective and are down here dating and generally annoying the people of Annapolis."

What the hell? "Where did you hear that?"

"From me. I said it to Wren, but it backfired because now he really has assigned me to you." Garrett touched the corner of the folder. "I do have other work, but you'd never know it."

Time to end this conversation. "No."

Garrett shrugged. "Take it up with the boss."

"I'm the boss." For some reason people around here kept forgetting that. Matthias never had that trouble in his office but it seems to keep coming up now.

"Uh-huh, sure."

"You've made your delivery, so now you can turn around and head back home." He leaned forward and pitched his voice low. "I'm not done here."

"Coffee?"

Matthias hadn't heard Kayla approach. She'd snuck

up on him with a coffeepot in her hand. No one got the jump on him. Almost no one. Certainly not like this. He was off his game and blamed Garrett's nonstop talking. "He's not staying."

"Yes, thank you," Garrett said at the same time.

"Anything else?" she asked as she poured.

"How's the tuna fish?"

This was fucking ridiculous. "Could you excuse us for a second?" Matthias managed to hold his voice steady until she walked away. Then he turned his attention back to the annoying man in front of him. "What are you doing?"

"Eating?" Garrett sighed. "Look, I'm not leaving until Wren gives me the okay, which means you're stuck."

That would make dinner with Kayla impossible. Might cut into his daily coffee talks with her, too. Regret tugged at Matthias. About the case, of course. Not on a personal level. But damn, he did want to make that dinner thing happen.

He needed to have a talk with Wren and look through the new information Garrett brought. As far as he could tell, he wasn't one step closer to leaving Annapolis. Maybe a second set of eyes would help to confirm. He'd thought about setting up a small camera in here and at her house. Those sounded like good Garrett jobs. "You can stay."

"Yeah, I know. I just said that."

Matthias pretended Garrett hadn't said anything, which was tough since he was always talking. "Just stay out of my way."

"Got it." Garrett leaned back in his chair. For a few seconds he didn't say a word.

Matthias knew that would never last.

Garrett picked up the fork again. "You gonna eat that pie?"

LATER THAT AFTERNOON Matthias found his way back to the café. It was near closing time. That usually meant Kayla would be leaving for her walk. She didn't vary that routine much. She hadn't used the same path in three days, which was smart, but the time of day and general plan didn't waver.

"Hey." He called out the greeting as he walked in.

She jerked at the sound and her head shot up. The mop she was holding dropped to the floor with a crack. "Two times in one day?"

"I needed a break." He bent over and grabbed the mop. Instead of giving it back, he held it. Ran it over the floor in the few places he could see she'd missed.

"From what?"

He sensed more poking around for information. No way was he making it easy on her. "Work."

"Ah, yes. The nondescript people-moving job."

He'd already said more than he intended, so he skipped offering up more details. "My back hurt from sitting. I thought a walk would do me some good."

"So you came over here from which office building . . . ?" She took the mop from him and planted it in the bucket.

"That would be an excellent dinner topic."

She shook her head and laughed. "I'm impressed with your refusal to give up."

"You have no idea." He could do this for weeks if he had to. He wasn't going to, but that was out of a need to get back to work and finish this off.

Pretty soon he'd abandon the soft approach and hit her head-on. The whole waiting-not-acting thing didn't really work for him anyway. He tried it because Wren suggested it, though what he knew about women didn't seem to be much. He'd stuck with it for three whole days because being with her, watching her, wasn't exactly a hardship.

The way she moved hypnotized him. Her calm enticed him. Everything about her compelled him.

His instincts didn't ping around her. Other parts of him did . . . and kept dinging. Dinged so hard that last night he'd needed a cold shower, and even that didn't work.

"Want to join me?" he asked, thinking they could trade dinner for a trip around the marina.

"What?"

"You like to go for walks, right? I thought you might want to join me."

Her smile froze. For a second she didn't move. Another man might not have picked up on the sudden smack of tension in the room or the sudden stiffening of her shoulders. He did.

"I have a meeting." She picked up the bucket and walked toward the kitchen. "Do you need anything before I lock the door?"

She still wore a smile but her mood had shifted.

There was no warmth coming off her, and her tone turned short and clipped.

The fucking walk.

He'd mentioned it and an invisible wall rose up between them. Because he shouldn't know she liked to walk. That was information he'd know if he followed her. Of course, he did, but she couldn't know that.

He'd screwed up. He never screwed up. Not on a mission. Informal or not, he knew better. He didn't even deal with people and gather intel like this at Quint, but he knew better.

"I'm good." He wasn't sure what else to say to tip the conversation back in his favor.

All the inroads he'd made, all the goodwill. Gone.

He toyed with the idea of coming clear, of launching into questions. He could throw her off balance and maybe catch her saying the wrong thing.

Then he looked at her face. The stern line of her mouth and wariness in her eyes. Yeah, they'd leapt backward. She wasn't running, but he sensed her internal struggle.

Standing there, he mentally debated strategy. He couldn't afford to let her race away and change names. Not again.

"Dinner?" She said the word and stood there.

She'd managed to flip him onto the defensive and he didn't like the sensation at all. "What?"

She leaned the mop handle against the counter. "A onetime offer. Daleo's. It's seafood, about three miles down the road. You're paying, by the way."

He would have been less stunned if she threw the bucket at him. "Tonight?"

This was a setup. A way to lure him to one place and race to another.

Impressive.

He didn't bother looking at his watch or asking about a reservation. He knew they wouldn't need one because they wouldn't be eating. This was a game and an intricate one. "I can pick you up at—"

"I'll meet you there at six."

Of course she would. *Right.*

Matthias shot her his best time-to-battle smile. "Perfect. I've been looking forward to this."

"Hasn't anyone ever told you to be careful what you wish for?"

One of the many trite words of wisdom he'd ignored over the years. "I don't listen to advice."

"I'm learning all sorts of things about you today."

He could play this game better than anyone. There wasn't a pivot she could make that he couldn't anticipate. "Imagine what tonight will bring."

"Oh, I know exactly what's going to happen next." She winked at him as she slipped into the back. "Be ready."

She played the role right to the end. Didn't give away her fear. He only picked up on the new wariness because he was watching for it.

Damn, she was good.

But he was better.

CHAPTER 7

He knew about her schedule. The walks and her routine. Kayla had sensed someone had been watching her. Now she knew the truth—Matthias was much more than a coffee date.

Kayla intended to get on a bus and slip out of town. That was the plan. That was always the plan. She had done this dance so many times that she knew it by heart. Rip up the roots she'd planted, only take what she needed and then run. Talk to no one. Don't leave any ties, no matter how much that hurt.

But this time she had someone she hated to lose. A friend. The only real one she'd let herself make in seven years. Lauren worked a few doors down from the café and had introduced herself immediately. Kayla had tried to maintain her distance, but Lauren didn't allow it. The first week she'd stopped by at closing with wine. The next day she showed up with a bad action movie and day-old cupcakes. That was four months ago and they'd been friends since.

Lauren didn't know the bits and pieces about the past, but she knew it had been bad. Deadly bad. Kayla appreciated that Lauren didn't push for more information. She talked and laughed, told ridiculous stories about her clients. Their friendship formed over all those nights and all that girl time.

Lauren ran a pleasure-boat crew and took couples, families and businesspeople out on recreational and fishing trips. Being on the water made Kayla need to heave, so she never went along, but she loved that her new friend intended to rebuild the place after inheriting it on the brink of bankruptcy.

Despite the burst of loyalty and pride, Kayla knew she should take off and leave Lauren behind. Calling or checking in once she changed her name didn't really work. She'd tried that with her dad, and the press and private investigators had hounded him until he died.

There also was the very real possibility that she could bring danger into someone else's life. She'd been threatened so many times over the years. All it would take would be for one person to act on the harsh words. And if Lauren was there, in the wrong place at the wrong time . . . She couldn't handle that, so now when she cut ties she shredded them.

None of that explained why she was standing at Lauren's door or why she'd zigzagged her way there from the marina, hiding behind bushes and on the lookout for the broody guy who left the ten-dollar tip for two cups of coffee. She still had no idea what Matthias really wanted or what he hoped to gain, but she knew the dinner date was a farce. She did not have the luxury of waiting around to find out more.

"It works better if you actually ring the bell."

At the sound of Lauren's amused voice behind her, Kayla spun around. "You're not inside."

Not the most intelligent response but her brain refused to function. She couldn't blink without seeing Matthias's face. His deep voice. The way he just showed up. Even when he wasn't there she thought about him.

"Man, you're quick tonight." Lauren laughed at her own joke but her smile soon faded. The gym bag slipped off her shoulder but she caught it from falling as she moved closer to the porch's bottom step. "What happened?"

"Nothing."

Lauren frowned. "Try again. You're pale and look like you're half a second from jumping in the bushes."

That sounded about right. "Well, I was thinking of trying to hide in the mailbox."

Kayla held her voice steady but her brain cells kept sputtering. She had a note in her hand. Short and not very clear, but it was something. A reassurance that their friendship had meant something to her, so if Lauren ever doubted that, she could read it and she'd have proof.

For whatever reason, Kayla could not get her fingers to unclench the crumpled paper and hand it over.

"That sounds totally rational." Lauren walked past her to the door. After a second of fumbling with her keys, she unlocked the door. "Come inside."

But Kayla didn't move. She stayed right there, standing on the faded redbrick porch. "Not a good idea."

"You're freaking me out. And since I spent an afternoon listening to a group of forty-something accountants pretend they were big-time sailors then squeal in terror at the idea of actually taking a fish off a hook, that's saying something." Lauren's eyebrow lifted. "I managed not to drown any of them, so yay for me."

Kayla would miss this. The way they fell into comfortable conversation. Lauren's stories. "I just wanted to say goodbye."

"I'm not accepting that answer." All the emotion left Lauren's face and her mouth fell into a thin line. "Tell me what's going on."

Kayla glanced around before tightening her grip on the note locked in her fist. "There was an . . . incident."

"Define *incident*."

"The guy at the café . . ."

Lauren smiled. "Mike or . . . wait, that wasn't his name."

Kayla hadn't meant to mention him but he wouldn't leave her head. And now this. "Someone's following me."

"Then why are we hanging out here? Get your butt inside." Lauren didn't really offer an option that time. She tugged on Kayla's arm and pulled her into the small cottage. Slammed the door behind them and threw the two locks before setting the alarm.

"Uh, he's not here now."

"Who? You know the person who's following you?"

"Matthias."

Lauren spun around to face Kayla. "Talk."

"It's not that simple."

"Oh, please. You've been talking all your life."

Lauren dropped her keys on the table next to the love-seat and headed for the kitchen. "Besides, I'm not asking for your résumé. I just want to know why a guy you've been hanging out and having coffee with is stalking you."

"Maybe it's nothing."

Lauren grabbed two bottles of water and came back to stand in front of Kayla. "Maybe it's something, but I won't be able to tell if you keep talking like a bad spy movie."

"He got weird."

"Oh, my God. It's like you're trying to make me frustrated." Lauren held out one of the bottles. Shook it until Kayla finally grabbed it. "Are we talking handsy or dickish or he put a fork in his hair . . . what?"

That was Lauren. She didn't ruffle. She couldn't be thrown offtrack. And she could shoot a deadly stare like no one Kayla had ever met.

"He knows what I do after work. I don't know how to explain it." She didn't. It all jumbled in her head. "It almost felt like he knew I wasn't always Kayla and was testing me."

"That's more than annoying."

"My past refuses to stay buried."

"This past that clearly includes a stalker." Lauren sighed. "And you still sound like a spy movie. Just so you know."

Kayla stuffed the note into her shorts pocket and grabbed on to the water bottle with both hands. "I'm not trying to be cryptic."

"You're failing, but that doesn't change the facts. We need to call the police. Do you have a last name for this guy?"

It sounded like the most logical step, but Kayla knew better. "That won't work."

"Look, I get that things happened that you can't talk about, or won't or aren't ready to. I respect all of it and am not going to push. But"—Lauren pointed to the chair as she sat down across from it on the loveseat—"I am not okay with you being scared."

Kayla started peeling off the bottle's label. "Look, I—"

"Nope." Lauren eyed the open chair again. "Stop acting like you're going to run and make a Kayla-sized hole in my wall. Sit."

Kayla couldn't help but laugh at that. "You're bossy."

"That's one of my nicer traits." Lauren put her bottle on the coffee table and leaned in with her elbows on her knees. "You are private and tough. I love that about you, but do you know what you're not?"

"What?"

"Running away. From what I can tell you've spent years in hiding and, damn, Kayla, that has to stop. I'm exhausted for you." Lauren sat back on the loveseat. "And you're not going anywhere while you still owe me twenty dollars from that bet about that guy I hired two weeks ago."

"Paul what's-his-name? You told me he gets motion sickness, so I never thought he'd make it on your crew for more than three days." Kayla thought about the water and her stomach flipped over. "Trust me. That constant need to heave is not fun."

"Paul probably would have left if I'd actually made him go out on the boat."

She should have known. "That's cheating."

Lauren tapped a finger to her forehead. "You need to be a smarter gambler."

"Who knew the bet was fixed?" But it made sense. Lauren was hypercompetitive and completely steady. It was what helped her survive an upbringing with a suicidal mother and the shock of a husband who drowned at sea.

Lauren snorted. "As if I'd part with twenty dollars without a fight."

After what felt like a lifetime of tamping down her feelings and refusing to care about anyone deeply enough for the pain of losing them to so much as sting, Kayla's heart ached. With Lauren she'd lowered the wall and now . . . "I'm going to miss you."

Lauren sank even deeper into the loveseat cushions. "You're not, because you're not going anywhere."

"It's not that easy." Though it was cute that she thought she could just order it and make it happen. Kayla used to have that sort of confidence. Then it faded. Now she just operated in survival mode.

"We all have demons, Kayla."

"Not like this." She winced after she said it because it was a jerk move to assume her pain was somehow greater than Lauren's. "Sorry."

But Lauren didn't flinch. She actually smiled. "Give it a week and we'll see if we can't solve this."

A week might be too late. Hell, a day could be too late. Still . . . the temptation to stay and force her stalker into the open. To make him or her finally try to follow through on the threats or maybe stop forever. "Look at you being all optimistic."

"What does this Matthias guy look like?"

It took Kayla a second to catch up in the conversation. Her mind had gone back through the years and all the notes and promises to make her bleed. Now it snapped to the guy in the café. The walking definition of *tall, dark and smoldering*. "Why?"

"So I know to kick him in the balls if I see him."

And she would. Kayla *could* bet on that. "He might not be guilty of anything."

"He scared you. That's enough."

Kayla's mind shifted in a totally different direction. An unwanted one. A hot and dirty one. "Not at first."

"What do you mean?"

"I'm not sure." All Kayla knew was that when she saw him, when she first felt his stare, she needed to stare back. Wanted to strip him down.

Yeah, he was definitely dangerous. She just wasn't sure how.

MATTHIAS HUNG UP his cell and tucked it in his back pocket. His car keys clanged together in his hand as he watched the clouds roll in. He had more than one problem to deal with, but Kayla had his focus now.

He'd put a tracker on her car earlier, lodged it near the back tire. As expected, she didn't go anywhere near the restaurant or their supposed dinner date. He made the mistake of checking in with Garrett, who insisted on tagging along. Now they both stood outside his car, a few houses down from the one Kayla had entered more than a half hour ago.

Damn, real-life surveillance was boring. No wonder he hired people to do this shit now.

But he had to handle this job on his own. He'd promised to check in and give his mother a status. With that done, the air had changed. The thick humidity gave way to a cooler breeze as the spring storm prepared to hit.

Mother. He hadn't thought of anyone as that for most of his life. Even now the word sounded wrong in his head. He got the part about her being young and desperate and alone all those years ago. The issue with drugs. All of it.

Feeling bad about all she'd gone through did not mean he wanted to connect. Not at thirty-four. But he could give her closure on Nick.

Garrett reached for the door on the other side of the car. "Who called?"

"Not your business." Matthias was not in the mood for a game of show-and-tell. He certainly wasn't ready to talk about his mother, or the only way he could think about her—as Mary. Not yet. Not when knowing her was still such a new and not all that pleasant sensation.

She talked about Nick all the time. The sadness and despair pulsed off her seven years after his murder. Except for those moments when her fury took over. She wanted Carrie Gleason—now Kayla—to pay and she expected he would make it happen. Almost demanded it the day after she burst into his life and announced she was his birth mother.

Garrett rapped his knuckles against the hood of the car. "You are a hell of a conversationalist."

"You can always leave."

Garrett tried to open the passenger door but it was locked. "I actually can't since I can't get in the damn car."

When Matthias hit the button and the locks opened, Garrett still didn't move. "How about now?"

"That's no longer an option. I called Wren."

Not a surprise. Matthias figured he wasn't the only one with an obligatory check-in tonight. "And?"

"I explained how you're even worse with women—and other humans in general—than he is." Garrett opened the door. Also took off his suit jacket and hung it on the hook in the backseat. "When I told him about the walk and the messed-up date he told me I might be babysitting you forever. He also said to have bail money ready at all times."

Matthias hated all of it. "You tattled on me?"

"I'm trying to believe you, a grown man, and a lethal one, just used *tattled* in a sentence." Garrett's expression said *what the fuck*, but he didn't actually say the words.

"Admittedly the walk thing was a slip." One that Matthias knew he should have kept to himself. That would teach him to report anything to Garrett.

"Since when do you have slips?"

Almost never. Since he wasn't accustomed to having family issues, or even a family, he wanted to chalk the aberration up to that. But on some level he sensed Kayla was the issue. She was this mystery he wanted to unravel. In bed, out of bed. He actually wanted to have a real dinner date, which made no sense at all.

But he'd already overshared with Garrett and wasn't about to do that again. "I am human."

"I'm pretending you didn't say that." Garrett gave a quick look around them. "For the record, it's not just the walk. It's how blinded you get near Kayla. You're watching her, having coffee chats. I mean, come on. What the hell?"

"I didn't do anything abnormal back at the café." A guy couldn't talk to a woman without everyone having an opinion about it.

"That you think that has me concerned."

"Now you sound like Wren." Matthias hated to admit it, but he wished Wren were there. He might have some newfound female insight. "Did you at least get me a room at the inn? I need some clothes and other items. After a night sleeping in my car, I'm ready for a change."

Garrett made a face. "Fuck you. Am I your travel assistant now?"

The reaction eased some of the frustration pounding inside Matthias. There was something about seeing Garrett, usually in control and cracking jokes, lose his temper that made the world spin right again. "I can continue to sleep in the car, if needed. I'm not soft, like some people."

Garrett scoffed. "Or you could go home. You live less than an hour away."

True, but she was here. Kayla, the one he was sent to track and interrogate. The same one who made his dick twitch just by talking to him. That sexy voice practically licked across his balls.

"I'm staying here." Until he figured this out, got some answers or lost his mind. One of those. "I need to talk with Kayla and I need to make sure she doesn't run."

Garrett shook his head. "Damn. My cat is going to die if we have to stay away that long."

"You have a cat?"

"Cats are cool."

Matthias really couldn't refute that. Any animal that had honed the fuck-you stare like a cat did deserved his admiration. But the rain had started and Matthias wasn't in the mood to stand in a downpour and talk kittens. "The room?"

Garrett took out his phone. "Right. We may as well get used to this town, since it looks like we're staying."

"For now." For however long it took.

CHAPTER 8

Kayla stepped out of the café kitchen the next afternoon and slammed to a halt. The grilled cheese she was carrying slid across the plate, right to the edge, but didn't fall off. No skill involved. Just plain luck, which she hoped meant a streak had finally kicked in.

She'd survived the café's version of a morning rush as some of Lauren's clients came in to pick up their prepurchased boxed lunches. Then the summer camp showed up. Twenty kids in matching red T-shirts, all screaming and jumping and otherwise excited for a day on the water as they ate breakfast and collected their lunches for later. The usual crowd that stopped in after that then buzzed out again.

Now this guy.

She dropped off the sandwich and managed a half smile for the man sitting by himself in the corner booth. A quick circle back and to the counter and a pretend drop on the floor and she spied her gun, needing the reassurance that it hadn't moved. Then she picked up the coffeepot before heading for Matthias. The pot in her hand and the pen in her pocket served as her only weapons. She'd make them be enough.

Fighting back every instinct to take off for the front door, she stayed steady. Walked until she stood right next to him. "Did you get my text?"

He glanced up from his cell. "The one you sent this morning to cancel dinner last night?"

"Something came up." But she did take a second to peek at his cell. Lines of characters. It looked like gibberish.

He put his phone on the table facedown. "Uh-huh."

Fine, they'd do this the hard way. She glanced at the empty booth across from him. "Where's your sidekick?"

The corner of his mouth lifted. "It would drive him apeshit to hear that description, so please call him that."

Just that little bit, the flash of perfectly lined white teeth and the way his face lit up for a second, threw her off. She gave her body a little shake and tightened her grip on the handle of the pot. It would absolutely work as a weapon if she needed it to.

Time to broach the subject. "I shouldn't have made the dinner date."

"Why did you?"

Him being here . . . she had no idea what that meant. He didn't look angry or annoyed. His expression matched the one he'd worn since she met him. Determined and rough around the edges. In control even though she'd treated him kind of shitty yesterday.

So, she went with a partially true response. "I got the sense you were playing a game and I wanted to end it. Maybe send you away with a bit of a sting?"

"But I like the coffee here."

This guy did not pick up on obvious hints. "So?"

His smile grew wider. "Is there anything I can say that won't piss you off?"

"Doubtful."

The tension snapped. She waited for a shot of fear to hit her, but it never happened. She couldn't explain it. Maybe it had something to do with his deep chuckle. It echoed around her, vibrated through her.

"I feel as if I can't win this argument," he said.

Enough. She had to get a grip. She kept finding him a little charming, and that was not okay. Not on top of the wild attraction her burst of fear hadn't killed last night.

Today he wore a white dress shirt, unbuttoned at the top. No suit coat but dark gray pants. The informal business attire didn't fit the rough-and-tumble vibe he gave off and really didn't fit with his choice to eat at a casual sandwich place by the water. Despite that, he looked at ease and self-confident. He didn't blend in because a guy with that face and an intense stare didn't fade into the background. No, he commanded attention, and he sure had hers.

But she noticed more than the clothes and the attitude. The short black hair ruffled either by the leftover wind from last night's storm or his fingers. Eyes so dark she couldn't see his pupils. The broad shoulders. Yeah, those were tough to miss since they took up most of his side of the booth.

"You know I take walks. How? Are you watching me?" She couldn't ignore that fact or afford to downplay it.

"Nothing nefarious. I saw you go two days ago and thought it might be a good way for us to talk." He shrugged. "Clearly mentioning it made you antsy."

She needed to keep her defenses up and in place until he either left town or she understood his motives. Something about him didn't add up. She wasn't buying the in-town-working-and-flirting-on-the-side story of his. For now, she'd keep the attitude. She could always surrender it later, when she knew she was safe.

"What do you really want?" She leaned against the outside edge of the booth across from him. "And if you say coffee, I'm dumping this pot on you."

He glanced to where she tapped her fingernails against the side of the pot. "Fair enough."

"Yeah, I know." When he didn't say anything, she tried again. "I'm still waiting for an explanation."

He nodded toward the open seat across from him. "Sit down and have a cup of coffee."

She'd bet that kind of thing usually worked in his world. He ordered and people obeyed. Not her. "Nope."

"Why?"

"You may be *a* boss, but you're not my boss." No, that title belonged to a very eccentric and lovable artist, an older woman who was out of town taking care of her even older mother. Kayla guessed Cecelia was about seventy-five. Since Cecelia insisted her mother had given birth later in life, Kayla had no idea how old the mother could be.

Cecelia checked in every other day, and the idea of running and leaving her without someone to keep

Gerald in line in the kitchen and the bills paid was another source of guilt for Kayla. She hadn't thought about the problem in her flurry of activity last night. She'd thought about it all day so far. The café opened from seven to three. Breakfast and lunch but no real dinner six days a week, which left a lot of shifts to cover if she raced out of town.

"And coffee isn't possible because I'm working." She actually hadn't meant to add that. Not at all.

He leaned forward and balanced his elbows on the edge of the table. "Then agree to talk with me on a break. We've done that several times." He held up his hands in what looked like mock surrender. "No ulterior motives. Promise."

The lack of anger in his voice struck her. Most guys who were left waiting in a restaurant would not come back for a potential second whopping. She'd never describe him as relaxed, but he didn't pulse with rage. He remained the imposing figure with a husky voice and strangely welcoming look in his eyes who'd intrigued her from the start.

She didn't trust him, but for the first in a long time she didn't trust her instincts either. Her read on him kept bouncing and shifting, and she hated the confused sensation. "I can't figure out if I'm supposed to hit you with a frying pan and call the police or . . . something else."

"I vote we try the 'something else' option." He sat with his fingers linked, palms together.

Her gaze bounced down to his watch. She'd noticed

it before. Nothing fancy. A black band that didn't look like leather. It was big with a dark face. "If this is some big revenge dating move, you should know it sucks."

"I like to think I can be smooth."

She hummed. "That's not my experience."

His smile came roaring back. "Let me buy you that cup of coffee and prove I'm not a scary guy. Right here. In the open. You can hold a pan, the coffeepot, a spoon. I don't care."

God, why was she tempted? Less than four days ago something in his affect, in the way he moved and how anger blanketed him, warned her. The suffocating tension had her ready to run, and she would have if not for the calming talk from Lauren. But now the thought of sitting down and talking to him tugged at her. Maybe he was a bad guy or one of the good ones. She was just so tired of not being able to recognize one from the other and constantly looking over her shoulder.

Still, she'd lived hard for seven years and was still breathing because she was careful. Exactly because she did not give in to idle curiosity. "Coffee's not a great idea."

"What are you afraid of?"

"Not you." But his unblinking stare did start a trembling low and deep inside her.

He didn't move except to nod. "Good to know."

"Really? Because I got the impression you wanted me scared." He sure as hell had her all jumpy.

"You don't strike me as someone who shakes easily." His gaze wandered over her, down her body.

She put a second hand on the side of the coffeepot to keep it from rattling. "Very perceptive of you."

"Thank you."

"Let's just say I have trust issues." Understatement of the decade.

"Hello." His sidekick slid in without a word. He stood next to her, glancing down at her. "Is he bothering you?"

"No," said the "he" in question.

She shrugged. "Sort of."

"I tend to believe her." The sidekick held out his hand. "I'm Garrett."

She took it then glanced at Matthias. "After a failed date attempt last night—"

"Caused by you."

"—Matthias was asking me out for coffee."

Garrett's eyebrow lifted. "Sorry I missed that. Did he have any finesse?"

"Almost none."

This time Garrett nodded. "Just as I feared."

"Shut the fuck up."

Ignoring Matthias's outburst, she focused on Garrett. He struck her as the chatty one anyway. "Are you in town for business, too?"

"Why are you asking him?"

She finally gave in and talked to Matthias again. "I sense he'll actually answer me. You, I'm guessing you'll play word games that don't really tell me anything."

"She totally gets you, man," Garrett said.

Matthias glared. "Don't help."

A weight lifted off her. If these two planned to hurt

her or grab her, she guessed they would have done it by now. And they wouldn't be wasting time joking in a café in Annapolis.

With that little bit of emotional freedom, she relaxed. She didn't quite slip back into flirting mode like she uncharacteristically had when she'd first met the boss man, but she no longer strangled the coffeepot handle in a death grip. "The suits. The serious expressions. The repeated stops for coffee here even though you don't exactly look like boating types."

Matthias had the nerve to look offended. "I'm fine on a boat."

That made one of them. "Really? They make me sick."

He pointed in the general direction of the marina. "You said that before, but I will remind you the water is right there."

"The café isn't on it." She didn't get people's fascination with being in the water. Let the fish have it. *Stay off their turf* was her motto.

"We're from the DC area, here on business," Garrett said.

Now, that was interesting. She looked at Garrett again, hoping to keep him talking. "At the marina?"

"Yes."

Uh-huh. No way. "I believed you right until there."

She waited for the nerves to come back, but they didn't. She stood there, coffeepot in hand, feeling in control and free from panic. It was a stark contrast to last night when she'd sat in a chair in the middle of her small studio, fully dressed and listening for any stray noise.

"Smart woman." Matthias grew serious and stiffened when the guy with the grilled cheese across the room dropped something on the floor that made a clanking sound. Then he looked at her again. "Now will you have that coffee?"

Garrett made a strangled sound. "So smooth."

"I almost feel sorry for him." She didn't, really, but poking at the guy appealed to her on some level. Probably had something to do with trying to shake his in-control exterior.

Garrett winced. "He is kind of bad at this."

"I did fine for a few days and then . . ." Matthias shook his head. "Well, never mind."

"I would trust her to say that, but not you," Garrett said.

Matthias stared back at him. "You could wait in the car."

She enjoyed the byplay more than she would have thought possible. "And not very friendly."

Matthias exhaled nice and loud. "So, yes to coffee? We'll try again."

Garrett shook his head. "Wow."

New customers filed into the café. A couple sat at one table and two older men who came every day and made a piece of pie last two hours found a booth. Their presence meant it was time to get back to work, which she almost regretted.

Matthias kept looking at her and she took pity on him. He likely didn't want or need her charity, but he was going to get it. She gave in. "It's raining on and off, so I'll probably take a break in here after I handle these folks. If you're still around, you can buy me coffee." But she was not dropping her guard. Not today or any other day. "Just keep in mind you're on probation this time. I'll be holding the frying pan the entire time and I have great aim."

"I think I missed something," Garrett mumbled.

Matthias never broke eye contact with her. "I'll be here."

"I somehow knew you'd say that."

HE'D TRULY DODGED a bullet. Forget dinner; it had taken some fast talking to get another shot just at coffee. They'd taken a huge step back.

An hour later, Matthias managed to convince Garrett to go back to the room and work. Threatening him helped. So did Garrett's apparent realization that he could use the time to give Wren an annoying status report. Matthias was sure he'd get a smartass text about what Wren heard any second.

But, for now, Matthias was exactly where he wanted to be. In a café booth away from the window. One of only four occupied tables and the perfect spot for him to watch Kayla pack up what looked like carryout containers.

Once she had everything bagged and the food and coffee served, she headed over to his booth. Without him asking, she slid onto the bench across from him. Even put her foot up on the edge of the seat beside his thigh.

She flattened her palms against the table. "I'm still on duty, so if I jump up that doesn't necessarily mean you're in trouble."

He didn't have any coffee but decided not to point that out. "Understood."

"So . . ." She looked at her fingernails before glancing up at him again.

He had no idea what that meant. "What?"

She shrugged. "You wanted to talk."

Since the second he'd seen her, he'd wanted to touch her and taste her and see what she wore under that slim uniform. Now he wasn't sure how to respond without sending her racing away again. Just proved how fucked up his mind was right now, and he could not figure out why he kept spinning over her. "Right."

Her foot dropped to the floor but she didn't rush away or even sit up straight. "You do know how, right?"

Thinking about her foot led to thinking about her leg . . . and he had no idea what they were even talking about. "You lost me."

"Is this supposed to be a date or something else?"

He decided not to put a name on it and skipped forward instead. "I'm concerned."

"You have my attention."

The fact she didn't stall or evade impressed him. "I saw the way you reacted to me yesterday."

She winced. "You creeped me out."

There was that word again. Sure, he could be intimidating, but he saw that as a positive.

She continued to sit there. No fidgeting. No shifting around. It was as if someone had stapled her butt to the seat.

"I really like smart women." He had no idea why he

mentioned that. It was the truth, but this hardly seemed like the time.

"For the record, you still sound a little creepy."

Now she was just trying to annoy him. That had to be it.

He decided to ignore the attempt. "I run a security business. I can sense when people are in trouble and need help. My impression was that you were one of those people."

She sat up straighter and that one foot slipped to the floor. "Your Spidey senses malfunctioned."

His mind went blank. "My what?"

"Spiderman."

He'd somehow lost control of the conversation. "Still confused."

"You creeped me out and—"

He groaned. Wasn't quiet about it either. He might even institute a new office rule that no one was allowed to say *creepy* in his presence for at least a year. "Maybe we could use another word?"

"Anyway, I reacted to your odd *mood*. These smart women you claim to like so much also tend to be careful. I'm one of those."

No matter what really happened with her years ago, careful was a wise move. "I get it."

A man at one of the tables signaled for her and she nodded in return before facing him again. "So, are we done here?"

"Sure." He waited until she stood up. "Now we can start the actual date."

CHAPTER 9

The guy had staying power. She had to give him that. That was fine because she had a knife strapped to her thigh. He had his priorities, she had hers.

She'd hung the CLOSED sign on the door and needed to finish up in the kitchen. That meant unloading the under-the-counter commercial dishwasher. As the unofficial manager, she also had some bookkeeping to do, but that could wait until she didn't have a super tall hottie hovering over her.

She opened the drawer and started taking the glasses out. She planned to run through this and usher him out. For safety reasons, she made an effort to say hello to the guys on the pier stacking the contents from their most recent fishing run. She even sent a text to Lauren, along with a sneakily taken photo of Matthias, as a sort of proof-of-life thing.

Instead of coming up with an excuse or sitting down and watching her work, Matthias rolled up his sleeves and joined her in unloading. "Do I put them on the counter or somewhere else?"

She was too stunned to spit out more than a grumble.

He froze. "Is there a third option that I'm not aware

of? I could sit them on the floor, but I guarantee I'll step on at least one."

She didn't have any trouble imagining him stomping around as glass shattered. Not that he was the stumbling type. Quite the opposite, actually. He had perfect posture and seemed fully in control of . . . well, everything, all the time.

The long leg, long torso thing kept drawing her attention. Flat stomach or not, he wasn't a little man. Watching him handle the glasses, holding them with two fingers and setting them on the counter with a gentle clink, made her smile. She guessed he farmed out this kind of work at home.

"The option I expected was for you to make me do everything while you explain how I could do it better if I did it your way." That's kind of how it worked around here with Cecelia gone. The cook, Gerald, believed his role started and stopped with food. She and the part-time cleaning staff handled everything else, except when he wanted to offer advice, which was always.

"Huh." He returned to unloading. "Maybe we should talk about the men you know. They sound like they suck."

Not her favorite subject. Being on the run meant no real dating, which meant either hooking up with a guy who meant nothing or using her hand. She'd tried both and after the short-term thrill wore off, the emptiness settled back in. "That would be a short conversation."

His head shot up and his gaze met hers. "I find it hard to believe you don't date."

"Why?"

"Do you own a fucking mirror?"

The frustration building in her gut melted away and the harsh memories faded. "Are you back to flirting?"

She reached across the counter and turned down Gerald's radio. If they were going to talk, she preferred if they didn't scream at each other.

"I'm relieved to hear you noticed the first time."

Noticed. Liked it. Panicked about it. Yeah, she'd hit the whole spectrum of emotions on that one. "These eyes see everything."

"Good to know."

"Including the lack of a wedding ring." The words spilled out before she could hold them back. She was about to say something sarcastic to cover up the moment when a very sexy, very confident smile spread across his mouth.

"Definitely single."

She noticed he didn't ask about her status. That meant he didn't know or didn't care. Could also suggest he wasn't interested. But then why did he sneak a peek at her bare legs every time he reached into the drawer?

Either he was complex and she couldn't read him, or he had very simple tastes and she was trying to make this whole situation too hard. Every time she let her mind wander and thought about how hot and dirty they might be together, she remembered his scowl and menacing voice after the unexplained anger set in during their first meeting. He'd made her want to bolt then, and she was not ready to discount her initial instincts when it came to him now.

They worked in comfortable silence for a few minutes as they unloaded the remaining contents onto the counter. When they finished, she closed the door and stood facing him, not sure what to do next. The rumbling panic had left her gut. She almost missed it compared to her current state of confusion. She wanted to know more about him, didn't want him to leave. Both of those ticked her off.

"This is a strange date," he said in a deep voice that bounced around the small room.

She wondered how long it would take for him to say something else. He made it almost four minutes, which she had to admit impressed her. Nothing about him so far suggested he appreciated silence.

Still, she saw no reason to make this date easy on him. "You're not that bad."

That would teach him to basically demand one and linger until her choices were to kick him out again or concede. She guessed she could have ignored him, but he wasn't exactly an easy guy to overlook.

He shot her an unreadable expression. "What are you talking about?"

Well, he certainly wasn't lying to impress her. On some level that probably was a good thing. "It was a joke."

He rested a hand against the counter and focused on her. "Are you sure?"

Turning around, she leaned her butt right next to his and looked at him. Really studied every inch, which was not exactly a hardship. Even all ruffled from sitting around waiting for her, he looked pretty delicious. The whole dark hair and pale skin combination appealed to her. The air of grumpiness should turn her off, but it didn't. She had no idea why.

Her college years—the first time, before everything collapsed—had been filled with sunny, blond outdoorsy types. He was the exact opposite. So serious. Sometimes bearing an expression of boredom, sometimes blank. Always smoldering, and that's what kept her insides jumping.

She shouldn't be attracted. He shouldn't be here. And she got the distinct impression he wasn't telling the truth. She didn't know how this would play out with *both* of them lying about who they really were.

"You're sort of a literal guy." She crossed her arms over her chest and continued staring.

"You mean humorless."

And a bit touchy. "Did I say that?"

He exhaled. From anyone else it might have risen to the level of a dramatic sigh. From him it had a touch of *are you kidding* woven into it. "No matter what word you use, it's not the first time I've heard the complaint."

With that, he looked away. Started stacking the glasses in their place on the open shelf.

But she wasn't quite ready to let it go. Not that she really knew what they were talking about, but she liked the sound of his voice and the way he moved. If he left now she'd be a little disappointed. That was a big self-realization, since she spent most of her time convincing Lauren and Cecelia—and herself—that she preferred being alone. But that wasn't true. It had never been true.

"I wasn't complaining."

Some of the tension left his face. "Now, that is unusual. A great many people spend a lot of time telling me how difficult I am."

"Do you care?"

"Not even a little."

She would have bet that would be his answer. And, unlike her, he actually meant it when he said it.

"I'm sure Garrett is careful about telling you." He didn't strike her as a guy who held back. The few times she'd gotten near their table he'd come off as amused. He lacked Matthias's streak of darkness. "Being his boss and all."

"Not."

She'd been about to race onto another topic but that stopped her. "Excuse me?"

"He doesn't work for me. He's on loan." Matthias actually rolled his eyes. "Whether I want him or not."

So many questions popped into her head. "Businesses loan employees out?"

"Not smart ones."

He hadn't moved closer. Not really. He stood there, at least two feet away, with a palm balanced against the counter. But as he watched her, his gaze bouncing down to her mouth now and then, the air closed in on her. She could have sworn the walls were farther away two seconds ago.

Inside she felt all panty and short of breath. She refused to let that show on the outside. "Anyone ever tell you how you talk in circles?"

"I'm actually known for being pretty direct."

That time he inched closer. They didn't touch, but one shift—if she moved her arm even a little—and she could brush against him. She should hate that. She hated that she didn't hate it.

Without warning, the fan above her head whirled to life. A rush of cool air blew over her. Talk about perfect timing. "I'm going to find another topic."

"That sounds like a good call."

She nodded toward the empty sink. "Do you regularly do dishes?"

He shrugged. "I have skills."

That sounded like a warning bell that another conversational dead end lay ahead. She couldn't tell. Pity for him she wasn't in the mood to be ignored or brushed away. "Right now your skills seem to consist of standing."

"I can take a hint." He glanced around but hesitated on the shelves to his left. One by one he set the glasses on top of each other and lined the clean ones up in perfectly aligned stacks with the ones already sitting there.

"You're good at this." When he turned to look at her, she shook her head. "No, don't stop. Keep stacking."

"Is there any reason I'm doing this alone?"

"I'm supervising." Except for a moment's regret at both using him and engaging in some serious objectification while she mentally stripped him, she had no intention of pitching in. This setup worked for her.

"I see."

She did move that time. Inched closer. Leaned in close enough to his side to smell him. She couldn't place the scent. Like wood and orange . . . very distinctive, just like him. "You don't look like the cleanup type."

"I've taken care of myself for a long time."

Well, that sort of qualified as an answer. "So, no fleet of assistants or household staff?"

He set down the glass with a clink that registered louder than the others. "Are you kidding?"

Once again she seemed to be wading into touchy territory. "You don't exactly look poor." She waved a hand in front of him, taking in everything from his shirt to his shoes. "Of course, I can't tell if you're wealthy either. You're a bit hard to read. If you know what I mean." When he continued to stare, she launched into more babbling. "Like, you look nice in the suit, and I'm thinking that impressive sedan outside is yours, but who knows."

The amusement was right there in his eyes and around his mouth. "Let me know if you want me to jump into this conversation at any point."

Okay, that was her clue to stop. But . . . "You really do all your own cooking and cleaning and that sort of thing?"

"I don't like people in my house."

He'd elevated the nonanswer to an art form. Every time she ventured in and tried to pick away at his rough exterior, that shield, he threw up another. Not with nasty words, but he verbally blocked anytime she got close to anything personal.

She understood the tendency, since she employed the diversionary tactic as often as possible. But he was on her turf. He kept coming back, which meant she'd keep banging on the door. "Is that an answer?"

"Of course."

Sure, of course. "I guess I should have figured you'd kind of duck."

"Meaning?"

Only inches separated them now. When the hell had that happened? "You just seem so . . ."

"Yes?" He put a finger behind his ear. "Please finish that thought."

"Maybe I shouldn't."

"I'm not moving until you do."

"You're, well, formidable." When his head shot back she mentally rewound the conversation to make sure she'd used the right word. But, yeah. That's what she meant. "Why did your mouth drop open?"

"Your word choice."

"It's perfectly sound." She could think of rougher descriptions. To her that one seemed pretty benign.

"I'm not sure that's what you want a woman to call you while on a date. Or at all, really. A business associate, maybe."

She got stuck on the first comment. "This isn't a date."

It was a knee-jerk response but the right one. This could not be a date. She could not do this when she was ready to take off with nothing more than her packed go-bag and a preplanned strategy to get to a new location.

"Clue me in." He leaned forward "What is it then? We can call it whatever you want."

Good grief. His breath brushed right over her cheek.

"Fair question." And once she could breathe again she might answer it. "But since I don't know your last name or where you grew up, I'm thinking this is more of a case of you trying to prove you're not really creepy."

He groaned. "I'm growing to hate that word."

The deep sound vibrated through her. Actually spun right from her head to her toes. No matter what else was true, this guy was dangerous in a shake-up-your-world way. "Which is why I plan to keep using it."

"Interesting answer."

"If you're looking for a pushover, you have the wrong woman." Silence screamed through the room as soon as the words left her mouth. Lord, why had she said that? Before she could fix it, he opened his mouth.

"Clarke."

The word rattled around in her head but didn't connect to anything. "I'm going to need an explanation on that response."

"Matthias Clarke." He stood up straight. Right there, right in front of her with only a thin layer of air separating them. "I grew up in a bunch of places, mostly in Delaware, then moved to the DC area for college. Now I run Quint Enterprises."

She wanted to climb all over him. She, serious careful she, wanted that more than anything. "Okay."

"I'm in town for business but you make me want to make time for pleasure."

She tried to ignore the way her stomach tumbled at that last part. He wasn't the first smooth-talker she'd met. The most interesting, yes, because he didn't seem to even try. Just every once in a while he came out with a phrase that made her want to wrap her legs around his waist and hold on.

Go figure.

She swallowed a few times. Waited to make sure her voice would be steady before she talked again. "That's a lot of information."

"You asked."

"I'm not sure I did, but I'm happy to know." With her brain scrambled and her control sputtering, she grabbed on to the one part of the explanation she could remember. "What's Quint?"

His gaze swept over her face. "I thought I already told you."

Now she feared she'd somehow blanked out for part of this little talk. "Indulge me."

"Private security."

The words crashed into her. The heat left her body and a cool wariness set in. "You're coughing up more details but you know those words still don't really mean anything, right?"

"I have sixty-three employees who would suggest differently." A bit of gruffness edged into his voice.

There it was. He didn't look angry, didn't even move, but his defenses definitely rose. She could almost see them click into place. "Ah, I hit a nerve."

"No."

"You're angry."

"You would know if I were, and I'm not."

Like that, the mood changed. Gone was the easy banter. She tried to call up her memory of the room. Where everything was. What she could use as a weapon, if needed. Though she didn't feel danger. Something else had eased between them.

This guy's dating skills might be rustier than hers. "Is that supposed to be comforting? Because you got all clenched."

For the first time since she'd met him, he shifted his weight around. He moved with a minimum of effort. He didn't waste energy. But something had him visibly on edge. "The business is a huge part of who I am."

That wasn't really the answer she expected. She'd heard responses like that before. This close to power-hungry Washington, DC, she expected that. But up until now nothing about him had struck her as ordinary.

But she could handle this conversation. It was safer anyway. "So, your job defines you."

He touched his palm to the counter. Next removed the towel from the bar next to the stove. It snapped but he didn't seem to notice. "Are you taking psychology classes or something?"

Well, actually . . . "Why?"

"The way you phrased the job question. I had a flashback."

He'd gotten really close to providing personal insight right there. She tried to draw it out. "To what?"

"You act like being devoted to my business is a weird thing."

She hated the pivot. She'd knocked right up against something interesting and he'd moved away. It was hard to imagine him in therapy. But then it was hard for her to imagine how she would have survived those rough years after the murders without it.

"Yeah. I mean, I hear that sort of thing about 'business being my life' all the time. I just don't get it."

The comment wasn't a poke. She didn't want to start a fight. She honestly thought work-as-life didn't make any sense. Maybe it was because she'd come so close to losing hers. All she knew was that being that singularly focused on something that brought stress was beyond her. She had enough stress.

He looked around the room. Touched the frying pan sitting on the stove. "You're not tied to this job?"

The words ran through her head and she took them apart, looking for judgment. She didn't hear any, so she answered honestly instead of coming out firing and defending. "It's a way to pay the rent. Decent and respectable, but I'm not sure it says much about who I am or how I got here."

"I get that."

She doubted it. "Really?"

"How would you define you?"

That was easy. Dead easy. "As a survivor." When he didn't say anything, that defending thing kicked in. "Does my answer offend you?"

"The exact opposite."

"Really?"

"It sounds pretty damn sexy."

Tension zipped back into the room. Not the angry kind. No, the let's-use-this-counter-for-fun-times kind. The force of it whipped her up and shook her. Stunned her and left her stammering. "Oh."

He nodded. "Really fucking sexy."

No one had ever told her that before. Sure, a few odd murder-groupie types had found her before she got better at covering her tracks. In the years right after, journalists had pretended to be something else a few times and asked her out as a way to establish contact and build a story.

But being liked for who she was and all she'd overcome was not a sensation she ever got to indulge in. Not even now, because he didn't know the truth. No one in Annapolis knew.

She fell back on sarcasm because some days it was all she had. "I smell like pie and I think I have a french fry in my hair. Is that the sort of thing that does it for you?"

"Apparently." He didn't smile. Didn't frown. But he looked at her, his gaze dancing over her like he wanted to lick every inch.

Talk about sexy. "I don't get you at all."

"You've made that clear."

Still no anger in his voice, and she knew because she listened and searched for it. She knew how to handle that emotion. This, the intensity of his focus and excitement building in her stomach, had her stumbling. "You aren't telling me much about you that I couldn't read in an employment file."

He took a step. "Do you want to know more?"

This close she could see light brown flecks in his otherwise near-black eyes. And interest. She sure saw that. Felt it in every cell as the heat from his body rolled off him and pummeled her.

"It's too early to tell." She lifted her arm to pretend to look at a watch then remembered she wasn't wearing one. When her hand fell back, it landed against his arm. Balanced there.

Her voice sounded all breathy and swoony . . . and that wasn't weird and embarrassing or anything.

"Would it make a difference if I told you I've wondered what it would be like to kiss you from the first time you poured my coffee?"

She almost choked. "Coffee is a thing with you."

She'd hook him up to an IV if he promised to get on with it.

"Not before meeting you."

"I think you mentioned a kiss?" She tried to swallow but found that didn't work either. Her entire body and most of her brain had abandoned her. Nothing settled her jumping nerves.

"That's the G-rated version of what I want." He touched her then. Dragged the backs of his fingers over her cheeks in a gentle caress.

"Is there an R-rated version?" Because she really wanted to jump ahead to that one.

He slipped his thumb over her bottom lip. Back and forth. "Fuck yeah."

She was never going to survive this. "Let's start with G and see how it goes."

One second she saw the room behind him and the light above. The next he leaned in, blocking her view of everything, and his mouth covered hers.

He kissed like she knew he'd kiss. With all that power and confidence, he didn't waste time on little pecks. He swooped in, captured her mouth with his, and her head spun. Lips traveled over lips. The kiss was firm and sure, coaxing and full of promise.

Hell, if this was G-rated she could not imagine what

happened when he got his clothes off. But now she wanted to know.

When his tongue slipped over hers, her knees buckled. Strong hands held her while they roamed down her arms and around her shoulders. He touched her, kissed her, surrounded her.

Their breathing mixed and when she nipped at his bottom lip, he groaned. Then he took over again. Pressing his hard body against hers as his mouth crossed over hers again and again. A buzzing sensation filled her head. She craved more. Too much.

In a moment of self-preservation she lifted her head, but the daze wouldn't clear. "Alrighty then."

His forehead touched hers as his chest rose and fell on harsh breaths. "Only okay?"

She couldn't seem to unclench her fingers. She had his shirt balled in her fists. "No."

"Then we should close up and get out of here."

That was a terrible idea. Stupid and half dangerous, and she was neither. A kiss shouldn't turn her head any more than a strong chin did. But she wanted this, for her and just for now. So . . . "Let's go."

CHAPTER 10

Between the kiss and the obvious green light, Matthias's usual control abandoned him. He pushed back on the search for answers, and concentrated on the need punching inside his gut.

This was about getting laid. Pure and simple. Nothing more. He didn't seek out danger or have a thing for mysterious women. It had been a while for him, and the attraction to Kayla had been immediate. This was about two people, bodies, heat and a much-needed release.

He silently repeated that mantra even as his brain screamed for him to pull back. He should question her, put the truth out there . . . he should, but every time he opened his mouth to put the brakes on he stopped again. He wanted her with a force that was kicking his ass.

This could be a rare case of putting his needs first. He never took anything for himself. He did what he was supposed to do: got the job done. He found the answers and made the hard calls. Spent hours locked in his office and in strategy meetings. Trained, excelled and thrived. That's who he was, or who he'd been ever since he trained with Quint and met Wren and the others more than a decade ago. Before that he was on a downward spiral. Since then, he took pride in being rock solid.

He was only in Annapolis now, on Kayla's trail, out of a sense of loyalty to people he'd never known. He'd vowed to get the proof he needed, write her off as a killer and then turn her over to the police and walk away, but he couldn't get there.

He'd dealt every single day with murderers and socio- paths who enjoyed hurting others, sometimes within the law and sometimes not. He'd spent his life assess- ing people and ferreting out liars. She could be one, and he'd looked for her assuming she was one, but that voice inside him said something else was going on here. Something they should talk about . . . but not now. He wasn't in the mindset to be rational or smart. His usually reliable common sense vanished as he watched her move.

Damn, he wanted her. Here, at her place, in his room, in the inn. Hell, he didn't care where so long as he got inside her, and soon.

Just as he was about to reach for her again, she turned away. For a second he thought she might kick him out, but she grabbed her keys. She finished closing up while he followed around behind her, forcing his hands to stay at his sides and not touch her.

When she headed to the door that emptied onto the pier he followed there, too. He wasn't a complete dumbass. When a woman who looked like her, and had the balls to stand up to him like she did, made it clear she wanted sex, he didn't say no. Problem was he had to fight the urge to throw her over his shoulder and carry her back to her place. He doubted she would appreciate being hauled around in front of the people on the dock. He wasn't an animal—not quite—so he could hold off. For a few seconds.

Good thing getting to her house took less than three minutes. He'd toyed with the idea of checking the place out while she was at work this morning. Garrett insisted there were too many people at the marina to risk it. Said it several times in different ways.

Matthias finally agreed to hold off, mostly to get Garrett to shut up. But now he'd see inside her apartment. Not that Matthias intended to search it. He had other plans for the next hour.

Somehow he managed not to touch her again during the short walk. He reached for her a few times but pulled back. His steps thudded against the wood as they walked along the pier. The steady clanking of metal against metal rang out as the boats bobbed in the water next to him. The smell of salt and fish wound around him.

He considered himself a city guy. The whole life-on-the-sea thing didn't make much sense to him. Even now the warm sun beat down on him and sweat had his dress shirt sticking to his lower back. People weaved in and out, some making quick meaningless conversation as they passed.

He quickly discovered he wasn't really a mindless "hello" kind of guy either. He was barely a sunshine kind of guy. He preferred the secure walls of his office. The quiet of his house.

He spied the boat rental shop before they got there.

The two-story white building had a fake run-down look to it, the kind that came when wealthy people tried to make things look quaint. That's sort of how he felt about Annapolis in general. Nice to visit, if one was the visiting type, which he wasn't.

She said hello to a few more people while he settled for nodding. For a woman who was supposed to be blending in, she seemed to live her life in the open. People knew her by name, or the one she went by now. Many waved and even more stared. Her being with a guy in a suit appeared to fascinate many.

Matthias had no idea what to think about any of that, so he filed the reactions away to analyze later. But there was no question the idea of her being a recluse and on the run fell apart in his mind. She was sunny and friendly and hot as fuck. Even now as they headed up the stairs that ran along the side of the building he had a front-row seat to that ass. It was even better close up. The way her uniform skimmed her thigh had his brain misfiring. Letting her go first may have been a mistake because all he could think about was those sleek legs wrapped around his waist.

He cleared his throat, tried to act like he'd actually been with a woman before. "How did you find this place?"

She glanced at him as she stopped on the small landing just outside her door. "The café owner also owns this business. She basically owns the marina. Her other renter moved out, so she offered it to me when I took the job."

"That's quite a perk." That would teach him to think excellent training, health insurance and retirement amounted to a good benefits package for his employees.

"I think she was trying to make up for the shocking low pay and high level of responsibility that came with the position. She's not really in town all that much, so most of the noncooking work falls to me." Kayla smiled as she turned the key on the first lock. Then she undid the second. Finally she pressed in a number code on the modern lock that looked far too new and impressive for the state of the building and low crime rate in the area.

Now, that was more like it. Triple security. She was either afraid of someone or hiding from something. He wondered if the answer was both.

He was about to point out the redundancy but stopped. The wrongness hit him before she turned the knob.

"Wait a second." He reached out and put a hand over hers. The keys jangled in her fingers but she didn't move.

He could feel eyes on him. Not from the curious types like the people in the rental place or some of the guys in the marina who openly gawked as he walked with Kayla. This was a sensation borne from experience. One that came from being hunted.

She looked at his hand where it covered hers then stared up at him. "What's wrong?"

"Not sure." He inhaled and let instinct take over. He didn't know where, but he knew it was happening. Someone watched them from a safe distance. Far enough to prevent a physical attack but likely close enough to hit them with a bullet.

"Is this some sort of game?"

"Stop talking." He needed her to stop talking so he could concentrate.

She jerked her hand away and stepped back as far as the flimsy railing would allow. "Excuse me."

He didn't want to look around and tip the watcher off, but he didn't want her in danger either. With a hand on her elbow, he pulled her toward the door. "Get inside."

She tried to shirk out of his hold but it didn't work. "I'm not a fan of bossy men."

"Now, Kayla." He pushed on the door with his palm. "I'm not kidding."

"You better have a good—" Her voice cut off as he shut the door behind them. "Oh, my God."

He spun around ready to attack and defend. The studio looked as if it had been struck by a cyclone. He could see every inch, including most of the bathroom, since the door stood open. Smashed furniture, ripped cushions. Shredded papers everywhere. Food thrown on the floor and the refrigerator door hanging open. But the worst was the warning written on the wall above the loveseat.

YOUR TURN TO DIE.

"What the fuck?" He stepped closer to investigate. The harsh smell of the spray paint hit him first, then he spotted the can on top of what remained of a pillow.

He sent a quick message to Garrett to get over there and be careful about it. As he finished typing, the quiet stillness behind him had him glancing over his shoulder. Kayla stood there with a gun aimed right at him. He had no idea where she got it or why whoever attacked this place hadn't taken it. Those were questions for later. Now he needed to calm her down.

"Kayla, what are you doing?" He lifted his arms as he turned to face her. Not because he planned to acquiesce but because she didn't need another reason to shoot him.

He couldn't tell her skill level, but she knew how to hold a gun and her arms didn't shake. None of that made him feel better about the chances of accidentally having his junk blown off.

"I tried to push my doubts aside and just enjoy the night, but . . . I should have known."

"Kayla."

"This was you." Her voice held steady but her eyes were wild.

Forget that the leap of logic didn't make sense. He didn't want her mind moving in that direction. "No, I was at the café with you."

"You came into town and it started all over again."

"What's 'it,' Kayla? Talk to me." She hovered on the edge. He could see it in every line of her body. Fear and fury mixed inside her, and her mind had switched to protection. The instinct didn't worry him. The idea of having a hole blown through him did.

"You know." She didn't move the gun around or lose her cool.

Yeah, she'd had training of some kind. That was

good news, but verbal responses like that weren't going to get them anywhere. He needed her to focus on him and believe he could help her. "Someone is after you."

"You."

He couldn't exactly deny that. "I didn't do this. I would never do this, and I think you know that."

"How could I? I've known you five damn days."

"True, but you were going to let me touch you. Let me inside you." Her fingers tightened on the gun, but he kept talking. Maintained the soothing tone as he inched closer without giving away his movements. "There's a reason for that. Trust that instinct and hear me when I say this wasn't me."

The gun didn't waver but the frantic vibe she was giving off died down a little. "Tell me who you really are."

He continued to hold his hands up. "Matthias Clarke. Owner of Quint Enterprises. You can look all of that up and—"

"You know what I'm asking."

There was no way in hell he was telling her the truth right now. Not with a weapon in her hands. "We can talk about this if you lower the gun."

The last of the crazed fear left her eyes. A desperate sort of calm replaced it. "No way."

Something had changed. She'd downshifted to a place where she could at least listen, maybe hear reason. He watched the change come over her. The stiffness didn't ease but the tension whipping through the room had. "I don't want to argue with you, but I don't want that going off by accident."

"I know how to shoot."

"I'm not sure that makes me feel better." But it did. If her instructor or whoever taught her had been any good, she knew to keep her finger off the trigger unless she planned on firing. So far she had.

He had two guns and a knife on him but had no intention of bringing any of them out unless absolutely necessary. He needed to disarm her in the least intrusive way and figure out what was happening. Gaining her trust, even a little bit of it, would be a bonus.

And they had bigger problems to deal with. At first glance someone who didn't know better might think the scene was scattered and the person following her would be unfocused and easy to catch. But he did know better. He'd analyzed rooms like this for more than a decade. He knew how to read violence. This looked messy, but the person stalking Kayla wanted her terrified and on the move. This was calculated.

Could be she was a murderer and deserved the shaking up, or something else could be happening here. Either way, he'd figure it out.

"I'm going to put my hands down and—"

She shook her head. "No."

He did it anyway. Lowered them slowly and kept them well away from his body to keep from spooking her. "From the first time I met you I knew you were scared and possibly running from something. Do you remember that?"

"They didn't find me this time until you came around. I can add two plus two." She eased up on the hold on the gun. It now aimed at his chest instead of his head.

He didn't like losing that part of him any better than his head. "If I wanted to scare you or hurt you I've had a hundred chances, Kayla. We were all alone in that café."

"People were just outside and would have heard you."

"That wouldn't have stopped me." An understatement, but he knew he should end the explanation there. Describing how he would have bundled her up or taken her out without raising an alarm would not make her feel more secure.

"Is that supposed to be comforting?"

He thought it might be because she now pointed the gun at his legs. "Admittedly, I'm not great at sweet talk."

"Last time, Matthias Clarke. Answer me. Why are you really in town? And don't give me that bullshit answer about having business projects in Annapolis or security or whatever." She looked fully in control of her fear now. This definitely was the same strong woman who'd rejected him without blinking.

Good. He could handle confident Kayla. "Put the gun down."

She nodded to the area behind him. "Open the door."

That didn't make any sense. "Why?"

"So I can scream if you come near me." She shrugged. "Then people will hear the gunshot and come running. I figure that will give you a fighting chance to survive so long as the ambulance gets here in time."

"The person who did this might be right outside." When she didn't say anything, he tried again. "I assume you have all those locks on the door for a reason. You know danger. You've been living with it."

Playing the odds, he took a visible step forward. He wanted her to see him coming.

"What are you doing?"

She shifted but his training won out. He was a second faster and had the gun as she was still pivoting out of the way.

"There." He gave it a quick look before tucking it in the back of his pants. "Jesus, Kayla. It's not even loaded."

"I couldn't find the bullets in this mess." Her gaze darted around the room. "I barely own anything and this is—"

"Okay." As gently as possible he put his hands on her arms and held her steady. He needed her to stay with him for at least a few more minutes. She could break down later, though he really hoped she didn't. "I'm not going to hurt you. The weapon is away."

"I still don't trust you."

"Which is smart, but I do need you to listen to me." When she didn't run, he tested some more. "We need to get out of here."

"You do."

He needed fingerprints and surveillance. They'd stepped right into the sort of thing he did best. "I'm going to lock this place down. Bring my men in and have them . . . why are you shaking your head?"

She wiggled out of his loose hold and stepped back. When her foot hit against the overturned table she winced. "It's fine."

What the hell? "This is not fucking fine."

"No police or investigators."

"Listen to me." He ducked his head and stared at her until she returned his eye contact. "I get that you're scared and—"

"I'm pissed."

Damn, he liked her style. "Good. Frankly, it looks like you have a right to that feeling. But bolting and hiding isn't the right response."

"It's not that simple." She put a hand on his stomach. "There are times . . ."

He wanted her to keep going, to keep touching him, so he put a hand over hers and held her fingers against him. "What?"

"Sometimes you have to let go, disappear, before you can move on from the past." She started out slow, with a space between her words, but then the speed picked up. "I've been trying for years and the problem is I still keep this thin tether to who I used to be. Snapping that might be the answer if I want any kind of life without this."

"Sometimes the only way to get around whatever is haunting you is to move through it. Don't ignore it. Don't double back or even try to erase it."

"You sound as if you're talking from experience."

He'd spent his whole fucking life paying for his past. "I know all about trying to outrun demons."

She curled her fingers and balled his shirt inside her tight fists. "You don't know about this. You couldn't possibly know."

The yearning in her voice tugged at him. The pain in her eyes. He understood all of it. But this wasn't about him and they couldn't have this conversation now. Hell, he couldn't imagine ever unloading about the foster homes and the one time he didn't move fast enough. Didn't yell loud enough. Couldn't save a kid who needed saving.

They needed to stay on her. Focus on getting her to a place where she could open up and he could solve whatever needed solving. "Whoever did this has done it before, yes? That's what you're trying to tell me. This isn't the first time someone has come after you."

"Yes."

"How bad?"

She hesitated for a full minute before talking. "Notes, threats, for a start."

Jesus. At least she'd switched to some nameless "they" and stopped blaming him. He took that as at least partial progress.

"Then anywhere you go, this will follow." So much of the brightness had seeped out of her. She looked drained and discouraged. He'd bet she could still knock him over because even in this state there was nothing weak about her, but he wanted her to save her energy. "We'll talk about all of that as soon as we get you out of here and my men do their work."

"I'm so exhausted." She lowered her head to his chest.

He inhaled, drawing in the faint scent of vanilla in her hair. Wrapped his arms around her and for just a second warmed her body with his. "Then trust me."

"That's never going to happen." The anger had left her voice. She no longer fought him. It sounded more like she was trying to be honest with him.

Just like everything else about her, he found that wildly sexy. "The one thing in the world you can count on is that I'm not going to let anyone hurt you."

She lifted her head and stared up at him. "What about you?"

"I'm not going to hurt you either. I'd like to touch you, which I think I've made clear." With his hands and mouth. Push inside her. "But not tonight."

"It sounds like you're blaming me for killing the mood."

"On the contrary, nothing gets my adrenaline pumping like figuring out a puzzle."

She actually smiled. "So, I'm a puzzle now?"

"Yes you are, Kayla. And I promise you I'm going to figure you out." One way or another, using every skill he possessed. "You can count on that."

CHAPTER 11

Kayla heard footsteps coming up the stairs and froze. She expected Matthias to morph into a human shield and start shouting. But he stood there, holding her, being way too comforting and comfortable.

As the seconds ticked by she teetered between being wary about who or what was about to come through the door and very aware of the feel of Matthias's hands on her lower back. He brushed his fingers over her, back and forth, until every nerve ending tingled. His deep breathing echoed in her ear, drowning out everything else. Almost.

"Matthias, someone is coming." She said the words into his shirt.

He sighed and pulled back. "Garrett's timing sucks."

"What?"

Right after Matthias referenced him, Garrett opened the door. Stood there, taking up most of it and blocking the sun behind him.

"What the ever-loving f—" He went from scowling to wide-eyed as he glanced to where her hand still rested on Matthias's arm. "Hello."

Matthias broke all contact then. He stepped away as he rolled his eyes. "You can swear in front of her. She's a big girl."

Garrett's smile looked like he held it out of pure will and not because he found anything funny or amusing. "I'm a bit more civilized than you are."

"Like hell." Matthias pointed from one to the other. "Kayla, you remember Garrett."

Garrett's fake smile faded as he looked around the room. "What the hell happened in here? If this is your idea of dating, we should talk."

"Someone broke in." Her gaze slipped to the message on the wall and then away again. Seeing the words, knowing someone out there had tracked her down to hurt her, took away what little peace she'd established in Annapolis.

"Not exactly." Matthias nodded in the direction of the door. "Check the door."

Garrett dropped down on his haunches and studied the lock. "Looks fine to me."

"That's one of the reasons she thought I did this. I haven't checked everything, but it doesn't look like anyone tampered with the door to get in here."

"There's still a piece of me that thinks this ties back to you." That actually wasn't true. His reactions didn't come off as practiced or false. Even though she fought it at first, this didn't seem like his kind of attack. No, he'd strike head-on and be sure she knew what hit her. He wouldn't sneak in and write something on a wall.

But she sensed that Matthias was not a man you let off the hook easily. If she didn't speak up and stand her ground he'd just keep trying to run right over her as he did whatever he thought he needed to do to fix her life.

One thing she always had been clear about—she didn't need a savior. She didn't hope someone bigger or stronger or richer would rush in and make it all better. She wanted simplicity and freedom from fear. She knew that could only come from her. She just had no idea how to get there.

Garrett got up and stepped farther into the studio. Walked around with his hands on his hips as he shook his head. "Nah, this isn't Matthias's style. He'd be clean and strategic. No warning. Just put you in a hospital or body bag."

"It's fascinating that both of you think the right response is to say this isn't something Matthias would do." When Matthias just stared at her, she stared back. She refused to believe he didn't understand her point.

"I don't get it," he said.

Then again . . . "You're not saying you wouldn't attack. It's that you wouldn't do it *this* way."

The confusion on Matthias's face turned to a look that said *no shit*. "I wouldn't warn you first, that's for damn sure."

The man did not disappoint. The honesty made her twitchy, but she knew it was right. She thought Matthias would say straight out how he'd handle something like this, and he did.

Now if she could only pin him down on why he was in town. Then she could try to put the pieces together on why his presence seemed to trigger a new round of stalking and angry threats. Once she got there she might be able to pinpoint the person who was so determined to make every day of her life a nightmare.

"Time for a change of topic." Garrett clapped his hands together as he turned back to face them again. "Matthias?"

He turned to her. "Who else has a key?"

She didn't like him barking out questions, but she let that go. For now. "The landlord and my friend Lauren."

"We'll need her full name."

"Leave her alone. She didn't do this." Kayla didn't have any doubt about that. Matthias needed to move on.

"You can't know that." He dismissed her by looking away before she could respond. All of his attention focused on Garrett as he reeled off a list of new orders. "We need the names of everyone who lives and works around here and background checks. I have some of my people coming in from Quint. They'll handle forensics and the canvass and—"

She touched his arm and he immediately stopped talking. "Canvass?"

The word had *terrorize the neighbors* written all over it. She didn't like the idea. Didn't like what she thought it meant or where it might lead.

"They ask around the area, see if anyone heard or knows anything." Matthias ticked off the explanation and kept on talking.

She snuck in one word. "No."

"There might be security cameras on some of these buildings . . . wait." He blinked. Did a little head shake. "Did you say no?"

There was no question he was used to having all

of his orders followed exactly and without question. Well, if he wanted that then he'd wandered into the wrong café, because she was not that woman. Never had been and no matter how much life pounded her, never would be.

"I do not want your employees to stomp around and interrogate the people who work and live around here." A small part of her still hoped she could hold on to a life in this place. That somehow her cover would hold and she could attend those classes she'd signed up for and try to establish connections here.

None of that would be possible if men in suits stormed in, talking about her and being invasive. This part of Annapolis, right here by the marina, was, at heart, a small town. A welcoming and beautiful quiet place filled with good people who worked hard and a whole bunch of wealthy tourists who spent money like wildfire and helped keep the bills paid.

"My men are trained." Matthias's voice took on a rough edge, as if he was ticked off by having to keep talking to her about this topic.

Tough. "Was that my point?"

He leaned in until his face hovered right in front of hers and pointed toward the still open door. "One of those people you're trying to protect out there might have done this."

She pushed against his shoulders until he moved back. "No one did anything until you came into town."

His face flushed red. "Again with that?"

"Wow." Garrett stepped in between them. "You two are adorable. Truly."

Matthias shot Garrett a look filled with fury and a warning delivered through clenched teeth. "Don't make me kill you."

Those words . . . she waited for the panic to set in but nothing. Relief hit her out of nowhere. She wasn't afraid. He got jerky and loud, and instead of wanting to take her bag and go, she slipped into a fighting mood. It was as if the clock had flipped back seven years and a tiny piece of who she once was and how she'd reacted to stress survived.

A weight lifted and all of the tension spinning around inside of her slowed down to a nonvomit level. But she still didn't intend to let him get in the last word. "The gun isn't loaded. Remember?"

Matthias made a strangled sound. "As if I'm not carrying one that is."

"Talking about you being armed and dangerous is not going to get us where we want to be." Garrett clapped again. "Let's focus."

She was already sick of the clapping. He could stop that any time.

"No one has ever had to tell me that before," Matthias muttered under his breath as he walked toward the overturned loveseat.

"Well, see . . ." Garrett tucked his hands in his pockets. "You don't seem to be yourself right now."

Matthias didn't look up from whatever he was busy studying on the floor. "Meaning?"

"Yeah, I want the answer to that, too." She also wanted to know what had grabbed his attention. Something he moved around with his shoe but didn't try to pick up.

Garrett didn't blink. "Let's just say I have a lot of questions about what you were doing tonight in her apartment, but I'll let those go."

The words settled in Kayla's brain and she dragged her gaze away from Matthias and settled it on Garrett. "You're kind of nosy, aren't you?"

Matthias looked up then. "She's not wrong."

"No, I mean—"

"Back to the message on the wall." Matthias stood right under it.

Kayla tried not to notice. Tried not to read the words or think about the last time she saw red splashed against white paint.

"Right." Garrett's eyebrow lifted as he looked at her. "Any intel you can provide?"

Nothing she could say would make sense. "The threat speaks for itself."

"You can't leave it at that." Matthias walked back over to join them. It didn't take long, since the whole room was about fifteen by fifteen. "Not to be dick here, but no one breaks into my house and threatens to kill me."

Funny, he sounded pretty dickish right then and more than a little clueless. "I bet they think about it."

Garrett laughed. "Like you said, she's not wrong."

"This isn't a joke, Kayla." Matthias didn't laugh. If anything, his voice dipped lower, grew more serious. "Someone is specifically targeting you. Not me, you. If someone came after me, I'd have an idea why."

"You think I don't know this is all about me? You think this is the first time?" She'd done this dance so many times. Even when she finally worked up the nerve to unpack her bag in a place, she still never felt settled. Never got a refreshing night of sleep or believed the worst of the hounding might be over.

Matthias looked at Garrett. "I sent out a code to my office. I'll give more instructions when the group is on the way and will tell them to answer to you." His gaze skipped back to her. "How many?"

She understood what Matthias was asking and she knew the answer. Seven years, nine moves. "It doesn't matter."

She didn't always switch states or even towns, but she lost jobs and dropped out of more than one school. She'd been trying to finish her degree for seven years and never stayed anywhere long enough to make it happen.

This time she'd hoped she could at St. John's, the local liberal arts college. She'd even registered and started the process of transferring credits . . . The idea stuck in her head. Had that done it? Did someone track her through her old university records?

"Kayla." Matthias's voice softened as he called out to her.

That worried her more than his bark. When he flipped into understanding mode, her control crumbled. Some older naïve part of her still wanted to believe that she could trust and relax. But she knew better. "I didn't hire you. I don't really know you."

"That didn't bother you an hour ago when I was all over you."

Silence screeched through the room. Garrett froze. So did everything inside her.

It took another minute before she could form any words without spitting them out. "Watch it."

Her anger didn't seem to faze Matthias. All he did was nod. "We're going to the inn. We'll sit down and talk this through."

The man could win an award for stubbornness. "And you just assume I'm going with you."

"We'll stay on track. It will be all business this time."

He made it sound as if he was the one talking about work while she thought about other things. *Yeah, no.* "Do you hear yourself? I'm not talking about sex. I'm talking about not knowing either of you well enough to walk into that sort of situation."

"You can't stay here. Not unless you want to sleep in this mess and be in the way while my men work. Even then, I'll still be here, right by your side."

He made it sound as if she had two choices—him or nothing. "I have friends."

"Really?" Matthias had the nerve to sound stunned.

Garrett shook his head. "Yeah, that's not insulting."

She was about to side with Garrett when Matthias jumped in again. "I got the impression you were a recluse of sorts."

She half wondered if he ever dealt with actual human beings. He didn't seem very good at reading cues or knowing when to shut up. "Are you describing me or you?"

"You can't go to a friend's house." Matthias walked over to the door and glanced out before shutting them in.

Again with the confidence. He acted as if he knew what was best for her after one kiss and a bit of hand-holding. She couldn't imagine how he'd react after sex . . . not that they should go there or that she was in any frame of mind to make that decision. Still, commanding in bed, she approved of. Commanding in general conversation made her want to throw things. "You don't get to decide that."

"Do you want to put this friend in danger?" Whatever expression he saw on her face had him nodding. "That's right. You should look scared. Someone wants to hurt you. I'm thinking they've wanted to hurt you for a long time, so stop fighting me and let me keep you safe."

"Smooth," Garrett said as he glanced at his phone.

But Matthias had found the one argument that would stick. She'd already lost three friends to sense-less violence. She'd lived for seven years in the shadow of that guilt. Nothing lessened it, and God knew she'd tried to wipe that slate clean but only ended up feeling empty and worse. She absolutely could not live with more blood on her hands.

"Fine." That was all she could say and even that killed her to concede.

Matthias's eyes narrowed. "Is the plan to pretend to agree with me and then take off as soon as my back is turned?"

The man was determined to tick her off. "You know, Matthias, when you win an argument you should stop talking."

After a second of hesitation he nodded. "I can do that."

She truly doubted it. "Prove it."

Instead of firing back, Matthias turned to Garrett. "You stay here and wait for the crew. I want hourly updates."

Garrett slipped his phone into his back pocket. "Is this the part where we pretend I work for you?"

"Yes. Actually, I need to see you alone for a second before I go."

She was being dismissed. Wasn't that just great. "That is the least subtle thing you've ever said."

Matthias frowned at her, which was starting to become a habit. "Just stand in here and don't listen."

More orders. She wondered what it would take to force Matthias to come up with another go-to move. "Not going to happen, stud."

Garrett smiled. "I like her."

Matthias pointed at the wall. "Someone doesn't."

Her gaze followed his and the reminder smacked into her with the force of a punch. Okay, he could win this round. "You have two minutes."

Matthias waited until they got out on the small porch and closed the door behind them to start talking again. Even then, he dropped his voice to a whisper. Something already had Kayla all riled up again. Every time he opened his mouth she shot back with some new refusal.

If he hadn't found the whole strong-woman-standing-her-ground thing so fucking sexy he might have really gotten pissed. Instead he battled back his need to kiss her and focused on his duty to keep her safe. She might not think he had one, but he did.

Garrett's obvious amusement didn't help the situation. Even now he stood there smiling and otherwise silently begging to be punched. Matthias held back because he had a bigger issue he needed handled. "All the files on her and her case are in your room, right?"

"Yes, I moved them before coming over, just like you asked. But I'm still trying to believe she agreed to go with you."

Matthias was stunned by that, too, but tried not to show it. He'd hit a nerve. Now he knew where to push if she refused again. She cared about other people. Once again, not a trait he'd expect in someone who'd supposedly killed her college best friends for no clear reason.

The story about her continued to unravel. He now saw her as one more victim of a horrible night. Actually, he saw her as a survivor. He recognized the skills because he shared them. "I think her curiosity about who I am trumped her sense that I can't be trusted."

"I feel sorry for her."

That made him realize Garrett didn't get her at all. Kayla was not weak or needy. She had every right to be both with her past, but she didn't slip into that way of thinking. Not at all. "Pity me because she is not going to let up until she knows the truth."

Garrett exhaled loud and long. The sound telegraphed his impatience and frustration. "Then tell her."

"Not yet." She'd know soon enough that he had come to town to find her and interrogate her. Now wasn't the right time.

"You're going to earn her trust by lying to her?" Garrett snorted. "That's a great plan."

Matthias wondered for the hundredth time since he got to Annapolis why he didn't just call Wren and demand he call Garrett back home. "I'm going to tell her part of it."

"Want to tell me why you were in her apartment in the first place?"

Make that a hundred and one. "No."

"Are you sure? Keep in mind if you don't tell me I'll just make up a story then call Wren and get his view."

Garrett wanted the words—fine. "Don't be a dumbass. You know why."

All the amusement left his face. "You can't sleep with her."

Matthias almost laughed. He damn well could, but there were limits that even he recognized. "Well, no. Obviously not right now."

The door flew open behind them and Kayla stood there holding what looked like a pile of clothes. "Time's up."

"You shouldn't take anything out of the apartment." Matthias was about to launch into an explanation of forensics and concerns about contaminating the scene.

"Tough." She slipped out onto the small porch and stood between the men before looking up at Matthias. "Are you ready to talk?"

The lecture faded from his mind. He couldn't call up one word except the obvious one. "Me?"

"This is my life we're trying to protect. I decide who talks first." She winked at him. "I pick you."

Garrett shrugged. "She's got you there."

"Shut up." Matthias barely spared Garrett a glare, not even when Garrett traded places with Kayla and moved into the entrance of the apartment. Matthias's whole focus, all his energy, centered on her. "This isn't a game."

"I'm not playing." She went down one step then looked up at him. "Are you coming or not?"

"If I don't you'll probably get yourself killed." And that would totally piss him off.

"That's the spirit," she said as she went down another step.

She didn't look back. She was off . . . and damn if he didn't follow her.

CHAPTER 12

They made it to the inn in record time. Kayla didn't relish *the talk* and trying to pull information out of Matthias. She didn't exactly look forward to figuring out how to spill enough of her past, more than she ever did but not more than she could live with. If he really was going to help, he'd need some details . . . unfortunately.

But that's not why she walked quickly along the dock or practically ran to get into his car. No, the idea of someone being out there, watching and waiting—again—spurred her to move. He would protect her. For some reason, even with the limited time she'd known him, she'd bet she could count on that. This guy was a protector. He'd throw his body in front of hers. He didn't scare easily.

Being near him also made her heart race and her brain cells sputter, so she wanted to get inside and calm down as fast as possible. Or at least that's what she'd told herself during the last fifteen minutes. Now that they stood just outside his door at the inn, her stomach performed backflips. She hadn't eaten, and time had zoomed by from just after café closing to almost sundown.

Lost hours and scattered thoughts. That could be her theme song.

She inhaled, trying to regulate her breathing as he swiped his card and the lock clicked. Before she could move inside, he held up a hand. That fast her thoughts went from fumbling and zipping from topic to topic, to on edge. Tension pulled her muscles taut and had her teeth slamming together.

When he disappeared inside, she wanted to follow. Being alone, even for a few seconds, didn't calm her nerves. Her gaze skimmed down the hallway and across the worn blue carpeting. She turned to slip into the room.

He popped up in front of her. "Come inside."

She didn't argue. Not this time. She was too busy taking in every inch of the room. Make that suite. To her right sat the king-sized bed, with the comforter pulled tight and wrinkle-free. Forget bouncing a quarter on that. Her retired Army colonel father could have bounced a car on that thing. She'd lost him for good three years ago and only now could she call up memories and smile instead of cry.

Since Matthias stepped to the right and into the small living room area, she followed. There was a doorway at the far end near the couch. Through it, she spied another bed. "You guys are rooming together?"

"I'm not twelve." Matthias closed the door, shutting down her view to the other space.

That left them alone in a room with a big bed and

a mile of misunderstanding between them. Questions whipped through her head, about him and who he was and why he cared about her life even a little.

But she wasn't ready to deal with any of that yet. "I don't even understand that answer or why you sometimes get upset for no apparent reason."

He dumped her gun on the table. Then came his phone and another gun, one she hadn't seen before. It had just appeared without her knowing where it came from. One minute he stood, and then he started unloading. She wasn't sure what to think about the weapons, about Garrett, about the adjoining bedroom. So many questions.

"The team will be sending photos and forensics," he said, ignoring her earlier confusion. "And I do need you to write out that list of names. No stalling on that."

"That's not what we're going to talk about." She didn't even want to think about his topics and how his men would march into town and rip her life apart. There was just no way anyone associated with him, or who looked anything like him, could come and go unnoticed.

"Agreed." He sat down on the small couch and motioned for her to take the chair across from him. "That message on your wall."

"Is something we'll talk about *after* you tell me why you're here." When he started to talk, she raised her voice and kept going. "And don't try to sell the whole *I saw you and you looked scared and I'm a big strong man, so I stepped in.* Nope."

He leaned back into the cushions. "Wow."

"Start talking." She wanted to ask about a bottle of water, and sitting down really was tempting, but she'd made her stand so now she'd . . . stand.

"People don't normally speak to me like that."

Since he stretched an arm along the back of the couch cushions, she guessed he wasn't really all that concerned about her attitude, which was good because she didn't plan on changing it. She'd almost recovered from seeing the newest threat. Now she had to survive a talk with him.

"You've pointed out that you've had plenty of chances to hurt me, if you wanted to." In fact, he was a bit too eager to mention that. She thought they could just have a silent agreement on that at this point.

"I don't."

She believed him. She wouldn't be here if she didn't. "Then talk."

His gaze wandered over her face as he seemed to study her. "You're not afraid of me at all, are you?"

Oh, she had flares of fear. She also experienced a sensation that had nothing to do with fear whenever she got near him. That scared her more than anything. "Should I be?"

He crossed one leg over the other and sat there in a full male sprawl. "Most people are."

She'd bet he stoked that, encouraged it. "That's an annoying nonanswer."

"You sure don't sound afraid." He smiled. Not something he seemed to do often even though it softened his face.

Then again, she guessed that's why he generally

skipped the smiling. He'd be the type to enjoy making others feels uncomfortable. In his line of work—though she still wasn't a hundred percent sure what that was—it likely proved to be a handy skill.

She sat down on the armrest of the chair. It let her sit higher and gave her a feeling of being in control. "Tell me what's happening."

He lowered his foot until both touched the floor again. "I'd rather talk about the threats and what we can do to stop them."

"I bet, but you're not in charge."

"Are you sure?" He sounded almost amused now.

"We're going round in circles." When she realized she was rubbing her palms up and down her legs she stopped. The friction made her hands red and her legs hot. "I'm thinking you can do this sort of thing for hours."

"Kayla, listen to me." This time he leaned forward with his elbows balanced on his knees, all traces of lightness gone. "I deal with danger and death every day. I've seen shit I wouldn't wish on anyone. Nothing you can say is going to shock me."

That sounded good and a bit more tempting than she wanted to admit, but those were the words people said before they knew better. She'd lived this life and made difficult choices. She survived a bloodbath and shouldered through while most of the people she knew and once trusted blamed her.

She had secrets and regrets he could never know.

"You think I'm worried about disappointing you?" she asked.

"I didn't mean that."

"Maybe I want to forget." There was actually no question about it. That's exactly what she hoped for every single day. "Maybe I'm tired of reliving the worst moment of my life and being blamed for making it happen."

He didn't move. Nothing in her words seemed to surprise him. "Did you?"

She searched his tone for prejudgment but didn't really hear any. He sounded more clinical than curious. Not one in a long line of people hoping to crack the case by getting her to cough up the one piece of information that would change everything. Of course, he didn't actually ask her what happened, which was more telling than he seemed to realize.

"No, but it doesn't matter. The truth gets trampled in a case like this. It's a question of what people will believe. The whispers. The rumors." And those built and combined until they dealt a deafening blow.

"The threats."

"Yeah, that will teach me to live when everyone thinks I should have died." She waited for him to jump in with a million questions, but he just sat there. The lack of a real reaction to her harsh words meant something and she knew it, but she was just so grateful for the reprieve. Her entire body relaxed until it took every ounce of energy to continue to sit there. "God, I am just so tired."

"Okay, let's try this." He held a hand out to her. "Come here."

No way could she grab it. Her defenses had lowered

and touching carried such a risk. "Isn't it your turn to say something?"

"That can wait." His arm stayed out there like a lifeline. "Come here."

"I thought you wanted answers and . . ." She groaned as she slipped her fingers through her hair. She closed her eyes for a second then let her hands drop back to her lap. "I can't even remember what I wanted to say."

"Later."

When he issued orders, her anger rose and she met him as an equal in an argument. But she had no barriers, no defense, against this side of him. Against the caring and soft lilt to his deep voice.

"I don't trust you. I'm not sure I even like you." If only that last part were true, then she could write him off and forget him. But from the first time she saw him, something sparked. She could feel his heated gaze on her and instead of rolling her eyes or growing wary, she wanted him to look. She stole peeks and it felt good for him to return them.

Before her brain could kick in and all the reasons why she should hold back piled up, she reached out. Touched her fingers to his and slipped them together. The warmth of his palm erased the chill racing through her.

"Totally understandable. You've had a shitty night, except for the date part, of course," he said as he gently pulled her off the armrest and brought her down on his lap.

Not on the couch. Not beside him. No, she settled against his chest. This man she barely knew and had allowed to get close, or close for her, in a matter of a day.

She abandoned the struggle before it even started and leaned into him. Tucked her head on his shoulder and inhaled his reassuring scent. "Why am I so tired?"

"Burn-off after the adrenaline rush." One of his arms came around her, bringing her body even closer to his. The other stayed on her lap with their fingers entwined.

"I guess you know a lot about that."

He exhaled and his breath grazed her forehead. "Too much."

"How dangerous are you?" She used her free hand to touch the back of his. Feeling the strength that contrasted so sharply with their current position.

"To you?" He hummed and it vibrated through her. "I'm not."

"To other people?" She knew the answer, but for some reason she wanted to hear it. To see if he'd tell the truth.

"Very."

"That's oddly comforting."

"You should rest."

"It's not late." She actually had no idea what time it was. She tried to turn and look out the window, but she noticed for the first time that the curtains were shut and not a sliver of light snuck in.

"You're going to fall over if you don't take at least a short break," he said as he rubbed his hand up and down her back.

"I thought you had a million questions." Not that she wanted to hear one of them right now. It was so much easier to close her eyes and not think at all.

"More than that, but they can all wait until you're awake."

Sleeping here was a terrible idea. She should call Lauren and take a few minutes to get her thoughts together and get up. Sit in the chair. "If I rest, where are you going to be?"

"In the room, watching you . . ." His words rambled to a stop before beginning again. "Unless that sounds creepy."

She smiled but didn't bother to open her eyes. "It does."

"Then I'll be working."

For a few more seconds she just sat there, boneless as her body melted into his. She felt some shifting and expected him to stretch out or move her. He stood with her in his arms. Didn't make a sound or hesitate, just one steady whoosh and they were up.

She grabbed on to his shoulders to keep from falling down. "What are you—"

"Taking you to bed." He took one step then stopped. "In a non-naked way."

"That's a shame."

He froze. "Don't."

She could feel the tension in his arms and hands. He might be playing the role of the chivalrous hero but the naughty part of him hadn't completely disappeared. Which was good because she planned on testing those skills later, preferably when she didn't feel like curling into a ball and sleeping for a month.

He carried her over to the bed and set her down on the edge. His hands slipped behind his neck and loosened her hold. But instead of standing up again, he put his palms on the mattress on either side of her hips. The move brought his face close to hers.

"Go ahead and lie back." His eyes traveled over her face and down to her mouth.

Some of her sleepiness vanished. "Can your work wait?"

His eyebrow lifted. "What exactly are you asking?"

Not that, though the idea of bringing him down on the bed with her did keep running through her mind. He'd wake her up. He'd make her feel safe and cherished, if only for an hour. If only she could make that last.

She glanced at the closed curtains again and thought about the men stomping through her apartment and the whirlwind of the last twenty-four hours. No, he was right. She needed rest, not sex, right now. But she doubted she'd be able to drift off, unless she could get through to him. "You're going to make me say it."

"Apparently." He didn't pull back. "Go ahead."

"Can you just get on the bed with me for a few minutes?" She waved her hand between them and accidentally smacked him in the nose. "No sex or anything. And, really, I doubt I'll sleep."

He didn't fight her or debate. "Fine."

That was a good thing because she was about two seconds away from breaking into full-fledged babbling. She balled her hands into fists on her lap to keep from reaching out to him or fidgeting. "That's a yes?"

"Kayla?"

"Yes?"

He lifted a hand and brushed her hair away from her face. "Are you stalling for a reason?"

Because she wanted to curl into him. Up until that minute she'd forgotten about her hair and the fact her uniform was tugged to one side. He made her forget everything. "You confuse me."

He shot her one of those sexy smiles. "I know the feeling."

"Do you want to change or—"

"Kayla, lie down." When she didn't immediately do it, he helped her by kicking off his shoes and stretching out on the mattress. Instead of holding out a hand or asking her to join him, he reached up and brought her down with him.

For a second, she kept her muscles stiff and locked. Didn't lean back or accept his comfort. But the longer they lay there with only a few inches separating them, the more his body called to hers. She gave in to the dip in the mattress and rolled back into him. Her back touched his front from chest to thighs and his legs curled behind hers.

"I'd never take you for the spooning type." She made the joke to cut the silence.

"Close your eyes." His arm slipped around her and his hand spanned her waist. "You need to sleep for a few minutes."

"I'm afraid to." She looked over her shoulder at him. "Do you get that?"

"You scare the hell out of me but that might be a different thing."

If he meant it as a joke he didn't laugh. Didn't smile.

He pushed up a little and leaned in. This time his kiss was slow and lingering. His mouth brushed over hers. He lured her in and had her wanting more, but he pulled back.

She tried to hold his stare but gave in and snuggled closer. "Well . . ."

"You can trust me." His words vibrated against her.

"I hope so." But part of her still doubted it.

CHAPTER 13

Matthias made it through an hour of no-touching torture until Kayla finally slipped into a deep sleep. Instead of jumping up and getting back to work, he'd sat there on the edge of the bed and listened to her even breathing. Watched her. Put a blanket over her. Generally acted like someone else and he had no idea why.

The eventual expected call from Garrett broke his staring. Matthias had never been so grateful for his phone in his life. He even silently thanked Garrett from inadvertently stopping him from doing something weird like cuddling.

He had to leave Annapolis and get away from her, and soon.

HE'D BEEN OUT of the bed for two hours now. Kayla still slept, so he slipped into Garrett's room to collect the rest of the intel. His team leader had called about thirty minutes ago and listened to the assignments for tomorrow. Matthias had the four members check in to another hotel and suggested they try to blend in. Since he really didn't know how, he'd left it to Garrett to explain on the scene.

Now Matthias watched as Garrett moved around his room, putting his Kayla-related files in a pile. Matthias was pretty sure Garrett was drawing the whole oral report out. So far he'd talked about the fibers and other items the team collected. Also confirmed the footprint Matthias had spotted on the piece of abandoned paper on the floor as male size eleven. He'd used the bathroom, gotten water and checked his messages.

Matthias was ten seconds from strangling him.

Garrett must have sensed it because he finally put his water bottle down. "No fingerprints."

"Damn." Matthias knew the news was coming but he still hated hearing it.

Just as he feared. This break-in, the threats, came from someone with some skills. Matthias still didn't know how the attacker had entered, but he'd damn sure figure it out before he let Kayla anywhere near her apartment again.

Kayla . . . just thinking her name brought back a rush of memories. The softness of her skin. The kissing. She was impressive on that score. And she seemed to want him as much as he wanted her, which was going to be a problem. He needed one of them to exhibit some common sense and pull away.

He loved her enthusiasm and that she knew what she wanted, and that the "what" was him, but the baggage stacked between them would not be easy to unload. Matthias hated to admit it but maybe Garrett had been right to suggest he try the honesty tactic first.

Too late now.

"I mean, no fingerprints at all." Garrett took off his

jacket and tie before leaning against the chest of drawers with one ankle crossed over the other. "The place was wiped clean."

"All that destruction and nothing?" Well, that just pissed Matthias off.

"Whoever did this was pretty serious, which makes me wonder why it was made to look messy and erratic."

Matthias had the same issue. "A cover."

Professionals thrived on anonymity. They got in and covered their tracks. That was the point. But the attack on Kayla's place was meant to terrify. Someone wanted her uncertain and on the run, and Matthias couldn't think of what a stalker could get out of that.

Garrett balanced his palms on either side of his hips. "The other option is the person came in looking for something. The question is what."

"Only Kayla can tell us that." Though Matthias doubted she would without a fight.

"Speaking of which . . ."

Matthias jumped on the topic before Garrett took the conversation to an annoying place. "She's sleeping. The adrenaline caught up with her."

"It sucks when that happens."

"Right." Matthias paced the area between the end of the bed and the chair by the window. The energy pinging around inside him demanded release. The walking didn't help but neither did standing still.

"So, you guys come to any conclusions?"

He didn't like Garrett's tone. Not one bit. "About what? What the hell are you saying?"

"Does she know you came here to find her?"

The door separating Matthias and Garrett's rooms pushed open and Kayla stood there wide-eyed and giving off a furious I'm-going-to-bang-your-heads-together vibe. "She does now."

"Well, shit."

Matthias didn't think Garrett's reaction was nearly strong enough. "Motherfucker."

"Looks like I woke up just in time." She walked over to them, all rested and ready to fight.

Matthias took in her shorts and those long legs. Her tiny T-shirt and the way it showed off a slim inch of skin at the bottom. She'd changed and washed up. He didn't know how he'd missed the sound of water running or her moving around over there. Mostly, he cursed his inability to shut a damn door.

"I should go," Garrett mumbled as he stood up straight and took a step toward the door to the hallway.

She pointed at him. "Do not move."

"Right." He leaned against the chest of drawers again. "Yes, ma'am."

Matthias was not in the mood for another verbal battle, but it looked as if he didn't have much of a choice. "I thought you were sleeping."

"Unfortunately for you, I'm wide awake now."

"Clearly."

"Don't stall." She stood right in front of him, apparently unconcerned that he was taller and stronger.

He'd never hurt her, but she couldn't really know that except on some instinctual level. Which was what made her refusal to back down so compelling. She'd made it clear she would not be intimidated. Never mind that he'd defused rising military coups and once dangled a dictator out a window to get him to talk. She demanded he listen, and damned if he didn't obey.

So fucking hot.

"Stalling is not really my thing." He heard the edge to his voice. It had nothing to do with anger and everything to do with the ponytail and bare feet and how stupidly cute she looked.

Apparently he was into the whole fresh-faced thing now. That was news to him.

"Neither is the truth," she spit back.

No, she was not backing down. Little could she know how that accusation tore through him. How he took pride in just telling it like it is. He didn't like her version of him at all. "I haven't lied to you."

"Come on."

"Not overtly." He wanted that distinction to matter.

She sighed at him. One of those you-are-an-idiot sighs. "I'm going to throw a chair at you."

Garrett cleared his throat. "I'm happy I stayed."

"You're sharing the blame here, so don't look pleased with yourself." She pinned Garrett with a glare before returning to her original target. "Talk. Now, Matthias."

"I'm exactly who I said I was."

She made a dramatic scene of rolling her eyes. "Spare me."

Damn if he didn't find that sexy, too. He also knew that if he didn't cough up some reality, he'd never get the information he needed for her.

The next few minutes were going to suck. He decided to buckle in and take it. "I came here looking for you."

"Why?"

He glanced at Garrett, who nodded. Matthias took that as a sign to keep going; he'd figure out how to live with the fallout later. "Three coeds are dead."

An unblinking stare was her only response. Seconds ticked by in the quiet room as she stood there. The limited traffic noise from the street had all but disappeared. Matthias couldn't hear voices or much other than the sound of his own breathing.

"I know. I was there." When she finally spoke, her voice was soft. Almost a whisper. "Who hired you?"

"I'm looking into this on my own." Which actually was the truth. Sort of. Mary Patterson—his mother, a term he'd never get used to—had asked him to get involved. He told her that he would look into it, but on his terms.

Kayla continued to stare. "Like a Good Samaritan thing?"

That response signaled danger, but he forged ahead anyway. "Sure."

"Try again." Her mouth flattened and some of the light left her eyes. "Just know that you are about to break the bullshit meter right now."

"The what?"

She looked at Garrett. "Is he kidding?"

"Probably not." Garrett shrugged. "He's a bit challenged when it comes to human interaction."

"Don't talk about me like I'm not here." That just pissed Matthias off, and he had enough to be pissed off about right now without adding new things.

"It's not fun, is it?" She snapped out the question.

"What else do you want me to say?" He'd come here for one reason—to collect information and get answers. Then he met her, talked to her, fucking kissed her and his world tipped sideways. No one had ever affected him this way, and he sure as hell didn't like the racing-out-of-control sensation she brought out in him.

"The truth." She shook her head. "Is that so hard for you?"

That's it. "Fine. Nick's mother asked me to—"

"Whoa." Kayla held out a hand and took a giant step back. "That woman?"

His defenses immediately rose. He hadn't known Mary very long and sure didn't trust her, because her story slid all over the place. Hell, she'd dumped him as soon as she gave birth to him. But she still did give birth to him. "What does that mean?"

"She's been investigating me for years."

"You're sure?" Garrett asked.

"She's followed me, called places when I finally did find work and then told lies so I'd get fired." She answered Garrett then switched her gaze to Matthias. "I know her and the type who believes her. No thank you."

"Are you ready to listen?"

"I'm done." She took a piece of paper out of her

pocket and dropped it on the floor. "There's your list of names, though I doubt you really need it since Mary doesn't care about the truth."

He scooped it up before she could grab it and rip it up. In her mood that seemed like a distinct possibility. "Okay, let's—"

"Save it." Kayla turned and headed for the adjoining door. "I'm leaving."

"Do not move." His voice boomed through the room.

"Uh, Matthias." Garrett winced. "This might not be the best strategy."

Forget that shit. "Kayla understands me just fine." Matthias closed the gap between him and Kayla. "Don't you?"

She lifted her chin and matched him glare-for-glare. "I think you should listen to your friend's warning."

He took another step and was almost on top of her now. "Nick's mother didn't hire me. She told me about Nick and her concerns about his killer never being found, and I said I'd look into it."

"Concerns?" Kayla made his comment sound like a joke.

"Why are you repeating random words?"

"She's hunted me down. Made my life a complete disaster." Kayla put a hand on his chest and pushed. "That's your benefactor."

She didn't actually have the strength to move him, but he got the message. She didn't want him in her space and even through the haze of frustration clouding his vision, he could respect that.

He never lost control but the combination of conflicting intel and possibly failing a brother he hadn't known he had, plus all his messed-up worries for Kayla, had him hovering right on the verge. Once he realized that, he took a deep breath and stepped back.

"She's not paying me," he said.

"I don't care about the financial arrangements. I care that I build a life, or start to, and she comes in and wrecks it."

Jesus, that all sounded real. He'd known Mary for months and there was something . . . something about her story and the way she talked about Nick that hadn't sat right with him. He'd ignored those doubts when he went to Wren. The need to "fix" a problem had overwhelmed the warning signs. He owed Nick that much.

Matthias wasn't sure what to think, but he needed to know one thing. "You believe she broke into your apartment?"

"There's a good chance of it." Her shoulders stiffened. "Did you tell her you found me? Give her my address?"

"Of course not." Garrett did a double take. "Wait, did you?"

Well, fuck. The idea he got played pissed Matthias off. "She knows I made contact. That's all."

Kayla groaned. "I knew I couldn't trust you."

"She didn't do this." Mary had called nine times yesterday. He fed her enough information to get her to calm down. Now he regretted his haste. Getting her off his back may have sicced her on Kayla, though Matthias still doubted it. "Whoever broke in was a pro, or at least highly trained. He or she infiltrated, didn't leave any evidence and didn't draw attention. All of that takes skills and patience."

"You mean the kind of skills and patience *you* have?"

No fucking way were they back to this again. "I didn't do it and you know it, so stop with that argument."

There was no way she could kiss him like that and still believe he was out to get her. And the fact he couldn't hold it together long enough not to touch her should tell her something about him. It pissed him off that she could think he'd hold her in bed one minute and set her up the next.

She studied him. Her gaze roamed all over him while the fury pounded off her. "I'm leaving."

So fucking stubborn. He reached for her, thought somehow that might help him get through to her, but then quickly discounted the thought. She may as well have a do-not-touch sign flashing above her head.

He fell back on reason. "You're still in danger. Here, I can protect you."

"And who protects me from you?" She glanced around him to Garrett. "You?"

The slight sliced through Matthias. He guessed that was exactly what she intended. "I know you're upset—"

"You figured that out?"

"The yelling clued me in." Before she could shoot back another response, he talked faster. "Let us finish collecting evidence and set up the surveillance to catch the person on video."

"Because when you figure out the truth you'll turn in your client and stop collecting a paycheck? Spare me."

She just wouldn't stop with this. "The money issue is a big concern for you, but since it's not real I'm going to ignore it and keep doing what I'm doing."

"Which is?"

"Trying to help you, believe it or not." He'd never met any human being who could outstubborn him. Until her.

"It's probably hard for her to tell that since you're both screaming." Garrett picked up his water bottle and approached them. "It's annoying, by the way."

Her gaze bounced back and forth between the men. "I'll stay but I get the bed." She focused on Matthias. "You can sleep in the hall for all I care."

"It's my room."

She turned and walked through the doorway, but not before calling over her shoulder. "Maybe Nick's mother will pay for another one for you."

The endless sparring with her was going to kill him. "You're exhausting."

"Right back at ya, stud. And stay out of my café, too." She slammed the door, cutting off anything else he might say.

Garrett stood there, staring at the closed door. "So, you handled that well."

"She makes me crazed." Matthias would have stormed into his room but she'd just start up again and he was done being accused of shit.

"Yep."

Matthias didn't find Garrett's reaction all that reassuring. "I have a feeling it's only going to get worse."

"I'm pretty sure you can count on that, since she doesn't know the mother part yet."

It was Matthias's turn to groan. "That's just fucking great."

Garrett laughed. "And for the record? You can't have this bed either."

CHAPTER 14

Kayla tried to work herself to death the next day. As ordered, Matthias stayed mostly outside. Garrett came in now and then, looking pathetic and ordering drinks and food. She seriously considered saying no. Toyed with the idea of telling Matthias to get back in his car and speed away. But something kept stopping her.

She'd known from the beginning his story didn't ring true. Hell, he half admitted being there *for* her. She reran every conversation, struck by how carefully he chose his words to walk just this side of the line from being a full-out liar.

The weasel.

Now, about an hour after the usual lunch rush, the café had cleared out. The sun tucked behind a cloud and the world outside the window fell into a depressing gray. It seemed fitting to her.

She had a few takeout orders waiting for pickup. She expected more calls from business owners in and around the marina. A few more customers would likely stumble in. But for now she concentrated on cleaning the counter. She scrubbed until her fingers turned red and raw. Put all of her frustration into erasing every bit of grime. After she conquered that, she'd start on the floor. Anything to keep moving.

The bell above the café door dinged and she looked up. Lauren stood in the doorway. "Hey."

Kayla couldn't exactly question the openmouthed stare. It wasn't as if she liked cleaning. She'd whined to Lauren more than once about this part of the job.

"If you scrub that any harder you might dig through the stone," Lauren said in an amused voice.

That only made Kayla rub harder. "Sounds good to me."

Lauren made it across the room in a few steps. "What's going on?"

The sponge squeaked across the shiny surface. "Nothing."

"Oh, my God, Kayla." Lauren reached over and grabbed the sponge. "It's easier to get answers when I talk to my television."

"Good thing you're not prone to exaggeration." Kayla slumped back. She stood but she really had no idea how her legs still carried her.

She'd been in nonstop motion since she got up this morning in an effort to keep her mind clear. Thoughts had bombarded her all night. The anger had flowed over her and she'd flip-flopped all over the mattress with the things she should have said to Matthias. All the unanswered questions running through her mind.

"Sit." Lauren threw the sponge into the small sink along the wall near the kitchen.

"Nice shot."

"Talk."

There was no ignoring Lauren now. Kayla didn't even try. She plopped down on the barstool and tried to think of how much to say and if she should weigh the words. But seeing the concern in Lauren's eyes convinced Kayla to just spit it out. If she wasn't going to run—and she'd temporarily put that on hold thanks to Matthias—then she may as well nurture the one friendship she'd manage to hold on to and truly cared about.

"I was robbed." That really didn't cover it, but she figured it would get the conversation started. "Sort of."

Lauren didn't disappoint. Her hands came up and she gave Kayla a quick hug. Then another.

When she finally stepped back the worry was right there on her face. "What? When?"

Kayla touched the back of Lauren's fingers and brought Lauren down on the seat next to her. "It happened last night."

"Why didn't you call me?" Lauren's voice sputtered out for a second. "I would have come over and done . . . something. At least been there for you."

"I didn't want—"

"Warning." Lauren squeezed Kayla's hand. "If the end of that sentence sounds anything like *to disturb you* I'm going to be furious."

They huddled together on the barstools. After so many years of not sharing, of refusing to let anyone in out of fear of a fresh new hurt and an emotional scab that would never heal, of being so disappointed she couldn't move, it felt good to at least say something. It was a small piece of information, not even really all that important, but it amounted to the one step forward she was desperate to take.

First Matthias. Now Lauren.

Kayla waited for the panic to overtake her and her brain to shut down. But it didn't happen.

"It was weird and it all happened so fast." That was probably an understatement.

"What did the police say?"

This was the harder part to explain. "Actually . . ."

Lauren wore one of her patented you've-got-to-be-kidding-me frowns. "Please tell me you called the police. You need to file a report."

"An investigator was there."

Lauren's head shot back and her eyes narrowed. "That is the most careful sentence anyone's ever uttered."

No kidding.

The bell above the door dinged a second time and a man walked in. Elliot Gardner six foot and lanky with a baby face. His smile was big and warm. And he wore the boating uniform—khaki shorts, polo shirt and deck shoes. Kayla was pretty sure some store handed that trio out at the Maryland border, because she saw it on almost every man in the area over the age of twenty.

Lauren had been thrilled to sign up Elliot. She said he was about thirty and determined to learn how to sail. Very enthusiastic and not a jerk. He paid her a significant fee and tipped well. That made him Lauren's current favorite client. He'd retain that title so long as he never threw up on her boat.

He glanced around the empty café before his gaze settled on Lauren. "Are you ready?"

She barely looked at him. "In a second."

"It's okay." Kayla let go of Lauren's hand and plastered on a big smile to welcome Elliot. "Is it time for another lesson?"

"I think I'm early." He swallowed a wince as he started to back out of the empty café. "I can sit down outside for a few minutes if you guys need to talk."

She shook her head. "No."

"Thank you," Lauren said at the same time.

Elliot laughed. "Okay, I admit I'm not sure what the right answer is here."

"Sorry about that." Kayla stood up but stopped to give Lauren her most serious woman-to-woman *get to work* expression. "We're good. We'll talk tonight."

"I'm not going to give you a choice."

"Which is why I love you." Kayla returned to her safe space behind the counter. From there she could serve coffee and get to everything easily. It also acted as a shield if she needed to fidget and have it go unnoticed or reach for her cell and dial Matthias or Garrett, numbers Matthias had added this morning while glaring at her, silently daring her to object. "So, Elliot, is this the second or third lesson?"

"Second." He slipped a bottle out of his pocket. "I brought suntan lotion this time. Learned my lesson the hard way the first time around."

Lauren jumped up, her professional sunny attitude back in check. "First rule of boating, Elliot."

"You did warn me."

Lauren shot Kayla a smile over her shoulder. "You heard him admit that."

"I did." The relaxed mood and Elliot's enthusiasm were contagious. "Have fun."

Elliot walked outside but Lauren hesitated at the door. "You sure you're okay?"

"I am. I'll see you tonight."

THE DOOR HADN'T been closed two seconds before Matthias stalked in through the kitchen. Kayla heard him coming because his presence made Gerald shout. The cook served as the ultimate warning system.

Matthias nodded toward the closed front door as he walked into the room and stood next to her behind the counter. "Who was that?"

"People I know."

He glanced down at her. "That's not a helpful answer."

"It does remind me that I need to add a few more names to that list." She thought about Lauren's clients and the part-time assistant and helpers that showed up at the marina for only a few hours at a time. Knowing Matthias, he'd want all of those.

"I need everyone who has been in and around the marina since you've been here." He smiled. "Garrett's tracking down the names of all the boat owners and slip renters right now. You should hear the whining."

"I don't blame him. That's a lot of people."

"When it comes to your safety I'll err on the side of doing too much."

She hated the lightness that burst through her when she saw him, as she listened to him. So annoying. And how was it possible he was even better looking today? The whole windblown-hair look suited him. The dress pants pulled tight across his hips also worked. Didn't hurt that the low waist showed off his trim stomach and highlighted his chest.

But with the business attire he could not look more out of place if he tried. Drop him in DC and he'd be fine. Here, he looked like a salesman who'd taken a wrong turn somewhere near Virginia.

"I thought I banned you from the café." Forget how happy she was to see him or how she'd looked through the back door all morning, sneaking peeks as he walked around the other businesses at the marina.

"I assumed the keep-out order was a joke."

"Then why have you been standing outside and away from me most of the day?" During those same hours she spent most of her energy trying not to think about him.

"Watching my team."

She expected a more exciting answer. "What?"

"See, you didn't even notice them out there." His gaze traveled to the cake on the stand by his elbow then to the individual homemade strawberry pies sitting right there.

She snapped her fingers in front of him to bring his attention back to her. "Did your boss get here yet?"

"What are you talking about?"

"Mary Patterson." Sure, she felt a bit childish, but she had not forgotten last night. He needed to know that. "I figured she'd want to come and catch you in action. It would be good, since she tends to hide in the shadows. I've never actually met her, but I do have some things I'd like to say to her."

He shook his head. "Are you done?"

"With what?"

He put a hand on the counter. The move brought his face closer to hers. "I came here for one reason but now I'm here to help. Do you get that?"

She refused to let his hotness charm her. "Me or her?"

"You are on fire today."

"Can you really blame me? You tried to sell the whole you-look-so-sad-and-I'm-your-hero garbage." Just thinking about that day made her want to smash the cake in his face. She'd been set up and lured in from the beginning.

"I never said anything like that."

So stubborn. "Why are you inside right now? There's a public bathroom at the end of the pier."

"Clearly I'm here for your welcoming charm."

She bit back a smile. "You're not allowed to be angry."

He had the nerve to shrug at her. "Okay."

"Or cute."

His eyebrows lifted. "You think I'm cute?"

"I'm serious, stop trying to be adorable or whatever this is. You were the one at fault last night." She kept trying to conjure up the same level of anger that had ruined her night but the well refused to rise.

"Did I miss the part where you told me about the message on your wall and why you think it's there?"

He certainly didn't sound contrite. "Since you seem to know so much about my life already, I didn't bother."

"You have a comeback for everything."

"I do." Her voice practically bounced off the walls. She dropped it much lower to prevent an unwanted showdown with Gerald. "So there."

Matthias pushed away from the counter and glanced at the desserts again. "Can I have pie?"

That proved too adorable to resist. "It will cost you double."

"That seems fair."

She pointed at the stool on the other side of the counter. "Sit and don't push it."

Turning away, she went to work on the pie. Got the dish and cut him a big slice. She moved around without a word. Gerald's radio played in the background. She didn't recognize the song, but then she never did.

The plate clinked against the counter as she set it in front of Matthias.

His eyes grew wide and that smile said appreciation. "Thank you."

"Uh-huh."

Before she could think about the fact she was serving him, she grabbed the coffeepot. Poured them both a cup and put one in front of him. Black and burning hot, just like he'd ordered in the past.

He swallowed a piece of pie then used his fork to scoop up another. He held it out to her. "Do you want a bite?"

His voice sounded like sex. "I don't like sweets."

"What?" His arm dropped and the fork hit the counter. "How is that possible?"

"Not a fan of sugar."

His face screwed up in a look of horror. "What the hell is wrong with you?"

She couldn't help but smile at that reaction. "Gerald asked the same thing when I started here."

"The guy in the kitchen?"

"The fifty-year-old cook who thinks I talk too much, should stay out of his kitchen and don't unload the dishwasher the right way."

Matthias picked up the mug but stopped before taking a sip. "Technically, I unloaded the dishwasher last night. Does he want to come out and fight with me?"

"You're such a tough guy."

He slowly lowered the mug to the counter. "I can be whatever you want me to be."

The air shifted in the café. In the short space between sentences, the mood changed. The staccato banter faded away until the need to launch across the countertop and grab him nearly overwhelmed her. "I want you to be straight with me at all times."

"I'm trying."

She actually believed him. "From anyone else that would be a weird answer."

"From me?"

"It's probably honest." She grabbed the coffeepot and topped off his mug. "I assume you're not used to sharing."

"Correct. I do not share well."

She wasn't totally sure what they were talking about now, but she'd slipped right to the edge of babble. It happened when she got nervous, and everything about Matthias shook her. "Sounds like only-child syndrome."

"Something like that."

"I was, too. I recognize the type."

"Charming?"

He was and she kind of hated that. If he'd act like a dick she could write him off and ignore everything he said. But his smiles left her breathless and when he joked she felt this spiraling comfort that actually scared her. She'd survived for seven tough years by being on edge.

"Demanding," she said, filling in the blank.

"That fits you."

She couldn't really deny that. "Yeah, right. Just me."

The room slipped into silence as he played with the handle of the coffee mug. Ran his fingers back and forth along it in a move that was weirdly hot and sexual.

He stared at his pie until he glanced up and pinned her with an intense gaze. "Any chance you'll let me sleep in the bed with you tonight?"

Her stomach flipped over. "What makes you think I'm staying with you?"

"At the inn or your place, you aren't sleeping alone." This time he spun the mug around, letting the bottom clank against the counter. "That's not up for debate."

She wasn't arguing. She didn't have the strength

anymore. "Is that the bodyguard in you talking or something else?"

"I'm not sure yet." He picked up the mug but didn't take a sip. "That kind of depends on you."

"I'm still angry with you." She was but it decreased the more she sat there with him.

"Then I'll wait until later to ask."

She did love his tenacity . . . and his timing. "You think I'm just going to cool down and forget why you're really in town?"

"I get the sense you remember everything." And he didn't sound too happy about that.

"Very true."

"Then I'll just hope you remember how good that kiss was."

She almost lifted her hand to touch a finger to her lips. Tightening her muscles, she stopped herself just in time. "Don't you think a lot of yourself?"

"I was actually giving you all the credit."

Charmer. "You're trouble."

"Probably true."

And she was just about out of self-control. "Eat your pie."

CHAPTER 15

Three hours ticked by before they could throw the CLOSED sign. Gerald slipped out, mumbling something about needing to have a say in the hiring of even volunteer staff from now on. Matthias didn't take it personally. He continued to unload the dishwasher, knowing the faster he did that, the faster he could get her out of there.

He felt her gaze on him but tried to ignore it. If he gave in, even an inch, he'd be all over her. His control had all but snapped. He blamed the combination of that sexy little uniform and her fierce personality.

She dropped a dishcloth on the counter and turned to stare at him. "So . . ."

Much more of this and he'd be on the floor with his mouth trailing up her thigh. "That's a hell of a conversation starter."

"Let me finish."

"Of course." He put the last of the glasses on the counter and shut the drawer. "Go ahead."

"Since you stayed here all day I'm beginning to think you take this unwanted bodyguard position seriously."

That's what she wanted to talk about? "Very."

The radio played in the background. Hard rock. Not exactly the most romantic of tunes wailed through the room, but it's not as if he heard the words anyway. He was too busy watching her legs, one crossed over the other. Seeing the way the buttons on the top of her uniform pulled across her chest as she moved.

He needed to rein it in. There would be no touching unless she asked for it.

"It's hard to believe that you normally spend most of your days just walking around outside," she said.

He feared the casual chitchat might make his brain explode. He pretended to go along with it even as the need to touch her screamed through him. "Usually I sit in an office and order people around."

"I can totally see you doing that."

"I'm good at it." This, whatever this was? Yeah, he wasn't so good at this.

"Because you're bossy."

"That's not wrong." His hand knocked against the glasses and the clanking drowned out the loud music for a second. Not his smoothest moment. None of this was.

"You had to be bored." She reached over and turned off the radio. The move had her stretching across the counter and her uniform slipping up higher on her thighs.

Now she was just playing with him. That had to be it. Unless he'd totally lost it and was in this moment alone, she had to feel the pinging sensation and know every word and every move upped the tension. It thrummed off the walls and smacked into him.

"Since I spent most of the time today watching you, no." That wasn't a lie. He'd thought about fucking her all damn day. The job was to keep her safe, but that's not where his mind wandered.

"Ah, I see. Was that in your capacity as bodyguard or something else?"

"Mostly the former, but I did take a few peeks on behalf of the latter." *Few* meaning constant.

"And now you've unloaded the dishwasher again." She looked down at his hands where they rested on the edge of the counter. Slipped one of hers over one of his.

Oh, she definitely felt the pinging. He'd wager his entire net worth on that. But he kept his voice steady . . . somehow. "As far as skills go, it's not a bad one to have."

"Matthias." She sighed at him. "Any chance I could get you to kiss me again?"

Hot damn. "Is this for scientific purposes or—"

"It's for me. Because I want you to." She held his gaze. Sounded sure.

He turned to face her head-on but didn't touch her. Not yet. He wanted to draw this out and make every minute count. "I love a woman who knows her mind."

"Not too forward for you?"

It was as if she hadn't been paying attention. "You could strip naked and wrap your legs around me and I wouldn't find you too forward."

She winked at him. "Baby steps."

That's all it took. One shift in weight and he was on her. Had his hands around her waist and his mouth on hers. Not sweet and not charming. He dove in, branding her. He wanted her to remember this kiss. To feel it whenever she thought about him.

She didn't pull back. Didn't hesitate. She met him move for move. Toured her hands over him as her mouth pressed against his. She was so damn hot and responsive.

His brain said to ease on the brake but his body shouted something very different. His hands slid down her sides and kept going. When she widened her stance, opening her legs even further, he slipped his fingers past the bottom edge of her skirt. Skimmed over her soft skin until she trembled and even then didn't stop.

When he hit the edge of her underwear a warning signal blared in his head. He might have stopped if she hadn't moaned. The sound ran through him and his fingers moved higher. He touched her through her underwear. Rubbed back and forth until her hips pushed forward, matching his rhythm.

The click barely registered. It hit the back of his brain and sat there. Then his body jackknifed into action. He pulled back, just enough to reach for his gun. "What was that?"

Garrett walked in with his hands up in the air. "It's just me . . . well, now."

His gaze went to them, to Matthias's hand, which was still touching her.

Kayla punched Matthias's shoulder. "You didn't lock the door?"

"He's like fucking germs. He's everywhere." Matthias growled the response, assuming Garrett would get the hint and go.

But no, he just stood there. Smiling.

"That's heartwarming." Garrett's gaze went to Matthias's arm. "Maybe if you could take your hand out of her dress, we can talk for two seconds." His smile widened. "Unless you already told her your brilliant new plan."

Kayla groaned and not the good kind. "Is this going to tick me off?"

"Doesn't everything?" But Matthias backed up, gave her a bit of space.

Garrett pretended to cough into his hand. "Asks the guy who's currently feeling her up."

That made Matthias move faster. He slipped his hand out of the warmth between her legs and smoothed her skirt down. He aimed for chivalrous, but he had no idea if he hit the mark. "No one asked you for a play-by-play."

"My life was much quieter before you two came to town." Red still stained her cheeks but she sounded back in control as she turned and leaned against the counter.

"And more boring," Garrett said.

"Don't be so sure." She shooed them toward the dining room. "In the other room. We may as well find a table because I sense I'll need to be sitting down for this."

Matthias tried to ignore Garrett and his smirk as he walked past him. He continued into the dining room and stopped when he got to the first table. Someone stood at the front door and kept knocking.

"Who's that?" But he was pretty sure he knew. While following Kayla, he discovered her friend. He'd checked into her. She was a hometown girl, completely invested in the community long before Kayla moved in. There was nothing in the woman's past that raised an alarm with regard to Kayla.

"My friend Lauren," Kayla said to Matthias. "I told you I had one."

After delivering the comment, she tried to zoom past Matthias. He caught her arm just in time. Looked like they needed to have a conversation about the intelligence of running to open the door when a stalker was on the loose. But he'd wanted to meet this friend, so that meant getting her inside. He nodded to Garrett. "Let her in."

Kayla glanced at Matthias. Bit down on her lip. "She doesn't know."

The sentence was cryptic but he got the point. Kayla's need for secrecy extended to everyone. He knew about her past because he came to town armed with the information. That didn't mean Kayla had filled Lauren in. "If she's your friend, she might be in danger."

"Enough." Kayla held up her hand. "You made your point."

He let go of her arm then, but he really didn't want to. "Excellent."

Garrett unlocked the door and motioned for Lauren to step inside. "Hello."

She eyed him up as she slid past him and came inside. When she saw Matthias she came to a stop. "And you are?"

Kayla piped up before he could answer. "Lauren, this is Matthias. He's the investigator I told you about."

"When did that happen?" He'd been with her or watching her personally for all but a few minutes when he visited the dive shop and the place below Kayla's apartment. None of his men told him she'd had a visitor.

"He's actually more of a self-appointed bodyguard. This is his assistant . . . or something." Kayla waved a hand in Garrett's direction. "I'm not clear on their work relationship."

"Neither is Matthias. I'm Garrett." He shook Lauren's hand and then they all stood around a four-top.

"What's going on?" Lauren asked as her gaze moved around the table.

Matthias knew Kayla trusted Lauren. As someone connected to the area, Lauren might prove helpful in gathering information on the break-in, so Matthias was fine with providing intel . . . up to a point.

He nodded at Garrett. "Go ahead."

"The quick and dirty version?" Garrett asked. "Someone broke into Kayla's place, trashed it and wrote a threatening message on the wall."

Lauren put her palms on the back of the chair in front of her. "Wait . . ."

Garrett looked at Matthias. "Do you want to take it from here?"

He wanted to take this a bit slower so he could assess Lauren and her reactions and give Kayla a second to breathe. It was her life they were in the process of unraveling. "Everyone sit down."

Lauren slid out a chair and dropped into it.

The rest of them obeyed, too. Matthias figured he got lucky with that because it wasn't like Kayla to blindly agree to anything he said. Even something as simple as this.

"The big secret is . . ." Kayla's voice trailed off as she looked at him.

He slipped a hand over her knee under the table and gave it a reassuring squeeze. "If you're ready."

But she didn't just bluster forward. Sometimes she talked fast and rushed out her words. Not here. Not this time. A full two minutes ticked by. More than once Lauren started to talk but stopped again when Matthias shook his head.

At minute three, Kayla inhaled a deep breath and began. Her words came out low and sounded pained. "There was a murder while I was in college. A massacre, actually. My housemates. All of them. I'm the only one who survived."

"Apparently her continued living pisses someone off," Garrett added.

Kayla frowned at him. "I wasn't going to say it that way, but yeah."

Lauren blinked a few times. She shook her head, as if she were trying to force the words to make sense. "Murders?"

"Seven years ago and nowhere near here." Kayla rubbed her hands together over and over until the skin turned red. "We'd just started our junior year. Had moved into this fantastic old house about six blocks from campus."

Just saying the sentences seemed to make her body

cave in on itself. It was as if the weight of the words leaving her body deflated her. Matthias had no idea how to help her or make it better. For a man who spent his entire life saving so he could make up for the one time he'd failed to do so, watching the pain play across Kayla's face and haunt her eyes made him feel useless.

"So, the stalker you have now is related to the murders?" Lauren stopped there, but her meaning wasn't a mystery.

Matthias didn't know how much Kayla had told her friend, but obviously something. Clearly the stalker part wasn't news. It made him wonder what other intel Lauren might know.

But now wasn't the time to dig into that or ask about her clients and her business. Later.

Kayla slipped a hand under the table. Her fingers touched his thigh and he immediately reached out. Their fingers entwined and he tried with all his might to send strength to her through the simple touch.

"For the first few years right after, while the investigation was ongoing, there were all these questions and reporters." Her voice cut off. "After the police cleared my name the threats started. I've been followed around ever since. Every time I change my name and try to make a new life, someone tracks me down."

Lauren frowned. "Do you know who?"

That question could only lead to trouble, so Matthias jumped in. "We're going to skip over that question for now."

"Convenient," Garrett muttered under his breath.

Matthias didn't feel one ounce of regret for talking right over Garrett. "The point is, we're here to look into this and see if we can solve this once and for all."

Lauren's frown hadn't eased. "Solve what though?"

Matthias answered. "The murders."

"The identity of my stalker," Kayla said at the same time.

"Well, that was interesting." Garrett hummed. "Seems we have another communication issue."

"I think I'm a little lost, but I'll catch up." Lauren glanced around the table one more time before her gaze landed on Kayla. It hesitated there before moving on to Matthias. "Tell me what you're doing now. What exactly is the plan?"

There was only one thing that could happen, in his view. "I'm going to move into Kayla's apartment and pretend to be her boyfriend. That will—"

"What?" Kayla's head shot up and she dropped his hand. "Hold on."

"Impressive how you slipped that in there," Garrett said.

Matthias shrugged. "I tried."

Lauren leaned across the table toward Kayla. Reached an arm out toward her as she looked at Matthias. "Who are you again?"

The protective gesture eased some of the tightening in his gut. Lauren looked ready to throw her body in front of Kayla's. Matthias would never let that happen, of course, but the show of loyalty almost made him smile. "Her bodyguard."

"Hired by?"

She was almost as tenacious as Kayla. "Not relevant."

"There's an interesting answer."

Yeah, he definitely understood why the women got along. Neither of them ceded ground during a discussion. "The point is that I don't want her alone. I also need her to continue on with her daily life, not act like she's on edge or in danger."

"But she is," Lauren said.

Since Kayla looked a bit too stunned by his bombshell to take over, Matthias kept talking. Besides that, he had no intention of having his plan change, arguments or not. "To date, this stalker has thrived on ruining Kayla. Running her out of town, making her change her life around and hide. If she stands her ground this time, we can flush him out."

Kayla shifted in her seat next to him to face him. "That's really the plan?"

"That's ridiculous," Lauren said. "She'll be a target."

"But I'll be there." An obvious point and one he thought they'd get without him highlighting it.

"Are you immune to bullets?"

Kayla would pick this moment to snap back into the conversation. Lucky him. "Not really."

"Kayla." Lauren put her hand over Kayla's on top of the table. "Come live with me. We'll call the police or the FBI or . . ." Her gaze moved to Matthias's face and stayed there. "What's with that expression?"

"The you're-not-going-to-win thing?" Garrett scoffed. "He's really good at it."

"If she goes with you then you'll be in the way and I'll have to guard two of you instead of one."

Kayla pinched his thigh. "Matthias."

Apparently that wasn't delicate enough. Fine, he got the hint and tried again. "And Kayla doesn't want you in danger."

"Better," Garrett said.

Kayla put her second hand over the one already holding Lauren's. "Matthias is absolutely right about one thing. This has to end. I really can't take much more."

"I get that and I agree, but you've gone from this lone wolf to having a stalker and now these two and . . ." Lauren shook her head. "God, how did you survive?"

Matthias had the same question. He knew what it was like to be alone and feel abandoned. He understood guilt and pain. He got through because he had a group of men, like Wren, who forced him to redirect his frustration and not just wallow. Somehow, Kayla managed all of that on her own. He respected that and he didn't respect that many people.

"The killings? I was in the shower." A sharp whack of silence hit the room. The chairs didn't move. No one shifted around in a seat. "You can all stare at me, but it's the truth. I heard a noise, turned off the water and went downstairs to find . . ."

When her voice broke, Matthias took over again. "Okay, that's enough of that for now."

"Are you sure you can keep her safe?" Lauren had asked other questions but this time her eyes were filled with concern.

"Yes." Matthias didn't sugarcoat the extent of his

protection. "Her and by extension you. Now that I know Kayla cares about you, I'll have someone from my team stationed outside of your house and with you round the clock."

Lauren waved him off. "That's nice and all, but not necessary."

Matthias recognized the gesture because Kayla did it, too. He didn't like it coming from either woman. "Someone could try to get to Kayla through you, so it's happening."

"Fine." Lauren glared at her friend. "And this is not an excuse for you to run, so don't even think about it."

Garrett whistled. "The women in this town are made of strong stuff."

"She goes out on a boat every day. If she didn't have healthy self-confidence she would have thrown one of her male clients overboard by now." Kayla smiled as she reeled off Lauren's skills.

Matthias didn't need further convincing. He was impressed as hell with both of them. "I'll have my people take you home and then they'll shadow you."

"How will they do that out on the water?" Lauren asked.

"We'll investigate all of your clients and have a boat stationed nearby in case." That was just common sense, but Matthias didn't add that. He guessed Lauren would be as undeterred by his safety messages as Kayla seemed to be.

Garrett nodded. "You should do that regardless of the Kayla issue."

Kayla eyed Garrett. "I'm an issue now?"

"I'm not the one in danger," Lauren said.

"Being out there is dangerous." Garrett wanted to say more but was smart enough to stop there.

"And vomit inducing." Kayla held up her hands in what looked like mock surrender. "But hey, if they protect me, they protect you."

"That's emotional blackmail."

Matthias didn't know a whole lot about women, but he sensed the issue had been settled. "My people will meet you outside. I'll text them instructions."

"I feel like I've been dismissed," Lauren said.

Garrett stood up next to her. "Matthias does that sort of thing a lot."

"What are you going to be doing while I meet with your people?" Lauren pushed back her chair and stood next to Garrett.

Matthias had an easy answer for that one. "Convincing Kayla to fake date me."

"I'll walk you out because I'm not sure I want to see this." With that, Garrett guided Lauren to the door.

Matthias waited until the door shut behind them, closing the two of them in the diner alone, before turning to Kayla. "Well?"

"That's how you convince me?" Kayla leaned back in her chair.

He had no idea what the comment and the body language meant. The blank stare didn't give him any hints either. "You know my proposal is the right answer."

"The same proposal where I get to be a target."

He didn't like that word one bit. It sliced through him, burning as it went. "You could trust me."

"You're asking a lot."

Garrett slipped back inside and locked the door behind him. Then he started talking, clearly oblivious that he'd interrupted a conversation. "What's her story?"

But his question did grab Matthias's attention. "You're interested in Lauren?"

"I wasn't talking to you."

"A few years ago her husband went missing during an excursion. Both the deckhand and the husband were never seen again." Kayla sounded like she intended to say more, but her words rolled to a stop. "What?"

Matthias glanced at Garrett. Knew exactly what the other man was thinking. But getting into this would take them way offtrack. "Nothing."

Her gaze zipped back and forth between them. "You two are doing that thing where you look at each other and communicate without speaking."

"Did he have debts?" Garrett asked. "Maybe also a girlfriend Lauren didn't know about until later?"

"Why?" Kayla sounded more confused than ever.

Matthias took pity on her. "Lost at sea is a pretty common way for people to try to disappear. It generally doesn't work for long, because it's also the worst way to disappear. It's too obvious. It's the excuse novices use, which immediately makes it suspect. Add in the Coast Guard and its expertise, and getting away with it becomes difficult."

Kayla's mouth dropped open. "You do this for a living?"

He didn't really understand the question. "Disappear?"

"Don't be an ass. Answer me."

Garrett took over. "Let's just say we're familiar with the type of guy, usually a guy, who wants a life do-over."

"You think that's what Lauren's husband did?" Kayla sounded dazed. More so by her friend's possible predicament than her lifetime of fear.

Women confused the hell out of Matthias.

"We have no idea." He glared at Garrett when he snorted. "And I can only deal with one disaster at a time, and right now you're it."

"The way you said that almost guarantees you're going to stay in the bodyguard zone tonight."

That fucking sucked. "Damn."

Garrett frowned. "What does that mean?"

No way was Matthias answering that or letting her explain. "It's time to go home."

"Okay, I'll go along with this—"

"You don't have a choice." She seemed to be confused on that point and he had no idea how.

"—so long as you two buy new clothes."

Matthias stopped in the middle of standing up. "What's wrong with our clothes?"

She tugged on his pants. "You look like FBI. Worse, you look like sad FBI guys who got the wrong directions to a raid and were separated from the rest of your group."

Nothing said *you're not going to get laid* quite like when a woman pointed out a man's wardrobe failures. Even Matthias could figure that out. "You might watch too much television."

Garrett made a face. "What show would that even be?"

"No one is going to believe I'm dating a starchy dude in a suit. Find jeans or shorts or something," Kayla said, talking right over both men in the room.

"I can just take everything off." Matthias thought that sounded like a fair compromise.

She handed him her keys. "It's clearly time to go."

CHAPTER 16

They somehow made it back to her apartment. Good thing it wasn't far away because Kayla could barely concentrate to walk. She'd been dreading the return and having to deal with the idea of someone pawing through her things and spewing hate in the one safe space she still had.

As they got closer, Matthias tangled his fingers with hers. The simple gesture of holding her hand was ridiculously romantic and so out of character. He likely did it because it would make it easier to toss her into the water if he saw danger lurking and needed to act as a human shield. But it grounded her and was still sweet, and that was not a word she usually associated with him.

She let him lead her up the stairs and pretended he wasn't basically dragging her. The kiss had been so good back at the café that for a short time it wiped out the reality of what she had to face behind that door. The cleanup and coming face-to-face with all that fury being directed straight at her.

While on the small porch, Matthias reached around her. "I got this."

Before she could comment on the keys and locks, and all the other things she'd ignored for two days while she was gone, he had the door open. With a gentle hand on her lower back, he pushed her inside.

In panic, her eyes slammed shut as she crossed the threshold. Silence surrounded her. To maintain her balance she leaned into his strong body. Soaked in some of his strength.

It took her another second to work up the nerve to open her eyes again. When she did she could only blink. Everything was in order. Even the broken furniture looked as if it had been repaired. New pillows sat on the loveseat. Not the same ones she had, but similar colors, as if someone had tried to replicate her old place postattack.

"The apartment is back in order." She meant to think the words but heard them come out as a stunned whisper.

"Of course." He locked the door behind them. He held a stack of keys in his palm that jingled when he moved.

Reality crashed into her. "You did this."

"My people are very good at their jobs." He separated the key chains and held one out to her. "On that note, here you go. All new, so you'll need to decide if you want to give Lauren an extra set or not."

The wave of relief crashing over Kayla wiped out any concern about that comment. All that strangling tension finally eased.

She'd spent so much of the last few years on her own, depending on no one and ready to bolt. She didn't have people who took care of things for her, and generally didn't want that, but for this moment the reassurance of knowing he was there filled her with a humbled gratitude she didn't know how to express.

She inhaled, trying to kick-start her brain and wipe out the last bits of panic that had threatened to swamp her as she walked up those stairs. "What about the alarm code? There's no way you could break that."

He winked at her. "I love when you say stuff like that."

That ego annoyed the crap out of her sometimes. Not today. "I forgot who you are and what you can do."

He nodded as he walked around the apartment. He checked behind the few pieces of furniture and looked in the closet and bathroom. She knew it was a subtle security check. He was trying to make this easier on her, and she loved that.

He stopped at the bar that separated the kitchen area from the living area, which was not to be confused with her bed. That rested against the far wall to the left. "I like Lauren."

The change in topic shouldn't have surprised Kayla. This was what he did. As part of his job, he even tried to protect her from harsh conversations. "Me, too."

"Having someone"—he made an odd grumbling noise—"helps."

That bit of insight was new. She'd assumed from his body language and all that talk about "his team" that he viewed his work as his life. "Are you saying that because Garrett told you or because you believe it?"

"What does that mean?"

"Aren't you the ultimate loner?" She didn't mean it as an attack. Most people would list her in that column as well.

"Not really." He tucked his set of her keys into his pocket and headed for the loveseat. "I have friends. There's a small group of people I trust. Very small, but I do have them."

When he sank into the cushions, she staked out the coffee table in front of him. Without a word from her, he opened his legs so hers would fit between his as she sat down. They seemed to move in unison, neither balking at the comfortable silences between sentences.

"You give off this impression. Like, you sit alone in an office all day, go home for a few hours then head back to your desk and don't move. Rinse, repeat." That image fit him so well at the beginning. Now, not as much, though she still picked up a bit of a savior complex. Not in the dickish way. This seemed to come from the honest belief that he had a duty to protect her despite no one hiring him to do that.

"I don't deny the workaholic tendencies. I learned my work ethic by watching. There was this man . . ." That's it. Matthias didn't say more.

She'd never craved the end of a sentence so much in her life. "Who?"

"Never mind."

She knew if she didn't say anything else he would leave it there. They continue to run around in circles, never going deeper. For the first in a long time, she wanted more than a few minutes with a guy or the promise of being safe, if only for a little while.

She put her hands on his knees and leaned in closer. "If we're going to have sex, I want to know more about you."

He sat up a little straighter. "Wait, are we having sex tonight?"

No question. She'd made that decision during the lunch rush. So many secrets still spun around them. They had trust issues and she got the distinct impression he had much more to tell about why he was really in town. All of that suggested they ignore this thing between them. If for no other reason than self-protection she should back off and be extra careful.

Solid reasoning, which she planned to ignore. "I guess that depends on if you decide to confide in me."

"There's a sex test?" He held up both hands. "Don't get me wrong. I plan to pass it. I just need to know the ground rules."

His eagerness destroyed any last bits of doubt running through her head. "You might not like them."

"I like what I'm hearing so far."

The excitement in his eyes and the way his whole body snapped to high alert. This was one of those times she found him extra adorable. "You know everything about me."

"Not true."

He knew the worst and hadn't taken off, so that was something. She couldn't tell him all of it—not the worst part that no one knew—but she could try to explain who she was back then. "Before the murders I was a pretty normal college coed, completely self-centered and so sure I would get a business degree, move overseas and live this glamorous life. All while running in marathons and generally being awesome."

He laughed. "Sounds like a typical twenty-something."

The rich sound spurred her to continue. "I had a lot of confidence and a very supportive dad."

"Your mom?"

"She left long ago. I actually have no idea where she is." Before Matthias could offer the usual "I'm sorry" response that made her head spin, she pushed on. "The point is, everything was normal for me until the day it wasn't."

"I don't really know what normal is, but no matter who you are, stumbling into that scene had to be horrifying." The regret was right there in his eyes. "I'm sorry you had to live through that."

She guessed he'd seen the photos or at least heard enough to know this wasn't a case of kids dying in their sleep. It had been a bloodbath, with defensive wounds and a fight to the death. All things that made her the prime suspect for so long because no one believed that she didn't hear the commotion just one floor down.

But she didn't want to talk about her. "So, who are you, Matthias Clarke?"

"What you see is what you get with me."

Disappointment pummeled her. She'd expected him to play fair. "You're cheating."

"You know exactly what to say to get me talking about things I never talk about. I hate being accused of not playing fair."

"So then?"

He rubbed his hands up and down his thighs. "My mom gave me up and I never knew my father. Never had a huge need to track him down."

"Were your adoptive parents nice?"

"Well, that's the thing." He rubbed those hands harder. "There was an issue about the consent forms and trying to find her, so instead of a clean adoption I ended up back in foster care. There was a hearing to terminate parental rights but it scared off the people who planned to adopt me. After all the time and legal maneuvering I never got out until I aged out."

Her heart ached for him. She wanted to reach out and say things that she'd mean but she knew from experience he'd find them empty and not all that helpful. She'd sat on his side of this type of conversation before, on the receiving end of pity, and it lacked any sort of restorative power.

But knowing even that bit about him provided some insight. He was a man who had to fight for everything and never really knew where he fit in. So much of who he was fell into place.

She wanted to know more but not make the wounds deeper, so she went for what she thought might be an easier subject. "Who was the man you were talking about?"

Some of the tension left Matthias's shoulders. "His name was Quint. He rounded up a bunch of us, young men with potential and a strong need to have their skills focused into legal work."

She thought that was a good thing but couldn't be sure. "I don't know what that means."

"He ran a security company. The one I now own because I bought it from him when he retired."

"So, he was your mentor."

A small smile crossed his lips. "He was everything. He stopped all five of us from doing stupid things that would have landed us in jail or in the ground."

Every new piece of information cracked open his shell but led to more questions. "What exactly did he stop you from doing?"

"Taking revenge." He reached out and took her hand. "And I'm thinking that's enough show-and-tell for tonight."

The need for more pounded her but she bit back the thousand questions spinning around in her head. "Agreed."

They had other things to do tonight. Things that she thought about until she couldn't concentrate or sleep.

He turned her hand over. Ran a fingertip along the inside of her palm. Caressed every inch of skin. "So, is sex still on the table?"

"I'd prefer if we used the bed rather than a table." She lifted his hand and slipped his finger into her mouth. Twirled her tongue around it.

"You are so fucking hot."

"Tell me all about it while you take my clothes off."

"Deal." He leaned forward and planted a quick kiss on her mouth then stood.

He didn't move back. His legs were right in front of her. So close that she reached out and trailed a hand up the back of his legs and over his firm calf. "But I'm still dressed."

"For now." He unbuttoned his shirt. He almost moved in slow motion.

She watched as he revealed inch by delicious inch of skin. He slipped the material off his shoulders and dropped it next to her, but she couldn't look away from him. From the broad chest to those sleek muscles.

When he reached for his belt, she batted his hands away and took over the task. The belt buckle jangled as she slid the other end through. First came the button. Then the zipper. Her hand dipped inside his fly and wrapped around him. "Every part of your body is impressive."

His fingers slipped into her hair. "Wait until you see what I can do with it."

"So sure of yourself." She pumped her hand up and down a few times. Power flowed through her as he grew in her palm.

His fingers traveled under her chin and lifted her head so she could look at him. "I'm sure of you."

She wanted to push him into the loveseat. Take him in her mouth. But she needed his hands on her even more.

She somehow managed to get to her feet. She wasn't sure if she stood up or he pulled her, but she was in his arms. His hands moved over her, igniting a path as they went. Heat swept over her and her muscles pulled tight. And when his hands went to the buttons on her uniform, her breath caught in her throat.

"Yes." She leaned in until her head rested against his cheek. Looking down, she watched his strong hands brush aside the uniform and slip inside the flimsy material of her bra.

He cupped her breasts and let his thumbs flick over her nipples. In just a few touches her body caught fire. By sheer force of will, she stood still. But when he lowered his head and swept his tongue over her, back and forth in slow sensual torture, her knees buckled. Fighting to stand, she balanced against him for support.

His breathing echoed in her ear as his tongue slipped behind it. The shiver running through her had every bone shaking. The way he licked her, took her in his mouth and sucked on her soft skin, had her head falling back. She forgot how good this could feel.

A hand traveled down her body, pushing the rest of the uniform aside. Between kisses and touches, she shoved it down and off. Standing there in nothing more than a pair of blue bikini underwear, need overtook her. She wrapped her arms around his neck and practically jumped on top of him.

Without even a sway, he caught her. His fingers gripped the back of her bare thighs as she locked her ankles around his waist. The room spun around her. The walls came into focus again as her back hit the bed. Then all she could see was him, over her, touching her from chest to knee.

He kissed her, stealing her breath all over again. The taste of him was like a drug to her. She almost fought him when his mouth moved down her body to her chest. Her breasts ached from the attention and everything inside her started to pull tight.

The foreplay drove her wild. She craved his fingers lower, inside her. She was about to tell him, but he was already shifting.

His mouth traveled over her stomach. While his lips touched the top of the elastic band of her underwear, his finger slipped inside. That tongue skimmed over her through the cotton. Back and forth, tongue and fingers. He rubbed and caressed until her back lifted off the bed.

"Take them off." She tugged at the side of her underwear, trying to pull them off or at least give him easier access.

He trapped her hand against the mattress while his mouth continued its work. He nuzzled the material aside and his tongue found skin. She tried to open her legs to give him more access but the material still wrapped around and limited her movements.

She slipped her fingers through his hair and tugged until he lifted his head. "Matthias, please."

She didn't think he heard her until he moved to his knees between her upraised thighs. The mattress dipped, but he never lost contact. His hand skimmed over the front of her underwear then he pulled them down. Dragged them over her legs and threw them on the floor.

Then he was back. He reached into his back pocket and took out a condom. "I was hopeful."

She couldn't laugh because she couldn't find her breath. Air refused to fill her lungs as her heartbeat hammered in her ears. She wanted this—him—so much. This wasn't about needing to feel something. It was about needing *him*. His touch, his body, his kisses.

The realization slammed into her. She lay there totally naked, with her hands dropped beside her head. Open to him and willing to give him anything. "Do it."

"Hell, yeah." He put the condom between his teeth and shifted his weight.

She didn't realize what he was doing until he shoved his pants off. The mattress bounced, but she couldn't get up. She watched those muscles strain. Every part of him was so sleek and firm.

He slipped the condom on then opened her legs even wider. His finger slipped inside her again, pumping in and out. Her head rolled to the side as she waited right there on the edge, inches from flying apart. All it took was his fingers and mouth. She was wet and ready and . . .

"Matthias." His name escaped her on a sigh.

He pushed her legs back, closer to her chest. The front of his thighs touched the back of hers. And he entered her. Inch by inch, he pushed inside. Her tiny muscles squeezed around him as her body adjusted to his. He went so deep then began to move.

He plunged in and out, picking up speed as her breathing hitched in her throat.

Her muscles tightened and a rush of heat blew over her. Sweat collected on his chest and she fought the urge to lean up and lick it off.

When he slipped his finger over her, hit her with the double punch of touching her and being inside her, her back arched. Her hand pressed against his, guiding his fingers to exactly where she wanted them. Anything to bring his body closer.

Need spun through her. Excitement ratcheted up. She was so close that his final push started her orgasm. She came on a rough exhale of breath. Her hips bucked and her fingers locked on his hips.

The room blanked out around her as her body took over. She moved and shifted until she didn't have any energy left. She could hear him groan and tried to wrap her body around his, hold him as he came, but her arms wouldn't lift. Every muscle ignored the orders from her brain. She slipped into a state of relaxation as his body shivered and moved one last time above hers.

His elbows seemed to give out and his weight came down heavier on top of her. She didn't complain. The warmth of his body felt so good against her. His heavy breathing brushed over her neck.

She trailed her fingers over his back while they lay there in silence for a few minutes. His fingers played with the ends of her hair as his body cooled.

"Damn," he said without moving.

The sound of awe in his voice was one of the sexiest things ever. "That's what I was thinking."

He pushed up on an elbow and stared down at her. "What is it about you?"

"I'm not sure I'm all that special."

He took her mouth in a kiss that ended with him sucking on her bottom lip before letting go. "Wrong."

God knew he did make her feel special. "You should show me."

He groaned. "Woman, I can barely move."

This side of him, all satiated and cuddling, made her smile. She slid a hand over his ass and squeezed. "Are you sure you're done for the night?"

"I know I never said that."

"So, you want—"

His hands cradled her head. "Stop talking."

CHAPTER 17

Matthias still didn't know what hit him. The sex . . . sweet damn. The first time made him see double. The round in the shower had him rethinking his view on the subject. He wasn't a huge fan before her because he'd spent most of the time trying not to slip or fall. Not with Kayla. She got on her knees and he lost the ability to form sentences.

He loved that she knew what she liked. Hell, he just plain liked her. Not a sensation he was used to. He'd always been more of a sex-for-companionship-or-release kind of guy. With her, he actually wanted to stay over. The desperate need to race from the bed and get home didn't hit him in the middle of the chest.

The only difference he could identify was her. All of her. He'd had great sex before and had known a lot of amazing women, but the intensity of his feelings—hell, the fact he had real feelings—ran deeper this time. Chalk it up to the attitude, the strength and the very real sense she was a survivor. A kindred spirit. He actually thought about telling her things about his past he'd never said to any other woman. He craved the unburdening. That confused the hell out of him.

She showed him how she wanted to be touched and didn't hold back when it came to pleasing him. And that mouth . . . damn. After a night with her, he wanted to please her, which probably explained why he was wearing faded jeans and a gray T-shirt today instead of his usual business clothes.

Two men on his team actually did a double take when they saw him wearing the jeans. The stunned expressions almost made up for letting one of his guys go into his house and grab some clothes. The guy picked up Garrett's things, too. Which was why neither of them looked recognizable while sitting in the middle of the café the next afternoon.

"Look who's here."

At the sound of Garrett's voice, Matthias looked up from his cup of coffee. He didn't know what he expected to see but Wren heading right for them definitely wasn't it. "What the hell are you doing here?"

Wren stopped at the side of the table. He had a file under his arm and wore a severe frown. "What are you wearing?"

"We're blending in," Garrett said between bites of pie.

"With what?" Wren pulled out a chair and sat down. "This is an interesting way to conduct surveillance, by the way."

"We're on a break." Garrett swallowed then wiped his mouth with a napkin. "Which reminds me, baby-sitting Matthias here is a pretty good gig."

Matthias hoped this conversation ran out of steam soon. He decided to help it along. "Why are you in Annapolis?"

"Garrett told me there was kissing." Wren dragged Garrett's near-empty plate over to him and studied the last few bites and pile of crumbs. At the sound of footsteps, he glanced up. "Well, not between you two, but with . . . her, maybe?"

Kayla stopped right behind Matthias. "Oh, good. Another dude in a suit."

He would pay money to see her force Wren into casual clothes. Matthias was pretty sure Wren wore a black suit to bed. "Kayla, this is Wren."

She looked amused by the three of them sitting together. "Is that a first name or a last name?"

"Honestly?" Wren shook his head. "That's not really important."

Kayla sighed as she moved around to the side of Matthias's chair. "Apparently all your friends have that mysterious and annoying thing going on."

"If it's any consolation, he doesn't have that many friends," Garrett said.

"Understandable." She talked tough but she put her hand on Matthias's shoulder. Massaged it.

Matthias didn't hate that. "Wren is Garrett's actual boss."

She made a pffft sound. "I don't really understand the business relationship of any of you. And please don't spend two seconds trying to explain it."

Wren grabbed the last piece of crust off Garrett's plate. "It's fluid."

She hummed as she glanced at Matthias. "Wow, he's more cryptic than you are."

Now, there was an understatement. Wren was the

most paranoid person Matthias had ever met. "You have no idea."

"I brought some information." Wren's gaze bounced to Kayla then back to both men. "Should we . . . uh . . ."

"No." They were way past this point. She knew about his life. He knew about hers. Parts only, sure, but those fundamentals formed a bond of sorts. Matthias was not about to wreck that now. "It's her life."

"Good answer." She squeezed his shoulder. "You're learning."

"I have some skills."

"One problem." She pulled out the chair next to him and sat down. "When did you plan on sharing the big news that your friends are investigating me?"

"Never, since I didn't know." He'd specifically told Wren to keep out of this. He tracked her down but Matthias was determined to handle everything from there.

"I'm investigating the underlying murders," Wren said as he put a file on the table.

Garrett cleared his throat. "This might be a good time for me to mention that neither Wren nor Matthias have any people skills. Wren is getting better because his girlfriend is making him, but as you can see he still has a long way to go."

"I think I want to meet this girlfriend," she said.

"We all do." Matthias planned to do exactly that once he was back in DC. It would teach Wren to interfere with someone else's personal life without permission.

"Enough of that." Wren tapped the folder. "Back to the murders."

Matthias looked around. There were three full tables

and someone sitting at the counter. No one seemed to be watching, but there was no reason to invite strangers into their conversation. "Maybe don't yell that."

Wren stared at Kayla. "Doug Weston."

She tensed. Matthias was in tune with her body but he would have picked up on the move without having seen her naked. The full-body cringe stuck out. That was especially interesting since he remembered reading the name in one of Wren's files on her. "What about him?"

"Who?" Garrett asked.

"He was a friend of all of yours in college." Wren's deep voice rang out even though he whispered, or performed his version of a whisper. "He disappeared about two years after the murders, right after graduation. He'd been on the suspect list before then."

She balanced her elbows on the armrests. "How do you know all that?"

Wren shrugged. "I have an *in* at police headquarters."

"In Syracuse, New York?" She snorted. "I don't think so."

"Everywhere, actually."

She fell back into her chair. "Yeah, I don't get that answer. Like, at all."

"He collects information then passes it on to me to act on it," Matthias explained. "It's more complicated than that, but think of that as the general rule on how our businesses work together."

Garrett glanced at her. "Move on. Trust me."

"As if I have a choice." She looked at Matthias. "I thought the goal was to find out who was stalking me."

While Matthias knew some of the information Wren

just passed on, mostly because Wren texted bits and pieces to him, it was hard to see how it could be anything but relevant. "It's logical that the original killer is the one hunting you. Maybe he or she thinks you saw something."

"No, you've got this wrong." Her chair creaked as she turned to face Matthias. "Listen, I haven't seen or heard from Doug in years. I left Syracuse after . . . after they died."

He heard what she was saying but didn't understand how that absolved Doug of anything. "But why not him?"

"He's not smart enough to break into apartments without tripping alarms." She sighed. "I dated the guy for a year. He could barely undo my bra strap without an instruction manual."

But that didn't mean he couldn't fire a gun. Matthias knew from experience being basically useless didn't prevent someone from also being dangerous. "Kayla—"

She nodded toward Lauren and the man with her as they walked through the door. "I have to get back to work."

Lauren smiled at Kayla. "We're about to head out, but I wanted to pick up the food."

"Right." Kayla got up and double-timed it to the counter. "Hold on."

"Lauren." Garrett added a nod to his greeting.

Before anyone could say anything else, Kayla came back holding two large brown bags. "Here you go. You taking the barfer out on the water with you this time?"

"That's not me, is it?"

"This is Elliot, who's going out with me today." Lauren made the introduction as she reached for the bags. "The barfer, as Kayla so delicately puts it, is Paul, my assistant. And he's gotten better."

"Because he stays mostly on firm ground," Kayla said.

Matthias was done hearing about barfing. "Sounds like a good call."

"So, how did boating lesson two go?" Kayla looked from Lauren to Elliot.

He shrugged in response. "I didn't drown."

"Good for you."

The shot of jealousy surprised Matthias. Kayla's voice was warm and welcoming while talking with Elliot. Matthias loved her style but he loved it more when she saved those smiles for him.

He looked at Elliot, trying to remove the keep-away-from-my-woman bullshit from his voice because he didn't want to tick Kayla off. "Why?"

Elliot looked confused. "What?"

"Why do you need lessons?" Matthias asked, even though he thought the question was obvious.

Wren glanced at Garrett. "I see his people skills haven't improved."

Garrett shook his head. "Not even a little."

"I'm thinking about buying a boat . . . well, a small yacht." Elliot reached over and took the bags from Lauren. "I figure I should learn how to handle one before I put the money down."

"Or you could, you know, stay on land." Kayla

nodded her head when one of the tables motioned for her attention. "Remember, the water isn't our turf."

"How do you figure that?" Wren asked.

Kayla's eyebrow lifted. "Can you breathe underwater?"

"Okay, good point."

As soon as Wren answered, Kayla took off to handle the table that wanted her attention. From there she slipped behind the counter and got the coffeepot. Matthias followed it all.

With her busy, he figured this was a good time to drop an unwanted bombshell on Lauren. Thanks to all the people hanging around she'd have a harder time going off on him. At least he hoped that was true. "A few friends of mine will be out today. If they shadow you, don't get nervous. I told them you were a pro and they'd probably like to watch your moves."

Her smile flattened. "Interesting you waited until now to tell me."

"I'm not stupid." And while he was in the process of divvying up his team's resources . . . "Is the barfer staying back in the office?"

"Why do you ask?"

"Just wondering." Because he hadn't been able to track down Paul. The kid was always going out as Matthias was going in. Two of his men had the same issue, so Matthias was now determined to check the guy out himself.

Kayla came back just in time to see Lauren and Elliot go. She waved and then came back to the table.

Wren turned to Garrett. "Is that the one with the missing husband?"

"Really with this?" Kayla rolled her eyes. "Her husband is dead."

"Sure he is." Matthias didn't buy it either. The lost-at-sea story sounded too convenient and too familiar. Matthias was not a guy who believed in convenience.

Kayla stared at all of them. "Do you guys all take a class in being difficult?"

"It comes naturally," Garrett said.

"I'm going back to work."

She barely took one step before Wren stopped her. "What about this Doug Weston?"

"You've got the wrong guy."

That was it. She made the declaration and walked away. Kept going until she got to the door to the kitchen. Slammed her heel into it to push it open.

Clearly they'd hit a nerve. Matthias now wanted to know why.

Wren watched her go. "Interesting."

"The Doug thing?" Matthias knew that would poke at him until he figured it out. That guy should be the lead suspect. He'd vanished. So had Kayla, and maybe Doug had for the same reason. If so, Matthias needed to know the details.

"Her. I wouldn't have picked her as your type." Wren looked at Garrett. "Right?"

Oh, shit. "Aren't you needed back in DC?"

Wren shook his head. "I've got time."

"He's into her," Garrett said.

This was the absolute last thing Matthias wanted to talk about. Ever. "And when you leave take Garrett with you."

"He stays here until we figure this out." Wren slid the file across the table to Matthias. "Hey, you're the one who asked for the favor."

"To find Kayla. Your work is done." Seemed obvious enough to Matthias.

"But I'm intrigued."

Garrett laughed. "Last time he said that he ended up with a girlfriend."

"Maybe this time you will," Wren said, sounding just as amused.

Yeah, no more favors. That was Matthias's new rule. "Shut the fuck up. Both of you."

"I almost wish I could stay." Wren made a tsk-tsking sound. "Any woman who can make Matthias Clarke turn his life around is a woman worth knowing."

Matthias shook his head. Made a noise. Broke out all the nuh-uh-sounding responses he could think of. "It's not like that."

Wren looked at Garrett then back to Matthias. "Then what is it like?"

He had been asking that since he woke up this morning next to her. "I have no fucking idea."

CHAPTER 18

Hours later, long after dinner and sunset, Wren left for DC and the marina settled down. Lauren and Elliot had come back in and the party boat of college-aged kids moved out after angry nearby residents called marina security there twice.

Now, a cool breeze blew through Annapolis and seeped in through the window. Kayla had left the curtains open just a sliver to take advantage of the fresh air. Not that she felt the cool draft. No, she was too busy enjoying the show on the other side of the bed as Matthias kicked off his shoes and reached for the bottom of his T-shirt.

He might not wear casual clothes often but he sure as hell looked great in them. She'd been mesmerized all day by the way the hem rested on his slim hips and rode up now and then to treat her to a peek of flat stomach.

She thought having him hang around would bug her. She'd been really wrong.

They'd fallen into a comfortable rhythm where he'd come in and out of the café during the day and she'd feed him. He never really had to ask and never got in the way. Several of the regular customers, older women who stopped by after book club and all their other activities, started waiting until they chatted with him before paying their bills and leaving. Listening to him make small talk with seventy-year-olds while he engaged in a bit of innocent flirting might be her favorite thing ever.

She lifted a leg and put her foot on the edge of the bed as she slicked moisturizer over her skin. "Have you noticed how many people have descended on the marina lately?"

"What?" He looked up then did a double take. His hands dropped and his gaze went to her legs.

Breast man or not, he was predictable on that score.

"Your people. Wren. All of Lauren's customers." She rubbed the excess lotion into her hands as she dropped her foot to the floor. "The person who wants me dead."

He winced. "Don't say that."

"I'm serious." She came around the bed and sat on the edge, facing him. "I moved here because it was quiet and homey. I could enjoy a small-town feel but be close to DC and not that far from NYC. Cities where I could easily disappear for a few days, if needed."

"Your ability to survive amazes me."

"We're alike in that way." The foster homes. Being passed around and never having a place to call his own. That had to change how a kid saw the world. Shape him. She couldn't stop thinking about that and aching for the boy he'd been.

"Are you telling me you're planning on running again?"

Man, he was not understanding her at all tonight. Which was interesting because everything about today had felt so . . . normal. "I'm saying it's getting crowded."

He'd stayed alert and played the role of body-guard even in jeans, but something between them had changed. A small switch, perhaps, but she no longer felt like he was in the way. He fit into her life. He didn't throw his money around. The expensive wrappings were just that with him. The man underneath was rock solid. Not entirely truthful with her yet, but since she hadn't divulged her ultimate secret—hadn't really told him about Doug Weston—she couldn't blame Matthias for keeping parts of his life private.

And it had only been a few days. If anyone had told her that she would open up a piece of her life, even a little bit, so quickly she would have laughed.

He unzipped his jeans and shoved them down, let-ting them drop to the floor. "I'm not going anywhere, so don't ask."

"I don't want you to leave." It almost hurt to say the words because they'd become true. In such a short time, she'd gotten so used to having him around.

She wanted to write the attachment off as a bit of loneliness and a lot of attraction. Most times she could. She'd look at him and think any woman would want him so long as he kept the bossiness to a minimum. But he was more than a compelling man with an amazing body, though he did have one of those.

His hands went to the bottom of his tee, but he froze as she talked. "That's a change."

This could be it. She'd been waiting for some weird anti-commitment gene to flare up. Not that she wanted a relationship . . . she actually didn't know what she wanted anymore. She'd spent years convincing herself being alone suited her. But having all these people around, spending time with Lauren, spending every other minute with Matthias, Kayla wondered if she'd just been compensating for all she'd lost. Lying to ease the pain.

Despite the risks and the very real possibility he'd put on his clothes and go sit on the porch, she dove in. "Wasn't that the point of telling each other some of our secrets? To establish some level of intimacy. Not just sex. Maybe to build the start of trust, though I'm not sure we're there yet."

His eyes narrowed just a bit and only for a second. "Sounds right."

Men. "Did my word choice scare you?"

"No." He threw the shirt on the bed.

No running. No signs of panic. Well, wasn't that interesting?

"Oh, really?" She picked at a string on the comforter. Tugged until it started to unravel then let it drop.

His gaze went to her fingers then back to her face. "Do I look scared to you?"

He looked hot and sexy and completely calm. Not what she was expecting at all. "Actually, no."

"Good. Happy that's settled." He walked over to stand in front of her. Shimmied his way in until he stood between her legs. "But I admit I'd rather not talk right now."

"What do you want?" She ran her palms up and down the outside of his legs.

"You." He leaned down and kissed her. Drew it out until her heartbeat rattled in her chest. "Riding me."

He knew exactly the right thing to say. She liked so many things about him, including that. "We still have too many clothes on."

"I bet I can solve that."

Before he finished talking he reached down and tugged on her top. Slipped it up and off her. She'd just changed into the pajamas after a quick shower but was happy to let him peel them off again.

His fingertips brushed over her bare shoulders and down her throat. Over her breasts. "You are so fucking beautiful."

She believed anything he said. With him, she did feel beautiful and powerful and strong. He didn't overpower her, unless she asked him to. And right now she wanted him to take charge.

She reached for his boxer briefs and yanked them down until they slipped just over his increasing bulge. The feel of the elastic on his sensitive skin must have done something for him because all she could hear was a soft grumbling sound at the back of his throat. That special noise he made when she ran her fingers over him.

He'd washed his face and drops of water ran down his chest. She caught one with her tongue. Licked his stomach as her fingers slipped the briefs the rest of the way off. Squeezed his erection and felt the steady thump of his heartbeat under her ear.

When she closed her lips over him, his hips dipped

forward. Strong hands held her there as she pumped him in and out of her mouth.

Then he pulled back and stared down at her. "I need to be inside you."

The words skated through her. "Yes."

Without saying a word he backed up and took her by the hand. Led her to the pillows at the other end of the bed and had her stand there while he crawled on top of the mattress. The nightstand drawer opened and banged shut again and she looked down to see a condom sitting next to his hip on the bed.

He reached for her. Strong hands landed on her hips and he dragged her over top of him, straddling him. "Perfect."

The position let her see him, all of him. Need pulsed off him and his erection rubbed against her. The fierce intensity in his eyes made her tremble. Not from fear; from anticipation.

She pressed forward, bringing her body tight against his while her mouth settled on his neck. She trailed a line of kisses around to his throat. Felt him swallow under her lips. She liked that so much she made him do it again.

Heat beat between them. When he slipped his hand over her ass and ran a finger along the cleft between her cheeks her stomach flipped over. Then his hand traveled lower, came around to her stomach, and a finger slipped down and inside her. Plunged in and out. Rubbed and caressed her until her hips pitched forward. When he added a second finger her brain scrambled.

With her mind wild with need and her body on fire,

she lifted her hips and reached for the condom. Drawing it out, she slid it over him. Taking her time until he growled in her ear. By the time she lowered her body over him, his moves had turned jerky and his breath stuttered in his chest.

The loss of control fueled her. She sank down. Felt him pulse inside her.

"God, Kayla." He buried his head between her breasts. "I need you to move."

"Not yet." She wanted to savor this. Enjoy every minute.

"Damn." He threw his head back. Strain showed in his neck muscles but he didn't take over.

Still, she waited. Shifted a little and did it again when a shot of pleasure spiraled through her. "You feel so good."

"You're so wet and warm."

Watching him hold his pleasure off was so sexy. She kissed him and even that slight movement had her internal muscles thumping. She needed to come. Wanted to feel him abandon all control.

She couldn't hold back.

With her knees pressed deep into the mattress, she pushed up then lowered her body again. Loved every second of friction. Craved so much more.

But her body refused to wait. She could feel the excitement revving up inside her. Her muscles shook with the force of trying to hold back, so she gave in. The rhythm overwhelmed her and she let it sweep her up. Let Matthias's hands guide her up and down on his length.

The orgasm ripped through her as she struggled to catch her breath. Her chest hurt from the force of it. She crushed her lips to his in a blinding kiss. Unleashed her moan in his mouth. Their bodies kept moving as the last ripples held her body in their grip.

To bring him with her, she squeezed her thighs tighter against his sides. His shoulders stiffened and she could feel him let go. His hips shifted and the heat continued to roll off him.

After riding it out, he dropped his forehead to her shoulder and bit down gently. The nibbling on her sensitive skin had her wrapping her body tighter around his.

It took another few minutes for their bodies to cool and the pulsing inside her to subside. Every nerve ending had sparked to life with electricity. They'd had sex several times now and it always felt like this. So secure. So empowering.

She lifted her head and stared down at him. She expected him to be half asleep. Instead, he studied her with an odd wariness.

The steady calm abandoned her. That look of his immediately put her on guard. "Are you okay?"

"I'm not sure."

She grabbed the comforter and pulled it up around her. Leaned back so some air could move between them. His words had splashed a bucket of cold water on her and she wasn't sure what exactly had gone wrong. "Are you having some sort of after-sex regret?"

"Not like you think."

That wasn't exactly a denial, but it was enough to make her move. She lifted up, separating her body from his. "I'm guessing this is where you become a dick. I should have seen it coming."

Things were going too well. Things never went well for her. Hell, they rarely worked out at all. That was the price she paid for surviving seven years ago. No peace. Not ever.

She jumped off the bed and looked around for her pajamas. Being naked struck her as wrong all of a sudden.

"Kayla." Before she could venture too far from the bed, he grabbed her arm. "This isn't what you think."

Sure, right. "Okay."

"I need to tell you something."

Terrible scenarios bombarded her brain. She landed on the most obvious one. "You *are* married."

"She's my birth mother."

The comment had Kayla sitting back down hard on the edge of the bed. "What are you talking about?"

"I need you to know the truth." He shook his head. "I should have told you before now. You deserved that much."

"Whatever it is, say it now." Because she had no idea what he was talking about.

"I came to find you because Nick was my half brother."

CHAPTER 19

His timing sucked.

Matthias was still thinking that ten minutes later when they were both dressed and Kayla's first bout of yelling had died down. She'd called him names as she paced around the small studio.

He didn't fight her or even answer back. He'd earned her wrath and now he would take it. He also hoped she would wind down at some point so that he could explain. There were no signs of that happening any time soon.

But he'd brought this on himself. Of all the times to tell her the truth, that had been the wrong one. He'd blamed the guilt running through him. He took pride in being honest, even when it hurt. For the span of time while they were having sex he could put it aside. He was pretty sure that made him a dick.

She'd talked about intimacy and trust and he still hadn't piped up and told her the one piece of his life that crossed with hers. The facts she deserved to know. No, he'd skipped to kissing. Didn't stop until he was inside of her.

The rest, about his life before and the body in foster

care. The years he spent hunting down the foster dad who thought it was okay to beat kids. She didn't really have a right to know any of that. He could maintain his privacy there without breaking any sort of unspoken code. He wasn't even sure he *could* share that and stay sane. But she'd needed to know about his connection to Nick so she could make a decision, and he hadn't given her that.

He'd fucked up.

She broke her five minutes of complete silence without looking at him. "Starting tomorrow I want a different bodyguard."

That was never going to happen. "Listen to me."

He didn't reach for her or try to touch her. She flinched anyway.

"We're done talking." Her gaze skipped to the bed. "Done doing anything."

He could wait for permission or he could just let it out. He went with the latter, knowing she'd storm out if she didn't want to listen. "I didn't grow up with her. I didn't even know who Mary Patterson was until the day she contacted me."

Kayla paced to the window and stood there, looking out. Ignoring him. "I don't care."

He knew he should stop but the words flowed out of him and he couldn't seem to shut them off. "She'd given me up. She was young and in no condition to take care of me. She talked about a drug problem and her attempts to get clean. Her family gave up. They didn't support her and my dad bolted, stand-up guy that he was."

Kayla's hand tightened on the curtain. "You can stop talking now."

"I'm not looking for sympathy here. I'm trying to explain." He stood in the middle of her studio in his underwear and he didn't care about any of that so long as she listened to him. "God, Kayla, I'd never had anyone and this woman burst into my insulated steady world, talking about how she'd changed her life and remarried. She'd found the right guy and got married then he died in a car crash. It was one horror after another, but she had this other son. The one she clearly loved when she'd spent a lifetime not loving me. Nick, the brother I never knew."

Kayla continued to stare out the window. "Nick never said anything."

"He didn't know." It was clear to him that Mary never intended to tell Nick or anyone that she had an older son.

"At least she loved you enough to give you another life."

"Mary Patterson is not the sweet lady trying to make amends. She came after me because she needed my money and access to resources." He remembered the initial conversation and how quickly it skipped from a description of who she was back then to how he'd made something of his life and owed her. She almost demanded that he step in and find out the truth about Nick.

He'd tried to build an emotional wall against her. Mentally insisted he didn't care that she'd found a life without him. Pretended Nick wasn't part of his past, so no debt to him existed.

But loyalty had won out. Matthias agreed after he'd looked into her, searched the records he'd purposely never checked. But that didn't mean he trusted the woman who gave birth to him. There wasn't a bond between them and she made it clear she wanted to maintain a strict emotional distance. She gave him up long ago and wasn't looking to replace Nick in her heart.

It had been a hell of an introduction to his only known blood relation.

But Kayla didn't need that level of detail. Matthias tried to choke off the words. Make the verbal unloading stop. But then Kayla turned and looked at him. She wore her pain like a blanket. It flashed in her eyes and dragged around her mouth.

"She told you I killed him." The hurt hummed under Kayla's words.

"She believes it." Matthias wasn't sure why. Even the little bit he'd read in Wren's file pointed to other suspects. To Doug Weston and another man who worked at the university and later killed his neighbors when his anger exploded.

There were hints about jealousy between two of the housemates. People in town had been interviewed. Still, Mary's anger focused solely on Kayla and he now saw that he'd picked up on that and silently blamed Kayla, too.

That was before he got to know her. Now, everything had changed.

Kayla shook her head. "So do you."

"I did." He had to admit that much because he couldn't lie to her about her life. "At first, before I met you."

Kayla stepped away from the window. She moved closer to him, but not within touching range. "You came here to hunt me down and drag me back. Your goal is to put me in front of a jury, regardless of the evidence. And for whatever reason, you being here made me a target. You don't think Mary is the one who broke into my place, but it sure feels like it to me."

He didn't want to argue with her about the last part, but he needed her to understand his motives. "No, I came here for answers."

That much was true. At one time he thought all questions would lead to her, but none did.

"Then, what, you couldn't resist me?" She let out a harsh laugh. "Is that what I'm supposed to believe?"

God damn if that wasn't the truth. "I didn't break in here. I'm not trying to find evidence against you. I absolutely do not want to hurt you. The exact opposite is true."

"What is this, Matthias? What are we doing . . . playing house? I really don't understand."

"I want to protect you." It was his go-to move. After a lifetime of providing the bodies and supplies to rescue people, it was a habit for him. He'd made a promise long ago. A pledge to step in whenever he could and not let another innocent person die on his watch.

"Why help me? Because it's what you do?"

"It's who I am and . . ." Part of him wanted to write off his feelings for her as part of that. She was one more person who needed him to put his body in front of her. She'd never asked to be saved, and she never would, but that didn't stop him from being him. The other part of him knew that he was there, in this studio, because he couldn't stay away from her.

"What? Finish that sentence."

"I give a shit about you." There it was. The hard truth. She was not a job. Not anymore.

"I don't—" Her voice cut off as glass shattered behind her.

Adrenaline kicked in along with his instincts. He wrapped his arms around her and they took flight. She groaned as they hit the floor. He tried to slip a hand under her head to keep her from cracking her skull. Also shifted so that she didn't take the brunt of their joint weight.

As soon as they were down, he dragged her body under his. Rolled on top of her as glass rained over his back. He felt the twinges through his thin shirt but ignored the pain. When he heard another sharp crack, he tucked her tighter against the floor and under him.

Gunshots. That had to be it. Someone had fired through the window and nicked the glass. Splintered it and now shards lay all over the floor all around them.

His mind zipped to the layout of the studio. He blocked out the memory of her standing right there, in the firing line, just a minute before. Thanks to their fight, his guns were over by the bed. He had one tucked in the loveseat cushions, but crawling to it meant leaving her unprotected and that was not going to happen.

She called his name as a siren wailed in the distance. That was the one thing he could count on. In a quiet tight-knit community, someone would hear the strange sound and call the police. The noise should scare the attacker away, but he couldn't be sure, and part of him wanted the person caught right now.

He eased up his hold on her, but she grabbed his arm and pulled him back down. "Don't leave me."

"Never, baby." He pressed a kiss to the back of her head and ran his hands over her. He didn't feel blood. Didn't hear any more shooting. "I think we're clear."

"I don't want to move."

He understood but playing defense was not his game. He put a hand against the floor, thinking to push up and look around. Glass dug into his palm. "Shit."

"What?"

"Stay here."

He needed a blanket and a way to move her that guaranteed her skin wouldn't be ripped to shreds. The siren grew closer. He thought he also heard voices, like maybe people were out on the pier. That was a dangerous game with a shooter on the loose, but he had to hope the activity had scared the person off.

He shifted his weight and leaned away from her. Kept stretching until he could snag the corner of the blanket off the loveseat. He shook it out best as he could from his position on the floor and wrapped it around her.

With a hand on her hip, he stood up. "I need you to wait here. Help is coming."

"I thought you were the help."

"Not tonight." And that pissed him off.

He took a step and more glass crunched under his bare foot. At this rate, he'd be in pieces before the ambulance arrived. That meant staying put and not running after the attacker. Grabbing a pillow, he put it under his good foot and stood up. Slid the thing across the floor in a half crouch as he looked for his phone in the new round of mess in the apartment.

He spied it on the table beside the bed and ignored every cut and strain as he went to it. His body seemed to move in slow motion and a headache slammed through his brain. He didn't remember hitting his head against the floor, but he must have.

He grabbed the phone just as the sirens rang out right outside. He trusted the police, but he needed his people on this. He looked down at the screen and the apps blurred. "What the hell?"

"Matthias?" Her soft voice carried through the room.

He looked down and saw her sitting on the floor in the blanket. The color had left her face and she stared at his arm.

He recognized the dazed look in her eyes and it scared the shit out of him. "Are you hurt?"

"You are."

He'd started to go back to her but stopped when she said that. "What?"

She scrambled to her knees. "There's blood . . . everywhere."

"I don't . . ." He touched his hand to his head. He could feel the wetness and see the red on his fingers. "Well, fuck."

"You've been shot."

CHAPTER 20

Kayla smelled rubbing alcohol and disinfectant. The combination brought back memories of another time. Another horror.

She grabbed on to the edge of the emergency room bed to keep from falling down. It was irrational and had nothing to do with the people, but she hated doctors and hospitals and police. It had been a nonstop parade of all of them during the last two hours and the voice in her head screamed for her to race out there.

"At least you didn't faint." Garrett sounded amused as he stood in front of Matthias.

"Go away." The white bandage wrapped around his shoulder stood out against his bare skin. He sat shirtless on the edge of the table with his legs dangling over the side. He'd come into the hospital wearing only underwear but now he wore scrubs.

Garrett shrugged. "We should probably talk about your bodyguard skills though."

"Shut the fuck up."

Garrett looked at her and smiled. "Yeah, he's fine."

Despite the good news, panic crashed through every part of her. She hadn't been able to sit still when the ambulance came or when she saw the blood running down the side of Matthias's head and pooling on his arm. So much blood. Her adult life had been painted with it and the smell made her want to heave.

She closed her eyes and tried to focus on what the paramedic had told her. Head wounds came with a lot of blood. That didn't necessarily mean anything. The doctors here in the emergency room insisted Matthias was concussion-free. But her stomach kept rolling.

"Are you sure you're okay?"

At the sound of his concerned voice, her eyes popped open. She looked at him, saw the frown and the worried expression and rushed to reassure him. There was enough trauma without her adding more. "A few cuts and a sore back from when we hit the floor, but I'm fine."

"Good." Garrett did that annoying clapping thing. "We got our story straight and delivered it."

She had no idea what he was even talking about. She'd been shaken up and thrown around. Her brain barely clicked on at this point. "What does that mean?"

"We're covered. We followed the story we discussed and agreed to."

"You basically ordered me to lie."

"Convincingly." Matthias shifted and winced. His hand went to his injured shoulder and stayed there. "And what's not to like about our cover? There was a party boat on the water and people drinking too much and having a good time on the pier. Someone went too far when celebrating and I got hit by a stray bullet."

"Never mind that the whole story is ridiculous. It's also not even remotely what happened." Enough with the cover stories. They needed protection and investigators. Everything she hated, but that was tough. People she cared about worked and lived near the marina. Customers and tourists deserved to feel safe. If anyone got hurt or the marina got an unfair reputation because of her . . . damn, she could not live with any more guilt.

"But plausible," Garrett explained.

"It's a good plan." Matthias brushed his hand over the bandage, back and forth as if he didn't even realize he was doing it. "We could sell it because security had been out there. I'll also have one of your men provide some witness testimony."

They sounded so sure and practiced, like they'd done this a hundred times before. Maybe they had. This might be routine for them but shootings were new to her. She did not want them to become a habit.

The idea of Matthias being a step too late the next time shook her. She knew with absolute certainty he'd always step in front of her. But one time he might misjudge. He might be too late or go too far.

No, this had to end—now—and she was the only one with the power to do it. "We can't play around here. This is serious."

Matthias stopped looking around the enclosed space and stared at her. "It's always been serious. Someone threatened to kill you."

She didn't need the reminder. "What I'm saying is that there have been threats in the past, but they were just that. No one acted on them until now and look what happened."

Garrett scoffed. "He's fine."

"He's not fine," she shot back.

"I actually am." Matthias put his hand over hers on the table. "I've lived through far worse."

She wanted to turn her hand over and slip her fingers through his. Wanted to plead with him and make him understand that she could not have one more body on her conscience. She settled for raising her voice. For getting angry. "Don't be flippant. Now is not the time for your He-Man impression."

He squeezed her fingers. "Kayla, listen to me."

That soothing tone. He brought that out whenever he wanted to convince her of something. She didn't know where he'd learned the skill but it worked. Every time it lulled her, made her think about giving in.

Not this time. "You're bossy even when you're injured."

He shot her a crooked smile. "It's an all-the-time thing. Get used to it."

"I'm furious with you . . ." Fear overwhelmed her frustration. "But this is different. You could have been killed."

"Wait, what did he do to piss you off before the shooting?"

Kayla was about to wave Garrett's question away when Matthias answered. "She now knows about Nick being my half brother."

He told Garrett the truth. She had not expected that . . . then the words hit her and she turned on Garrett. "You knew before me? Was there an article in the newspaper and I missed it?"

"You two don't need me for this. I'm going to wait

outside." Garrett grabbed a fistful of curtain and drew it back, making a screeching sound of metal against metal on the rod.

"Hey," Matthias called out, stopping Garrett in mid-flight. "Handle the police."

Garrett glanced at her. "I'd much rather have that job. Much easier."

Then he was gone, but not before he zipped the curtain back in place. There was not much privacy. Every few minutes a voice would come over the loudspeaker, calling out some doctor's name. Bells kept dinging and she could hear the mumbled voices of the people in the next waiting area. But there, enclosed in the circle of the curtain and standing tight up against the bed, right next to Matthias, it did feel like just the two of them.

She looked at their joined hands. "Are you going to handle me, Matthias?"

Silence stretched out. He didn't move, so she glanced up to make sure he was still awake and hadn't slipped back into that glassy-eyed expression he'd had right after she told him about being shot.

But there was nothing clouded about his vision. He sat there, half slumped over and holding his bandage, but he did not blink. "We used the cover story because if we don't they'll investigate you. You'll become the story. Your past will be splashed all over the press again."

For her. He was doing this all for her. "That's not—"

"Suspected killer found in Annapolis." His deep voice rang out with that horrible potential headline. "You won't be able to move. It will all be brought out again."

The words sliced through her. She doubted there would ever be a day when they didn't. So much senseless loss. She owned her part in it. She accepted that guilt, but she wouldn't accept all of it. "I didn't kill them."

His hand tightened on his shoulder and he leaned forward until his face loomed right in front of hers. "I. Know. That."

She had to touch him then. Slid her hand over his cheek and felt the warmth of his skin. Her fingers lingered. She would have dropped her arm again, but he turned his head and kissed her palm.

"Why did you tell me about Nick now?" Looking back, running every line and every conversation, she realized he'd made a choice she might not have made in his position. He could have ridden this out. Enjoyed the sex and then left town, never divulging his tie to her past. But he didn't and she needed to understand why.

"Because you deserved to know." He moved their joined hands to his thigh and held them there. "And because I want you to trust me."

He made it sound so simple, but in reality, he was asking for the nearly impossible. "You're asking a lot."

"Give me a chance."

Forget the warnings flashing through her brain. That was exactly what she planned to do. "I never said I wouldn't."

MATTHIAS'S MUSCLES SCREAMED for rest. They'd talked with the police and been to the hospital. It had taken hours and led to so many phone calls. Wren had checked in. He and Garrett had talked and Matthias listened.

The whole time, he'd ached to get back to this room, this stupid inn. There was so much he needed to tell her. They'd ended their argument on an awful note and with so much left unsaid. She'd been furious, down to the clenched fists and wash of red-hot anger in her eyes. As much as he'd like to think the bullet got him off the hook, he knew that wasn't true.

But wading through all of that would have to wait. His body was a mass of pains and cuts. He'd refused all but over-the-counter pain relievers to treat the gunshot wound. It was more than a nick and less than a solid through-and-through. The bullet had taken a chunk of skin and that would hurt like a motherfucker for days. He'd already suffered from limited mobility. He didn't need the added distraction of falling asleep in the middle of a gun battle, so no meds.

Kayla walked past him to the middle of the room before facing him again. "You got a cot."

It was folded up and tucked under the window but hard to miss. "Garrett asked for it because I knew we couldn't sleep at your place tonight. I suspected you wouldn't want to sleep with me. Not after . . . you know."

Garrett nodded. "You're welcome."

"You should get some sleep," she said.

Matthias hated that she didn't brush off the offer of separate beds. He might talk tough, but the idea of lying next to her did sound good. But that's what he wanted and he'd made a silent vow to focus on what she needed. "We both need a shower. You go first."

She stared at him for a second then nodded. Without a word, she grabbed some clothes out of the chest of drawers and headed for the bathroom.

"Are you really okay?" Garrett asked after the door clicked shut.

"Shoulder stings. The knock to the head was worse. I'm not even sure when that happened." It felt like an all-star team had been playing basketball up there. Pain shot through him every time he turned his head, and the light hurt. He guessed by tomorrow the shoulder would start thumping and make the headache seem like no big deal.

"The fact you have something like forty cuts all over you probably confused your brain into thinking you had other issues to deal with."

It was a miracle they weren't both sliced and diced. If it hadn't been for the back of the loveseat catching a good portion of the shards, they might both be in the hospital.

They'd gotten lucky. He didn't want to tempt fate a second time by offering her up as a target again. Anyone who wanted to get to her would need to go through him.

Just the thought of how close she came . . . Jesus. He never wallowed in fear, but he sure as hell got a steady shock of it tonight. "She was standing in front of that window right before the shots were fired."

"You think the person's aim sucks or that they missed on purpose?"

"I'm trying to figure out why he escalated from threats to shooting." After years of following her around and making her life miserable someone suddenly wanted her dead? It didn't make sense. There had to be an intervening event that increased the attacker's anger level into danger territory. Damned if he knew what it was.

"She."

Matthias knew he missed something in the conversation. "What?"

Garrett sighed. "This could be a she."

"Agreed." Matthias didn't know which "she" Garrett was thinking about, but tonight wasn't the time to hash it out. "Tomorrow we go through everything. I want every photo and every document we have. The players, their families. Wren started on this Doug guy, but he had family and friends. Let's find them. We uncover it all and start over again, specifically looking into the original murders while we watch for our stalker."

"This feels like my regular job."

Good, because Matthias needed Garrett working at top speed on this. "We wanted to draw this fucker out. Well, he's out and he's shooting, so it's time we fire back."

"Do you think the bullet was meant for you or her?"

"Doesn't matter." It didn't because anyone aiming at her would now hit him. He'd guarantee that.

The door opened and steam rolled out. Her hair was wet and she had a towel balanced on her shoulder. She wore those cute pajamas he liked to peel off her.

He almost groaned out loud.

"That was quick." More like the shortest shower ever.

"I couldn't listen in on you two talking while the water was running."

"Impressive use of deductive reasoning. You should do this for a living." Garrett smiled as he headed for the doorway to his room.

"Dodge bullets? No thanks."

When Garrett started to shut the adjoining door, Matthias stopped him with a shake of his head then looked at Kayla. "We'll leave the door open between the rooms. If you need either of us, you call out."

"Where are you going to be?"

Matthias checked to make sure Garrett got the point, but he'd disappeared into the other room. "On the cot."

"You should take the bed."

"This isn't up for discussion." He honestly didn't have the strength or the will to fight her on this.

"You don't need to be a martyr."

"I promise you, I'm not." Matthias slipped off the stupid sling that had been holding his shoulder steady. The doctor wanted to put the arm in something more stable, but Matthias refused. Anything that slowed him down was a no-go right now.

"I hate that you lied to me again."

Her words stopped him as he opened the drawer to get a change of clothes. "I never really lied to you."

"Not telling me facts is the same thing as lying." She sat down on the edge of the bed and stared up at him.

Not to him. There was a line. Admittedly a thin one, but he recognized it. "We can agree to disagree."

She leaned back with her palms balanced on the mattress behind her. "How can you be so stubborn even after all that's happened tonight?"

"A lifetime of practice." No lying there.

"Nick would have liked you." She smiled as she seemed to disappear into her memories for a second. "He was funny and charming on the surface but much more complex underneath. Had this sort of simmering anger. After I met your mother, I decided she was the cause."

Part of him wanted to ask about Nick. Part of him wanted not to care.

No part of him thought of Mary Patterson as his mother. "Don't call her that."

"Isn't she your mother?"

He never really had one of those. After what he'd seen and the foster parents he'd survived, he never had the urge to find the woman who gave him up. He'd blocked her until she showed up looking for him. "She's the woman who gave birth to me. Didn't want me then, which I can understand. But doesn't really want me now either, so I prefer to think of her as Mary."

"She creates a lot of collateral damage."

No fucking kidding. "You're safe."

Kayla nodded. "So are you."

"You're going to protect me?" No one had ever protected him. Not really. Not like this.

"Count on it."

CHAPTER 21

Kayla walked into Garrett's room the next morning, slightly refreshed and a bit less likely to scream at anyone who came near her. Her nerves were still a jumbled mess. She could also use a few more hours of sleep. Checking on Matthias ten times during the night did nothing to help her get rest.

But it was a new day and she was ready to handle both Matthias and Garrett, and whatever annoying we-laugh-at-danger plans they had for the morning. Well, she was until she saw that they'd changed Garrett's area into some sort of makeshift control room. Garrett ran around while Matthias barked out orders with his arm in a sling.

Where in the world did they get a whiteboard? There were names listed across the top and stacks of files. She saw the edges of photographs and something that looked like a map. It looks like they were just getting started, but this undertaking was no joke. They'd slipped into overdrive.

She stopped right behind Matthias. "I hate to even ask what all of this is."

He didn't jump or sound surprised. "We're intel gathering."

Well, sure. That cleared up all her questions. "Should I be seeing this?"

Matthias glanced over at her. Shot her one of those what's-wrong-with-you frowns he did so well. "You see everything from now on."

That sounded like progress. She wasn't quite ready to forgive and forget, but at least he'd stopped hiding things from her. Or she hoped that was true.

She circled around the desk. Some of the newspaper clippings looked familiar. She saw two names on the sides of files—Steve and Jillian. The other two friends she'd lost. The ones without family members poking around in her life.

A wave of sadness washed over her, threatening to plow her under. She shook off the memories and focused on the paperwork. She could handle papers.

The men had gone quiet while she looked around but she could feel Matthias's gaze on her. The man always stood by, on guard.

Her gaze traveled over the disarray that seemed to be in some sort of filing system she didn't understand. Garrett did. He dug through and took a note out of one stack and a photo out of another.

Something pulled her attention away from the information in front of her. She kept looking around until she stared at the whiteboard again. She silently read the names in her head as she read across. The last column was the issue.

Her heartbeat kicked up and panic gnawed at her gut. She glanced at Matthias and found him watching her. Studying her.

"There's a Doug section." She somehow managed to keep her voice steady.

Matthias's expression stayed blank as he talked. "The police found cigarette butts with his DNA on them outside of your house the morning after the murders."

"It's not a secret. He came over and smoked. We didn't like it inside, so he did it outside." He was also immature and jealous. When she broke it off he acted like she wasn't allowed to dump her or move on.

They had all hated him. Nick and Steve banned him from the house. They did her dirty work because she told them how Doug followed her around between classes.

"So, it wasn't a smoking gun." Garrett held up his hand as he shook his head. "Sorry, just trying to lighten the mood."

It didn't work. Tension swirled around her.

She grabbed for the nearest piece of paper. It listed the names and personal information of the slip renters at the marina. "What's this?"

Matthias hesitated before answering. "We're checking everyone in the marina, including boat slip renters and regular customers of all the shops and the café. In fact, we're waiting on more information right now. Some surveillance footage and videos from along the pier that might show us if anyone was lurking around or carrying a weapon."

This topic she could handle. The stalker. The here and now. "You think someone fired at us from a boat?"

"From the bullet trajectory we're looking for a building at about the same height as your apartment." Matthias stepped over to stand beside her at the desk. He sifted through the top documents and dragged out a photograph of the pier taken from a boat that had to be some distance out on the water. It showed the entire waterfront.

She picked it up and studied it, not sure what it showed. "I've never seen this."

"It's for perspective and it shows the shooter likely was in one of these three buildings." Matthias pointed out the other multistory buildings near her apartment.

"Wow, okay." She'd seen that sort of thing on television. Putting the forensic terms to real life proved far more interesting than she'd expected. She just wished they were analyzing someone else's life.

"You haven't made me forget about the Doug question."

"There's no story there." She dropped the photo on the pile and moved away from Matthias. He had so many skills, and she wouldn't doubt that human lie detector was one of them. She needed to stay far enough out of touching range not to find out.

"Then let me figure out where he is and what happened to him," he said.

That's exactly what she was afraid of. Enough of her past had come rearing up. She didn't need to deal with the Doug chapter. Not any more than she already did every single day.

Thinking maybe some facts would help, she spelled them out. "We were accused of being in on it together. Then people talked about love triangles and jealousy. We were hounded and had our personal lives ripped apart. He's been questioned as much as I have. Is it any wonder that he dropped out of public view? I did."

"Not completely." Matthias gestured toward the folders on the desk. "I was able to find you."

"Technically, I found you," Garrett said without lifting his head or breaking his stride as he moved around the room, organizing his paperwork.

"Either way, you're looking in the wrong place. The answer is Mary."

Matthias shrugged. "Maybe."

The woman who hated her. Kayla was very clear on that point . . . and on the need to get out of there. Fresh air and a few hours of mindless work might flush out some of this extra energy. She expected to get questions about the so-called accidental shooting from well-meaning people around the café. It would take a good half hour to prepare herself for that.

"And now I'm going to get ready for work. Looks like today is casual day because my uniforms are back at the apartment and, clearly, I need to stay away from there for a while." She wasn't sure she could ever go back. One incident she might be able to ignore. Two? Not likely.

Before Matthias could pepper her with questions or ask anything else, she slipped away. Kept walking until she got into the bathroom in Matthias's room. She finally exhaled when she leaned back against the closed door.

She had the very real feeling Matthias wouldn't stop until he knew everything. Then she was screwed.

MATTHIAS WATCHED HER leave. Hell, she practically ran. When the issue of Doug came up, her demeanor changed. She switched from self-confident and open to shut off. She wouldn't listen to reason about him. Wouldn't entertain any theories.

If she was trying to convince him that Doug was innocent, she was doing a piss-poor job.

Garrett looked up from shuffling papers. "You notice how she doesn't want to talk about the actual murders?"

"It's hard to miss." It was also all he could think about.

He knew exactly what he'd do if someone killed the people he cared about. He'd track them down and exact revenge. The suffering came after and he owned that, but nothing would have stopped him from searching out the truth.

This was more than loyalty or fond feelings for a first love. Doug could be the key to everything.

Garrett looked into the next room then shut the door partway. When he returned to the center of his room, he leaned against the edge of the desk. "She separates out what's happening now from what happened then. Doesn't even seem interested in figuring out who killed her friends and turned her life upside down in the first place."

"Yep." It was as if Garrett had read his mind. Matthias had been toying with the same doubts and confusion ever since Doug's name came up. "That leaves us with three theories."

Garrett counted them out on his fingers. "She did it. She was in on it, or—"

"She knows who did it." That's the only option that made sense. It had been spinning in Matthias's mind and he couldn't discount it.

"Then why not sic us on that person?"

"Good question." He was right there. He'd made clear he could investigate or get Wren to do it. Between them, they'd test every theory. Hunt down every body.

Garrett sighed. "Do you have any answer?"

"No, but I will."

IT WAS LATE in the afternoon before Lauren showed up at the café for her usual check-in. She'd been out with a group of businessmen. Now she stood outside, talking with Paul. Seemed to be giving him a lecture, which made Kayla smile.

She needed one of those today. If one more business owner or tourist asked her about the shooting she'd scream. Like scream and not stop.

She watched Garrett watching Lauren. That made Kayla smile, too.

Grabbing the coffeepot, she made her way over to his table and refreshed his cup. At least he blended in today. Jeans and a casual shirt looked right on him. "How did you get stuck with guard duty?"

If she didn't know better she'd guess that Matthias

was hiding from her. They'd had a rocky few days. Every time he talked, she basically left the room. It wasn't all about him, but he couldn't know that.

"Matthias got a call and had to go to the police station."

She almost dropped the pot. It took two hands to save her from dumping it all over Garrett's new outfit. "What? Why?"

"Wren is working his magic to make sure this gets written off without your identity being divulged."

These men never stopped working. "He can do that?"

Garrett barked out a laugh. "He's freakishly good at his job. They both are."

"Since I'm alive today and not recuperating from a gunshot wound I appreciate Matthias's skills." Talk about an understatement. She felt a lot of things for Matthias—many of them unwanted but none that could be described as simple appreciation. She'd zoomed way past that days ago.

"The guy is good. Wren uses Quint all the time for jobs." Garrett usually engaged in sarcasm but his voice stayed steady. Even held a bit of awe in it.

Clearly Garrett was impressed. So was she, but she didn't have the details. Life was easier that way. She had enough to be angry about. "I don't think I want to know."

Garrett peeked at her over the top of his mug as he took a sip. "I wouldn't tell you if you did."

"Is it a good idea to send Matthias in to deal with people?" He wasn't exactly a master communicator.

He'd turned out to be better at connecting than she'd first thought, but still.

"No, but Wren has it under control."

"Wren . . . the same guy who was in here in a suit?" It was as if they had a secret club or something. "I'll believe you."

Lauren picked that minute to storm into the café with Paul in tow. Kayla looked behind her and saw the ice cream guy from the truck parked around the corner walking away. Oh, great. Lauren had heard the shooting news.

"What the hell happened?" Lauren called out before the door closed behind Paul.

"Who's the guy with Lauren?" Garrett whispered the question.

Kayla barely heard it over the banging of pots in the kitchen. "The barfer."

"I really hope his mom named him that."

Lauren came to a stop right in front of Garrett's table. "Where's your—"

"Her boyfriend?" Garrett glared at Lauren as he spoke. "Matthias will be back soon." Some of the tension left Garrett's face when he turned to Paul. "I'm Garrett, by the way."

"Paul. Hi." That's all Paul said, and even that was more than usual.

He was a young twenty-something. Seemed shy. Always wore that baseball hat and barely made eye contact. Lauren said he had a super brain for numbers and worked really cheap. He also needed spending money and some experience. In other words, a typical student at nearby St. John's. The same place Kayla had once thought she'd finish out her degree, but she guessed that was moot now.

"He's my assistant," Lauren said.

Garrett nodded. "So I've heard."

Lauren balanced her hands on the back of the chair. "What happened last night and where was Matthias?"

"Some stray bullets from unruly party celebrations. We're fine." Kayla tried to keep her voice light and carefree but she suspected she failed when Paul threw her an odd look.

Lauren didn't seem to like it either. Her mouth flattened into a thin line. "Bullshit."

Sensing they were headed for an explosion, Kayla tried to turn the conversation. She smiled at Paul. "Are you going out on the water today?"

His skin turned a bit green at the mention. "Tomorrow, unfortunately."

"How exactly do you plan on being on board if you don't like the water?" Garrett asked.

"My preference is to run the office."

Garrett shot the kid a man-to-man smile. "Ah, got it."

But Paul was still wincing and otherwise looking like he wanted to dig a hole and hide in it. He turned to Lauren. "You told him?"

Now Kayla got it. This was a stunning case of male embarrassment. Paul didn't like having his seasickness known. Since this might not be the town for it, she understood.

Lauren didn't sugarcoat it. "You threw up in front of a pleasure-boat cruise. The word was bound to get around."

"There are meds for that sort of thing," Garrett said.

Kayla took pity on the poor guy. She knew exactly how it felt to look out over the water and want to unload your lunch over the side of the boat. There were all kinds of tricks about watching the horizon or patches. None of them worked. She could attest to that fact.

"I think Paul is wise to stick to dry land." She touched an arm to his back, careful not to invade his space too much, and pointed at the counter. "Hungry?"

He looked at Lauren and she nodded. "We have time for a quick bite before we dig into some accounting."

"Sounds wildly exciting," Garrett mumbled, earning him a scowl from Lauren.

"Have a seat and I'll join you in a second." Lauren kept the fake smile in place until Paul was out of ear-shot. Then she turned on them. "What the hell?"

Garrett lowered his voice. "You might want to re-member Matthias is undercover."

"And apparently not very good at his job."

Kayla didn't like that. She couldn't let anyone think Matthias had fallen down on the job. It just wasn't like that. "I'm alive, so he's actually great at it."

"I'm sorry. I just heard the news today . . ." Lauren rolled her eyes at Kayla. "A warning text would not be a bad idea from now on. For the record, that's what friends do."

That was probably true but Kayla hadn't known how else to handle this mess. There were things she could tell and things she couldn't. People lurked around and anyone who overheard could be her stalker. Not exactly an easy road to walk.

She went with the most obvious answer. "I'm hoping that was the last time it ever happens."

"Right." Lauren turned to Garrett. "So, you're on bodyguard duty today?"

"For a few hours." He took out his phone. "I'm going to need to collect some information from you about Paul and the pier and other things."

Kayla's head started spinning again. "Wait a second."

"It's fine." Lauren grabbed the cell from Garrett's hand and added her phone number. "Done."

"You don't have to—"

"You know, Kayla . . ." Lauren wrapped an arm around Kayla's shoulder. "This would be a good time for you to figure out you're no longer alone. I am going to do whatever I can to help and to keep you safe. So deal with it."

Said so honestly and without any ego, the words stormed through the last of Kayla's defenses. "Okay."

"Now, I need pancakes." Lauren's gaze moved to Garrett when he started to talk. "Yes, I know that's breakfast but I'm feeling like breakfast."

With a wink, Lauren walked away. She went over to the counter and sat down with Paul.

Garrett watched and didn't even try to hide the fact he was staring at her ass. "She's right, you know. There are a lot of people who care about you and want to help you."

She wasn't the only one on the team. Kayla knew that. "Matthias."

"He fucked up but he's trying to make it better."

The seriousness of Garrett's tone caught her attention. They may joke around but the connection was real. "I know but, honestly, sometimes I want to punch him."

The tension expired and Garrett laughed. "Oh, I get that."

"This just all needs to end."

He nodded. "Give it time."

Wrong answer. "I've given it seven years."

CHAPTER 22

Matthias was in the last place in the world he wanted to be, one of his satellite offices near the Capitol in DC. Wren summoned him. Told him they had a problem. Wren didn't make statements like that without meaning them.

By the time Matthias got there, he realized Wren was actually understating the problem. He'd been tracking Mary Patterson . . . and she was in town. Landed two hours early, only to be picked up at Wren's request.

His friend did know how to fix a problem.

Matthias stood with Wren, watching Mary through a two-way mirror. Matthias didn't use the room often; it was mostly for security protocols and to test his team on how to beat a lie detector. But the space did come in handy sometimes.

Wren clapped Matthias on his good shoulder. "Ready to say hi to Mom?"

He winced at hearing her called that. "Thanks for handling this."

"It's what I do." Wren didn't say anything else. He walked out of the room and Matthias followed.

The ten steps from one side of the mirror to the

room on the other were some of the longest Matthias had taken. He had zero interest in the upcoming conversation, except to figure out why Mary thought dropping in unannounced was a good idea. The timing with the shooting made him more than a little suspicious.

They walked in to find Mary sitting at a table, playing on her phone. She glanced up, looked down then her head popped up again. She looked at Matthias's shoulder sling then scowled.

Matthias assumed that qualified as motherly concern on her part. "I'm surprised to see you."

"What happened to you?" She didn't stand up. No hug. No kiss. No real hello. Didn't even put down the phone.

"I'm fine." Not that he thought she cared all that much about his state of mind or his health.

Since meeting Kayla, one thing had become very clear in his mind, the thing he hadn't wanted to admit or deal with before now—Mary's sole intent was to use him. Her "real" son was gone and she wanted answers. He understood that drive. Hell, he didn't even know Nick, except for the bit he'd learned from Kayla and the hero worship from the woman in front of him, and he wanted answers for the poor kid.

No one should die that way, carved up and left to bleed out. The forensics report made it clear Nick had likely taken both the brunt of the attack and the longest to die. The defensive injuries meant he'd been awake and saw his attacker.

He'd choked on his own blood as the life seeped out of him. It was shitty and violent. The crime scene reeked of overkill. The idea that Kayla walked into that without warning made Matthias fucking pissed.

But he had another woman to worry about right now. One with a secret agenda and a problem with sincerity.

Mary waved her hand in front of him. "Did she do this to you?"

"You think Kayla hurt me?" The idea was ridiculous. Even Wren smiled. "Come on."

Mary's face flushed red and anger poured off her. "You don't know what she's capable of."

Before she could wind up and start spewing, Matthias cut her off. "Why are you in town?"

He knew where Kayla was and why. She was not running from the law. If anything, she welcomed it after he got shot. Nothing Mary told him about Kayla had turned out to be true.

"You told me you found her. I needed to come and see for myself, but you didn't give me that address. I'd planned to go to Annapolis and call you to come get me." Her gaze shot over to Wren where he stood leaning against the only door out of there. "I didn't expect to be picked up and brought here."

"My friend can be dramatic." Even Matthias had to admit the fake airport pickup was a bit over-the-top for Wren.

Wren shrugged. "It seemed like the right thing at the time."

She'd stepped out of the airport, thought she was

getting into a cab, and Wren's people brought her here. They told her immediately, which showed even Wren drew the line at kidnapping an unsuspecting woman.

No matter how it all played out, she needed to go home now. Having her here would put Kayla on edge. She already didn't have much faith in him. Seeing Mary would not help that situation. Matthias had a big enough hill to climb when it came to Kayla.

He sat down across from her. "You should go back."

"No." She turned her phone facedown on the table. "I have waited for years to find her."

She was not great at subterfuge. Not very smart about surveillance either. Before he put her in a cab at the end of this talk his people would be able to hand over her phone records and tell him what she'd been doing on that phone before they walked in. The place had cameras and high-tech equipment everywhere.

It was in his damn office. He knew everything that happened in it.

He knew some other information as well. "You've found her before." Kayla made that clear even though Mary never admitted it to him.

Surprise flashed across her face but she quickly schooled it again. "What?"

Nice try. "This isn't the first time, right? But you lost her and couldn't figure out her new name, so you contacted me."

He hated that he looked at this woman who'd given birth to him and felt nothing. Not even a kick of anger. It made him feel like a heartless dick.

He felt sorry for the kid she once was. The idea of not having resources or an ability to take care of a kid made him crazed. But turning the corner and thinking of her as a mother? That wasn't happening.

"I thought you would want to find the woman who killed your brother."

"Half." The guilt trip was an interesting choice. That sort of thing worked because for whatever reason he did feel something for Nick. Neither one of them picked their parents. Matthias had to hope his dad had been decent.

"That distinction doesn't matter. Blood is not the point when it comes to loyalty." Her fingertips clicked against the table. "You owe him."

"I understand loyalty." The man standing in the room with him had Matthias's back. So did Garrett and all of the Quint Five, the original group Quint took in and trained.

He'd treated them like family. Respected them. Taught them about honor and brotherhood. Refined their skills and targeted their energy in more productive ways so that they could earn a living and not end up in jail. For the first time in his life, Matthias had been able to depend on someone other than himself.

So, yeah, he understood loyalty. He also knew it had to be earned.

Wren pushed away from the door and crowded in closer. "If you went to Annapolis she might see you and run again. You'll make things worse."

"That won't happen." Something about Wren seemed

to make Mary nervous. He stood just outside of her personal space with his arms folded, but when he approached she got jumpy.

Wren shook his head. "Don't underestimate Kayla. She's resourceful."

Mary pointed at Wren but talked to Matthias. "See, he knows how she operates."

And he'd had enough. "Wren's people are going to take you to the airport and . . . what?"

"I'm not leaving yet. I need to be here. For Nick." She choked on his name. "I'll stay in DC. I have a hotel room."

She didn't have any money. He knew because the money she did have had come from him. He'd paid off her debts and the mortgage she claimed strangled her and put her under a constant threat of bankruptcy. That left extra cash, but the hotel part still surprised him. "You do?"

"You investigate and I'll wait." She reached across the table and put her hand over his. "Me being here, ready to go find her, will be your incentive to hurry up."

He looked down at her hand. At the slim wedding band she still wore even though her husband was long gone. A wave of unexpected sympathy hit him. He may have missed a life with her, but she did have one once.

"I don't need motivation. I promise." He tried to make the words sound hopeful but he wasn't sure he pulled it off.

"I'll find someone who can take you back to your hotel." Wren went to the door and motioned for Matthias to follow. "Can I see you for a second?"

The second Wren's back was turned, Mary slipped her hand back to her side of the table. Once Matthias got up, she grabbed her phone and went back to scrolling.

She could turn it on and off. He hoped like hell he hadn't inherited that skill.

He stepped out to find Wren leaning against the wall. The ease with which he moved through the halls here suggested he owned the place. He actually didn't, but he had hit it big first and staked Matthias as he grew Quint and turned it into the powerhouse it was today. Matthias never forgot that assist from Wren, though Wren never mentioned it.

Wren exhaled. "Your mom is interesting."

Calling her that grated against his nerves even louder this time. "It's Mary, and I don't buy the story either."

"Any chance she's good with a gun?"

"I don't actually know her, but I doubt she has the skills to pull any of this off." She couldn't hide her desire to be on the phone. The idea that she could stage an elaborate plan and hunt Kayla and beat security didn't make much sense to Matthias.

"I'll watch her, but you should be careful." Wren held up a hand. "Look, I know about bad parents, but they can still pluck the guilt strings. That woman sounds like a pro on that score."

Since Wren's father was literally a killer, Matthias didn't ignore the advice. But he also didn't want his friend to worry or take all of his time handling Matthias's life. He was a big boy. "I'm good."

Wren didn't even try to hide his smile. "Are you?"

"I'm not sure what you're asking." But he knew. This was about Kayla's and Garrett's big mouth. The fucker.

"You told Kayla about Nick. You got shot." Wren made a face. "You've kind of had a shitty few days."

He'd also had some pretty great moments, but he wasn't about to share that. "I didn't have a choice."

"That's because you care about her."

Now that Wren was in love and acted stupid, he expected all of his friends to do the same. No thanks. "It's because she deserves the truth."

"That's it, huh?"

The tone. The stare. Matthias didn't like any of it. "You think because you're getting laid on a regular basis that you're now an expert on women?"

"I think I know a guy who's leading with his dick and not his brain when I see him."

Now, that just pissed Matthias off. "When have I ever done that?"

"And that's my point."

"I've got this." As soon as the words left Matthias's mouth he knew they were a lie. Fact was he did like Kayla. Too much. He'd been away from her for a few stupid hours and missed her. What kind of shit was that?

Wren nodded. "We'll see."

CHAPTER 23

Matthias didn't come to the café all day. He finally showed up in a suit just as Kayla and Garrett arrived back at the inn. Got there just in time for dinner, and Garrett must have known he was on the way because he ordered for three.

That was two hours ago. Garrett had just disappeared to his side of the space, leaving the door partially open as they'd all silently agreed to do.

Matthias sat sprawled on the bed in jeans and white T-shirt this time. All comfortable and not making a move. Not talking to her either.

She had no idea how to start the conversation. They'd barely spoken, except to talk about the investigation and practical things, since *that* night. Whenever she thought about Matthias's relationship to Mary and the way he dodged the truth about her, Kayla's head started to pound. The fury that hit her when she'd first found out had died down and she couldn't call it back up.

Ignoring him didn't work. Trying not to think about him failed. Being without him all day made her grumpy. She really couldn't win.

She decided to go with something easy and try to

open the gate that had slammed shut between them. She didn't mean it as a test because she really wanted them to get back on track. She also wanted to know the answers to the questions dancing in her head. "Where did you really go today?"

He lowered the pages in his hand and his eyes focused on her instead of the reading. "To the police and then to see Wren. He had more intel for me and my people had collected more to add to the piles out there."

"Ah." She stood at the end of the bed, hoping something more brilliant than that response would come to her. After a few seconds ticked by she knew it wasn't going to happen.

"I also ended up checking in with Mary, not that I had a choice."

Kayla thought her heart stopped. It actually ached inside her chest. "What does that mean?"

He put the pages on the mattress next to his hip. "Since I didn't want to use my people for everything, especially because my connection to Mary isn't known, I asked Wren to track her. He figured out she was on the move and asking questions. Calling people. I went to DC to listen to Wren's report then try to work it out with her."

"I guess the fact she's still pursuing me and keeping up her crusade shouldn't surprise me."

He let out a long, labored exhale. "She's determined."

Kayla didn't point out that it was a trait he might have gotten from the other woman. "To have me arrested."

"Something like that."

Kayla appreciated that he didn't bother to deny it. "What did you tell her?"

"To back off." He put his hands on his lap. "I want her to leave you alone."

"Because you're handling me for her." Kayla winced as soon as she said the words. She knew she sounded bitchy. Picking a fight was not her goal. But all these thoughts and worries rattled around inside her.

For so many years she'd tamped that sort of thing down—analyzing and running ideas by someone else. She put her needs aside. She didn't have anyone to share her dreams and fears with, and she pretended it didn't matter. But it totally did.

"Because you didn't kill Nick." Matthias leaned forward. "Hear me, Kayla. I believe you didn't do it. I haven't thought it was even possible for you to have done something like that since right after I met you."

"Really?" If so, he was one of the few people who'd trusted her word from the start.

"You didn't do it."

She knew it, but now she knew he got it. The pressure building inside her released. Tears threatened to spill but she inhaled and blinked and forced them back. This was what true acceptance felt like. She didn't have to plead her case or convince him that someone was after her. He listened to what she said and believed her.

She put a knee on the end of the bed. "You didn't have to admit you'd spoken with her. You could have let me think you'd cut off contact. Said anything else, even claimed to have an unrelated work problem that stole you away."

"I'm considered a straight shooter, Kayla." He shook his head. "I know it doesn't seem like that, but—"

"It does." After days together, she got him. He was a rescuer at heart and hated games. It was all so clear. "I know you are."

"The one part of this situation I hate is that I came into it without telling you everything." He lifted his hand and touched his bandaged shoulder. The sling was off but he kept it wrapped up. "The other part I hate is you being in danger."

She believed him. Not even one doubt lingered. There were things she couldn't tell him or anyone. Things about Doug and the terrible decision she made years ago. About how she really didn't deserve to find peace no matter how much she craved it.

But she could be honest with him, at least on this level. About them. About how she wanted to be with him and forgave him for holding back the information about Nick.

She slid off the bed again. "You put your body in front of mine."

"And I would do it again."

"I knew you'd say that." She walked away. Traveled to the other side of the room.

"Where are you going?"

She could hear Garrett's television and see him leaning over the desk to gather some documents. He was walking around and not paying attention to them. That wasn't quite good enough.

She stuck her head in his room. "Goodnight."

Her voice made him jump as he turned to her. He started to say something but she winked. Cut off the words when she closed the door, locking him on his side and her on the other with Matthias.

"Kayla?"

She smiled at the confusion in Matthias's deep voice at the other side of the room but smothered it again before she turned back to face him. "I'm coming back."

"But what are you doing? I thought we agreed . . ." His voice trailed off when she started across the room. His gaze moved all over her, traveling down her body to her legs.

The guy was a sworn leg man. "I thought we needed some privacy."

"We need to talk about where we go from here, and I don't just mean the case."

The time for talk was over.

She slipped her T-shirt over her head. The bra came next. She reached behind her and unhooked it, let it drop to the floor. "You sure you want to have a conversation?"

"God, Kayla. You don't owe me anything."

"That's what this is about? You think this is payback of some sort." She watched him sit up straighter, press his back deeper into the headboard. It looked as if he was trying to scurry away. That was new.

"I just want us to be honest with each other," he said in a voice that bordered on begging.

The words nearly broke her heart. She didn't think she could care about someone this much. That her fears would fuel her need to protect and push her so willingly into the role of caretaker.

"Good." She scrambled up onto the bed again but hovered at the edge. Gave him some time to get used to the idea of her taking control in bed, because the poor guy seemed confused. "Because I want you."

"I don't want a pity fuck."

Wow, he was fighting this with every ounce of strength he possessed. She wasn't offended. This wasn't about her. This was about him being decent and not wanting to take advantage. She really did get how his mind worked now.

But other parts of him were much more interesting. "Such a dirty mouth."

"I'm serious." His hand dropped to his side, palm up.

She never thought of him as vulnerable but something about the wariness in his eyes and the way he stalled getting naked got to her. He was holding back for her. Once again rushing in to protect. This time she definitely didn't want that. It was sweet but misguided.

Once they got a few things clear, she never wanted to think about the Nick issue again. "Promise you'll never lie to me about Nick or Mary."

He barely let her finish the sentence before answering. "Promise."

She crawled up the bed, up his legs. "Have you told me everything?"

"About them?"

"Interesting that you're trying to carve out an exception." Not that she blamed him. She had hard limits,

too. Things that couldn't be said even in the safety of
a dark room.

"I'm not a young guy. I have a pile of secrets."

She straddled his calves and slid down until her
thighs touched his jeans. The scratchy material rubbed
against her sensitive skin. "And you've been shot at
before."

"Yes."

"Hit before. That's the scar under your ribs, right?"
She remembered every inch of his body. She'd toured
it with her hands and mouth. The signs of battle im-
printed on his skin. Now he'd have cuts and a new
bullet wound.

"Yes." His voice sounded thicker that time.

"You have others." She could catalog them.

"Yes."

"I want to touch them all."

His breath escaped on a heavy sound. "Kayla."

She slipped her arms up and let her body fall along
his long legs. Her hand cupped him through his jeans
and he twitched against her palm. Rubbing, she slipped
her thumb back and forth over him. Loved the way his
erection grew under her fingers.

"Should I stop?"

"God, no." Air moved into his voice. His chest rose
and fell but he never broke eye contact with her.

She moved again, skimming her hands up his chest.
She lay fully against him now as she placed gentle kisses
around the edge of his shoulder bandage, careful not to
press too hard. The injury worried her. He needed rest
but the bulge in his pants said he also wanted release.

She'd help him relax.

With her hands balanced against the headboard, she hovered over him now. Brushed her breasts against him. Across his chest then up higher. She sighed when his hands slipped over her. To tease her nipples. To press his lips against the tips.

She touched her nose to his hair and inhaled the scent of his shampoo, fresh from the shower. She kissed his head while she cradled his neck in her palm. Then her mouth moved down to cover his. The stunning kiss sent a shudder through her as her body came to life.

They might not always have the right words, but their bodies understood this. On this level they connected.

She eased back until her thighs straddled his hips again. Her hand slipped between her legs to touch him. First she had to get rid of those jeans. The button opened and she slowly lowered the zipper. It was so quiet, the ticking sounds echoed through the room as she opened his jeans.

When her hand slid inside he exhaled a deep breath. "God, Kayla."

"Your job is to lie back and enjoy." She was in charge tonight.

His fingers tangled in her hair. "You're going to kill me."

"You need to hold very still." She winked at him. "Relax that shoulder."

"Fuck the shoulder."

"That is not quite what I have planned." She pulled the opening of his jeans apart. Shifting down, her mouth replaced her fingers. Her tongue licked up the side and across the tip.

A moan escaped him as his head fell back. "Yes."

She couldn't get close enough or touch him enough. Her mouth closed over him and she sucked a trail along his skin. The move had his hips lifting off the bed. She recognized the encouragement and took him deeper, pushing him to the back of her throat, slipping him in and out of her mouth.

His hand pressed against the back of her head and he opened his legs wider, giving her space to slip down between them. There was no resisting now. They touched each other in the frantic need to peel the rest of their clothes off. It was awkward and perfect. A moment of total abandon.

When she lifted her head to look up at him, she saw the long length of his throat and the muscles straining as he clenched his teeth together. Still so tough yet happy to let her set the speed.

His head dropped to the side and inhaled a deep breath. "I'm yours."

That's exactly what she wanted to hear.

"You're mine." Then she lowered her head again.

CHAPTER 24

Matthias couldn't shake the feeling that he'd dodged a bullet the size of a rocket. Kayla had every right to be pissed at him. He'd expected her to quietly move around the room last night, maybe watch some television. But she'd locked the door and climbed all over him.

It had been pretty fucking fantastic. When the blood ran to his dick and his shoulder started to throb, he'd ignored it and concentrated on her. Seeing her hair fall across his thighs as her hot mouth moved up and down on him nearly made him lose it. He held it together long enough to get inside her, but just barely.

And now he was stuck in a room with Garrett.

Garrett shuffled the papers in front of him as he dragged the laptop over and turned it on. The guy was in full multitasking mode. "Is she still in the shower?"

"You've asked that ten times already." And since Matthias would rather be in there with her, he was sick of the question. He also dreaded to think where this conversation was about to go.

"She closed the door between our rooms last night."

There it was. "Shut up."

"I'm just saying."

"So am I." The video loaded and began to roll. Not grainy but not the best quality either. This one sat on a pole right across from Kayla's apartment. The same apartment he hoped she never went back to because it was starting to feel like the place was cursed. "Is this the video from the dock?"

Garrett looked up. "There's no sign of the shooter on this one. It's more of a what's-happening-there thing. I think it's also from earlier that day."

"That's just fucking great."

"We do have a load of new surveillance and I can run through that on my own." Garrett flipped through the pages in the binder in front of him. "Your team did a pretty great job of tracking the comings and goings and identifying most of the people on it."

"Of course they did." That's exactly what he'd trained them to do and paid them so well to accomplish.

They did it for other people. The only difference was that this time they did it for him. Since he was in the field, which never happened, he guessed his team was doing its best work.

"So, why are we redoing it?"

Because that's what he did. He oversaw the work. He had a chain of command and didn't step on his employees or get in their way, but he did watch over everything. Those control-freak tendencies were hard to kick. "I want to touch every piece of paper and every bit of evidence myself."

"Okay then."

Kayla stepped into the room as she fiddled with the back of her earring. "Having fun?"

He found the entire female morning production fascinating. She didn't take a long time getting ready, but there were so many steps and she never missed one. The moisturizer, the hair brushing . . . the lotions and bottles of things he couldn't identify and had no idea she needed. There appeared to be an order and she never strayed from it.

"Not even a little fun, actually," Garrett said in a voice that came close to a whine.

Matthias had to agree. "This part is tedious."

"How hard is it to look at video . . ." She leaned over Matthias's shoulder. "Nothing's happening on it anyway. Wait, is that my house?"

When she reached for the computer keys, he held her hand before she could touch anything. Between the touching and smelling her, his body was ready to go. He ignored it. "That's exactly it. There are long stretches of nothing in this job."

"Huh." She tapped her fingers on the desk. "Then watch during the day when there are more people shuffling around. The boaters come in and out all the time."

That was an interesting strategy. Matthias couldn't help but comment on it. "Because stalkers only come out in daylight?"

"Smartass." She followed the comment by slipping her fingers into his hair for just a second, then the touch was gone again.

Garrett laughed. "As Wren would say, it's better than being a dumbass."

"Your boss is very eloquent." Matthias tried to turn his attention back to work and off of her. He pointed to the folder next to Garrett's hand. "Speaking of which, are those the files he had delivered?"

Garrett patted the top one but didn't open it. "The intel on the 'others' on the pier."

"What does that even mean?" Kayla leaned against Matthias's chair, acting as if she didn't have any intention of leaving soon.

"Some of what we talked about before. Intel on Lauren's clients, customers in the shops and the café. That sort of thing." There was more, but he figured that basically covered it.

"I don't even want to know how you got the names and information to search."

He nodded. "No, you don't."

Her face lit up as she pointed to the screen. "There's the barfer."

"Who?" Matthias followed her hand and saw the image. A younger man with dark hair. He wore casual clothes and walked with his head down and a baseball cap on. As they watched the screen, he walked along the pier, glancing at the water but never getting close.

Matthias didn't remember seeing him before. "That's Lauren's assistant? The one who got here a few weeks before I did?"

Kayla pointed again. "That's Paul."

That name Matthias recognized. He sat up straighter

and rewound the video a few frames. "That kid has been avoiding me."

"Well, he's right there." She leaned between Matthias and Garrett and touched the screen. Just as she did, Paul looked up. Stared into the air, clearly not knowing the camera was there, before looking away again.

The face hit on a memory. Matthias reached out and clicked the spacebar, stopping the video. "Wait a second."

"What do you see?" she asked. "Say it because I'm missing it."

That was exactly the point. They were all missing it. Looking in the wrong direction. Matthias snapped his fingers as he tried to remember where he'd seen the face. "Where's his file?"

Garrett looked at the notes in front of him. "He's been tougher to pin down. Wren plans to send the information he's collected on Paul later today."

The face. The age. It all clicked together in Matthias's head. It took a few seconds, but he pinpointed where he'd seen the kid before. "They don't need to. I mean, they do. But not for an ID."

Kayla had a hand on his shoulder and concern in her eyes. "What is it?"

"That's not Paul."

She laughed. "It really is."

She wasn't getting this. The kid wasn't some innocent, seasick boy. He had an agenda and it had nothing to do with getting a paycheck from Lauren. "His name is Ben."

Garrett stopped searching through the Paul file and looked up. "You know him?"

Knew him. Could identify him. Had likely just found Kayla's stalker. "Give me Doug's file."

She groaned. "Come on. Again with that?"

Matthias turned his chair to the side. He wanted to wrap an arm around her waist as he delivered this news. Try to soften the blow. But his shoulder wouldn't let him lift the arm at all.

He settled for getting closer. If he could body block this information, he would. "He's Ben Weston. Doug's brother."

"What?"

But he could see from the hunted look in her eyes that she got it. He let her process his comment without saying more.

"No, not possible." She shook her head and kept shaking it. "I never met him but I saw photos. That kid is . . . a kid. Doug's baby brother."

Garrett winced. "He was a kid seven years ago."

Matthias dragged Doug's file over in front of him and paged through it. It only took a second to find the photo. It captured his awkward stage. Back then the kid was long legs and all teeth. But the eyes, the mouth, it was Ben.

The guy did manage to blend in. Running away anytime the team tried to talk to him also worked to his advantage. Until now. "No wonder we've had some trouble finding Paul."

Kayla sat down on the armrest of Matthias's chair. "Doug's brother."

He could hear the shock in her voice. He got it. Getting walloped by the past was never fun. Especially when that past liked to write threatening notes.

That settled it. "It's time we say hello to Paul."

Lauren looked up as they all walked into her office a half hour later. She was in the middle of grabbing a jacket and had a piece of paper in her hand. A smile spread across her face the second she saw them. "This is quite a group."

Matthias wasn't really in the mood for mindless chitchat. "Where's Paul?"

"Right there." Lauren pointed over their heads.

Matthias turned around just in time to see the kid move into the doorway. Same hate and same look of trying to hide in plain sight.

Paul's eyes widened. "Shit."

He pushed off the doorjamb and ran. Took off with his sneakers thudding on the pier.

On instinct, Matthias sprinted after him. With each step the pain in his arm intensified and the sling wrapped around his throat. He tore at it and threw it off. Not having it strapped to him made it hurt more. It thumped and ached until he thought it would fall off.

Still, he ran, dodging around the people walking along the docks. Several called out and he could hear yelling behind him. His men shifted in their positions. Two took off, following them.

Matthias got close but couldn't close the gap enough to reach out and grab him. Hell, this Paul—or whatever his name was—should have a track scholarship. He jumped over a bench and nearly knocked an older man over. He swung around, heading toward the boat slips. Matthias knew he'd have him if the kid proved to be reckless enough to go there. But at the last second, Paul turned and ran up the small grassy hill, scrambling almost on his hands and knees as he flew.

"Fucking kid." Matthias was one arm down for that sort of crawl.

Between the meds, the lack of sleep and the gunshot wound, he was not at his best. He still outran men younger than him and Garrett hadn't appeared. But the hill slowed him down. Hearing Kayla call out his name also wrecked his concentration. But he could not lose sight of this kid.

He finally reached the top, but he'd lost ground. The space between them grew. They raced between buildings, down the steps and into the parking lot. Brakes squealed and a new round of shouting started.

Paul looked over his shoulder as the three of them on his tail closed in. Matthias saw the blur. A black car. He called out for Paul to watch out. At the last second, Paul shifted to the left as the car pulled in front of him. He slammed into the side and bounced off.

It turned out to be enough of a distraction for Matthias to grab him. He used his good arm, and his fingers clamped down on Paul's shoulder. Matthias spun Paul around. Just as he started kicking, Garrett got out and trapped the kid against the car.

"Enough with the damn running." Matthias coughed out the warning through harsh breaths.

"You okay, grandpa?" Garrett asked.

"Tough talk from the guy who drove here." Still,

Matthias fought the need to double over and suck in as much oxygen as possible.

The pain in his shoulder almost knocked him down. Blood pumped through him and the wound burned. Probably not the activity the doctor had in mind when he said to keep the shoulder still for a few days.

Kayla and Lauren raced in. A few of the team wandered close by.

With her red face and wide eyes, Kayla looked ready to kill him. She didn't throw herself in his arms, but she did rush up to his side and grab his good arm.

She shoved his sling at him. Pinned it against his chest. "What were you thinking? You're injured."

He didn't hate that she cared. "I'm fine."

Paul picked that moment to throw his body around. "Get off me."

Matthias stepped in and held him still with a hand to his upper back and Garrett's help. Even if the kid did manage to get away, three guys with guns waited right there. He might not know it, but Matthias both sensed and saw his team's presence. They were ready to grab the kid.

He'd settle for something calmer for now. "No one goes anywhere until we talk."

"I don't need to—"

Matthias leaned in closer. "And figure out why you're trying to be Paul when you're really someone else."

The kid shook his head. "What?"

Matthias turned to Lauren and Kayla. "Meet Ben Weston."

CHAPTER 25

Paul sat at a table in the café and fiddled with the water bottle Kayla had gotten them. They were all there—Matthias, Lauren and Garrett. Kayla had closed the café, so no one else was around. Most people were too busy talking about all the action on the pier.

Matthias stalled the calls to the police. He told the people standing around that he had the situation handled and wanted to keep it private to avoid giving the kid a criminal record, but he knew that excuse would only last so long. He had Wren monitoring calls to the police and ready to step in if they needed more time.

What Matthias really needed was medication. Every time he moved pain screamed down his arm. He wasn't sure what damage he'd done, but he'd done something. He couldn't even touch the bandage without wanting to yell a stream of profanities. He just hoped he didn't need surgery. If he did, he'd blame Paul . . . or whatever his name was.

The kid kept shifting in his seat. Matthias couldn't blame him. Lauren looked ready to strangle him. Garrett was stationed at the door, with more men just outside. And Matthias had planted his body in the chair right in front of Paul. Kayla stood behind him. That amounted to a lot of people cheering on the showdown.

Paul spun the water bottle on the table. "Am I under arrest?"

"No, but this will go faster if you drop the attitude." Matthias was running out of both time and patience.

"He's scared." Lauren paced back and forth in front of Garrett. Her mood bounced from angry to concerned almost every other minute.

She was trying to protect the kid. Matthias got that. Something about the way his shoulders curled in and he refused to look at them made Matthias feel something for him, too. He didn't think the kid was being a jerk. He thought he was terrified.

Smart choice.

But Matthias didn't need someone questioning him while he searched for answers. "Lauren, you're not helping."

Paul looked over his head, likely at Lauren. "I want to leave."

As if that was going to happen. "Why are you in town?"

Paul's gaze touched Matthias's face for a second then bounced away again. "I'm going to school here."

"Stop." He'd said that three times already. Matthias couldn't figure out what the kid's class schedule had to do with Kayla or this situation. Maybe Paul was stalling, but if he thought someone was coming to save him he was wrong. "The truth this time. Not just the pieces you feel like telling us."

When he continued to sit there not talking, Matthias pushed forward. Enough with the soft sell. He wanted this over and he was pretty sure he needed to see another doctor. "Your name is Ben Weston. Your brother is Doug Weston, the guy Kayla dated in college."

"What?" The shock was clear in Lauren's voice.

"I had a different name back then. Carrie Gleason." Kayla pulled out a chair and sat down next to Matthias.

He didn't love that she was right there for the questioning. He trusted her but that didn't mean he wanted her to hear anything more about that night so long ago. And if this guy was the one who broke into her apartment, Matthias didn't want her near him period.

Paul or Ben or whatever he was going by shook his head. "You've got the wrong guy."

"I have your driver's license. That's you with your real name, dumbass." Matthias reached into his back pocket and took out the copy. Threw the paper on the table. "Now, wanna try again?"

Kayla sighed. "Ben, I know—"

"Where is he?" Paul focused all of his attention on Kayla.

"Who?"

"My brother."

"You're here looking for Doug?" She shook her head and her voice lost all of its edge. "I haven't seen him in years."

"No one has." Paul leaned forward. The hate was right there in his eyes. He looked ready to come over the table and grab her. "That's the point."

Matthias put his good arm in front of her like he

might if he put on the car brakes too fast. "Let's be careful."

But she was already off and talking. "You broke into my place. Doug's not there. There's nothing from my time with your brother there or anywhere in my life."

"I'm not saying anything else to you until you tell me where he is." Paul crossed his arms over his chest and leaned back in his chair. The front two legs left the floor.

The belligerent act didn't make Matthias happy. It would only prolong the inevitable, so he tried to rush them there. "She doesn't know and we're not talking about her. We're talking about you and the break-in and why we shouldn't turn you over to the police."

"We should. We're not talking about picking a lock here. This was serious mastermind stuff," Garrett said from across the room.

"That's not me." Paul pointed to Lauren. "Tell them."

"But you're my tech guy."

Paul's mouth dropped open. "That's computers, not what they're talking about."

Matthias thought about Paul being the guy in the office and Kayla's extra set of keys. Finding out about that days ago put a target on Lauren. Matthias shifted it now to the guy who literally had access to the keys to the kingdom.

Without turning around, Matthias called out to Lauren. "Did you keep the extra keys to Kayla's place in your office?"

"In the safe." She stepped forward and her face fell. "I didn't give him access to that."

"But how hard would it be for him to see you open it?" Garrett asked.

Lauren's mouth dropped open as the color rushed from her face. "You stole the keys and the code? You used me to get to Kayla?"

"And destroy my apartment," Kayla added.

"None of this matters. My brother is missing and that should be a bigger deal than some tossed furniture and a note on the wall." Paul ignored the rest and talked directly to her.

Now Matthias had his confirmation. The twisting in his gut eased. He could at least resolve this part of the threat against Kayla. "Who told you about the note?"

Paul looked wild now. His gaze bounced around the room as he shifted in his chair. "Lauren . . . you guys. Everyone knows."

"No one does. We leaked the information about the break-in but left out the threat." It was a simple investigative trick but it was amazing how often it worked. That fact never ceased to surprise Matthias. Some people did not know when to stop talking.

Garrett laughed. "Oops."

Paul shook his head as he stared at Kayla. "Where is he?"

"He's not with me. We stopped dating long ago. We weren't even a couple when the murders happened." Instead of anger at his admission, her voice carried a note of sadness. She kept repeating the same lines. The ones that really didn't answer what Paul was asking.

Matthias cataloged each fact, each statement Kayla offered, and stored it away for later. He'd learned more about Doug in the last ten minutes than she'd shared in all the time before then, but he still didn't know much. The puzzle was coming together in his head and he hated the picture he saw, so he blocked it out and concentrated on the Weston brother in front of him. He'd deal with the other one later.

Paul didn't blink. Energy pounded off him. He was wound up and pulled tight and it showed in every line of his body and in the strain in his voice. "Did he do it? That was the accusation, and what everyone said, right? He did it for you or with you. He killed them and ran."

Kayla shook her head. "I didn't kill anyone. I didn't have anything to do with the murders. Not one thing other than being unlucky enough to find the bodies."

Matthias mentally winced. She was answering questions no one asked. Jumped right over the easy response and the obvious issue. All that ducking only made her story about Doug harder to believe. Matthias wasn't sure what had happened, but he knew it didn't roll out like she said, and now his brain wouldn't let it go until he had an answer.

But the immediate problem was no matter what she said, Paul wasn't biting. He stayed right on track. "You're telling me Doug did? My brother killed his friends."

"They weren't his friends." She bit her bottom lip. "Not really."

"How can you say that?"

"You've been hunting me, shooting at me. You hit Matthias." Kayla touched his shoulder. "You did this."

"Wait." Paul sat back. He made a face like he'd tasted something sour. Looked much more like the scared kid than the tough-guy image he tried to project. "I don't have a gun. I have no idea how to shoot. You can't pin that on me."

Lauren stood behind Kayla now. "We're supposed to believe you did one horrible thing and not the other?"

"I trashed her place. I wrote the note." Paul grabbed his water bottle again. Tapped the side against the desk. "This was a onetime thing. The rest? Not me."

There was a full admission of something in there somewhere. Matthias thought they'd get one, but not like this. Not by him explaining what he *didn't* do. But Matthias still had questions and one very big one. "Why? Why, after all these years, did you come at Kayla? Instead of living your life, you tracked her down. Her and not any other suspect in this case."

Paul shifted the bottle from hand to hand. "She's the suspect."

The rest of the intel was in there. Matthias knew he could pull it out. "So was your brother and you're not looking for him. Not directly. You're looking for her."

"Because I believed what she said." Paul made the comment as if they all knew who he was talking about.

Matthias feared he did. "Who?"

"Mary Patterson." Someone in the room groaned and Kayla sat back hard in her chair. Over the noise and the sudden discomfort wrapping around them, Paul kept talking, as if willing them all to believe and understand. "She's the only one who would talk to me. I got old enough to ask questions and no one had any answers. She showed me police records and newspaper articles. She has all of the information to support her theory."

Matthias didn't have to work hard to imagine how this all spun out. Paul . . . Ben missed his brother but everyone tried to protect him. In the end, they created a young man in search of answers, filled with energy and no idea how to control it.

Hell, Matthias had been that guy. Different facts but the end result was the same. So much undirected anger led to stupid choices.

"She told you I did it." Kayla didn't ask it as a question.

"And you were with my brother and now he's missing, too."

The facts did sound damning. Matthias could see how someone could twist them around, especially with a grown-up like Mary sitting right there, pushing her theory. "Did she send you here to find Kayla?"

"No. That's all me." Paul nodded toward Kayla. "I tracked her using college records." He snorted. "It's pretty easy to get those online."

One more question answered. Whether he meant to or not, Paul explained the keys and access to Kayla's address. He didn't need to be a mastermind for those two pieces because so many people were willing to dig around and find the information he needed and hand it to him. "You hacked the university computers."

"I asked the right questions. I knew from her old school that she'd registered at St. John's. It was easy to trace her information from there." Paul barely spared Kayla a glance as he talked about her.

"But you did it because Mary told you to." Matthias would have been impressed with Mary's tenacity if it didn't keep fucking up his investigation. If her goal wasn't to destroy Kayla.

"She'd spent all this time following her and . . ." Paul's words cut off. "Look, I only did it once then I stopped."

"Aren't you a fucking Boy Scout?" But Matthias believed him. The kid's skill set didn't match the shooting. His actions lined up with everything else, but not that.

His men had performed an initial search of the room he rented and didn't find anything except a few photos of Kayla. No gun. They might find something on his computer. Matthias would reserve final judgment on the shooting part until then, but he didn't see it.

"Then I came here." Paul's voice had gone low, almost to a whisper.

Matthias wasn't sure why. "And?"

"Everyone I talked to here liked her. None of what Mary said matched with what I saw. Lauren liked her. So did the guys at the boat rental place and the marina security." He didn't look at Kayla or use her name, but then he suddenly did. "Hell, you kept trying to feed me."

Matthias had heard enough. All the facts jammed together in his head. He thought he understood Paul. He now knew more about Doug. But that was a conversation he needed to have with Kayla—alone.

"Okay, we're going to go over everything Mary told you and all you think you know and everything you've done." But without him. Matthias didn't think he could sit there for one more second. This kid was going to have to own up to what he did in some way. Matthias hoped that didn't include the police because that wouldn't do anything to lessen Paul's anger.

Paul held up a finger. "Just the one time."

He acted like that mattered. Matthias would disagree. "That was enough."

"I had no idea." Lauren whispered the comment but they all heard it.

Kayla spun around in her chair. "Of course not."

"But I hired him."

Kayla reached out and grabbed Lauren's hand. "You didn't know. There was no way you could."

Matthias wasn't sure he agreed with that. Lauren's background checks failed. He'd talk to her about that later. Never mind that he was starting to have a lot of things he needed to do *later*. "We'll need whatever paperwork he gave you."

Lauren nodded. "Sure."

"Shouldn't we call the police?" Kayla asked Matthias.

"Do you really think he shot up your apartment?" It wasn't a real answer, but it was all he had right now.

Matthias's mind had started to wander. It zipped to Doug and to Mary. He thought about Lauren and her access to information. Then there was Gerald and all the other people who came in and out of the marina. So many suspects but it was all starting to gel in his head. This was how he worked at home, when he didn't have a personal stake. And he did this time.

Kayla mattered to him, and not just her safety. She wasn't a job.

"You're saying there are two people after her?" Lauren asked. "That's a wild guess, right?"

No, they'd moved past that point. "It's fact."

"I can't do this." Kayla stood up. "I want to go home."

They should. Garrett could take over and he'd tape it all. Once they reviewed it and figured out Paul's true danger level they could figure out what to do next. Maybe get him some help. He deserved a trip to the police station and criminal charges, but when it came down to it Matthias doubted Kayla would agree. She already had a note of sympathy in her voice even though the kid had wrecked her house.

"I'll go with you," Lauren offered.

Matthias stood up next to Kayla. "No, me."

Lauren had woken up. In the last half hour she'd flipped from stunned to angry to protective. "She doesn't need more questioning."

He didn't like the suggestion she knew what Kayla needed more than he did. "I get that."

Kayla held out her hands and stood between them. "Guys, I'm fine."

That was just it. Matthias no longer believed that to be totally true. "We'll see."

CHAPTER 26

By the time they got back to the inn, Matthias's mind was racing with theories. The police hadn't solved the case in seven years. He didn't think he could leap in and get it done in a week, but he did have an advantage. He knew more than they ever did. He had an inside track right into Kayla's mind.

He'd watched her under stress. Seen her caring and panicked. The smiling, the anger. Through everything, even while she sat across from Paul, she held it together on one point. One piece of information never wavered. She didn't build on it or elaborate. She told a perfectly crafted tale . . . and he feared he knew why.

As soon as they were inside the room and the door closed, she turned on him. "Before you start you should know I'm not in the mood for a lecture about Paul or Doug or anything else."

Tension spun around her. It was as if she could hardly hold it in. Some unknown worry ate at her and pushed her.

He knew it was time for her to let some of it out. Past time. But getting there . . . fuck, he had no good way to do that.

"Okay." He said that because he didn't know what else to say. Not yet.

"I can't believe he was right there all along." She paced near the end of the bed.

She'd always been a mass of energy. She moved fast and handled a lot of things at one time, but did it with ease. This was different. There was a darkness spinning off her now. Every muscle worked. She moved her hands while her legs took her back and forth.

He knew he had to let it play out. This had to be on her terms. "He's a messed-up kid."

She stopped and stared at him. "That's not really an excuse."

There wasn't any anger in her voice. No, this wasn't about catching Paul or worrying about who else was out there. Her world was unraveling and she was trying to keep it all in. He recognized the tactic because he'd used it himself every damn day.

In so many ways they were different. He wallowed and hid in the shadows. Even though she hid under an alias, she gave off light. He preferred quiet. She talked to everyone. But they both kept secrets. Horrible secrets. The kind that shouldn't be shared because once the words came out there could be no pretending.

Matthias had lived in that state for so long. That calm middle point where he didn't look back but didn't think he deserved to look forward with any great depth. He could dwell on work, but he didn't get to find happiness or any kind of peace. He'd forfeited that and kept the reason stuffed deep inside him.

So, he knew what she was feeling. That out-of-control sensation. The idea that on this one point she was all alone in the world and needed to stay that way.

As he watched her struggle and deny something broke loose in him. The need to help her overcame the need to hide his shame. He might lose her. Hell, he might lose himself, drop right into the abyss, but it was time to say something. With her, right now.

At first the words wouldn't form in his mind. He struggled to figure out the right way to say the right thing. When that didn't happen, he just gave in and talked. Stood in the middle of the room with one arm in a sling and the other hanging loose by his side. Uncomfortable and unsure where this would go. "I know what it's like to get caught up. Your mind gets warped and you think you're doing the right thing."

Her expression didn't change. "What are you saying?"

He started to talk then stopped again. A lump formed in his throat and he ached to swallow it back but it sat there. "There was this boy named Kevin."

That name. He never let it enter his mind, but he did now.

When she didn't say anything, he continued. "I'd been in good foster homes and some mediocre ones. A lot of good people tried and some not so great people pocketed the money and left me alone."

The churning started in his stomach and worked its way up to his chest. Memories flooded him. Being young and unsure and so unwanted. It all came rushing back, slamming into the man he tried to be now.

"Then there was the home with Kevin. That one

sucked." He couldn't describe it and didn't want to go into the details. The lack of food and the punching really weren't the point. "The father was mean in a sick and twisted way. He got off on hurting people who were weaker than him, and we were kids so we all fell into that category."

She took a step toward him. "Matthias."

He put up a hand to ward her off. If she touched him, came to him, he wouldn't be able to get this out. And he needed to say it. More than that, she needed to hear it.

"One day Kevin didn't move fast enough or had the nerve to eat a pretzel. Something that wouldn't matter to a loving parent but mattered to this guy." Kevin's face popped into Matthias's head. He never forgot that blond hair and those big brown eyes. He'd purposely forgotten so many of the people who peppered his youth, but not Kevin. "So, this guy picked up a bat. He didn't use it at first. He preferred kicking, but then he lost control."

Her hand went to her mouth. Matthias thought he heard a gasp but he couldn't be sure. His mind had gone to another place. The room with the paneling and the green couch.

"He swung and Kevin was dead. I was a kid but I knew what was happening. I watched the life drain right out of him. Tried to stop it but was too late. I didn't pull hard enough on the guy's arm or step up . . . something."

She wiped her fingers across her cheek. "You were just a kid."

"Ten." Old enough to understand what happened.

Not strong enough to stop it, but he should have tried harder. Now when the scene played in his mind he could see he had hesitated. Those precious seconds cost Kevin everything. "The police came and there were stories but no one really believed this foster dad. He'd had trouble before and there were reports but no actual findings of abuse. He tried to shift the blame, because that's what bullies do. So, I was removed from the house and was much harder to place after that."

She shook her head. "I don't know how you survived."

"Fueled by revenge. Pure and simple, I vowed to kill him." The words sounded harsh but Matthias didn't pretty them up. She needed to know that he understood how a person could break. "And when I was twenty, I did. I'd tracked him and knew the state had started giving him kids again. I couldn't let history repeat."

She winced. "You told the police?"

From her reaction, she knew. He didn't have to pretend because the reality of what happened that day had already formed in her mind. "I went to the house, but this time when he picked up the bat I was stronger. I knew how to fight back. There was no hesitation." A heaviness settled on his chest. Matthias rubbed it but the ache didn't disappear. "The guy was garbage and he deserved it, but see, it wasn't my call to make. I know that now but couldn't see it back then."

"Quint helped you."

The man who saved him. "He's the only other person who knows."

She wiped away a few more tears. "I'm so sorry."

He studied her, looked for signs of revulsion, but saw none. There was pity there and sadness for a boy she never knew. But there was a spark of something else. He grabbed on to that. "So, I know what it's like to take another life, even when you're protecting everyone else. I know that your whole body shakes."

"You don't have to—"

"There is no feeling like it. Bile rushes up your throat and you freeze. Every time you think about it feelings of hopelessness crash into you again. The guilt. The pain."

She took a step back and ran right into the end of the mattress. "Please stop."

"I know all about vigilante justice because I've been there." He couldn't get the words out fast enough now. It was as if after holding them back for so many years they now overflowed the mental wall he'd thrown up to block them. "You lose a bit of your humanity and you can never get it back."

Her arm shook. "I don't want to hear this."

Because she knew. She wasn't repulsed because she knew. "There's this aching inside you not so much because you did it, because you still think that was justified in some way. No, the ache comes from knowing you *can* do it. You're one of those people."

Tears ran down her cheeks now. "I can't . . ."

"But you figure out how to live with it. You punish yourself but you learn to breathe again, even as you cover your tracks and hope it will all go away."

She moved her hand as if trying to bat his words away. "We should—"

He took the final step and reached for her. Wrapped his fingers around her hand and held it to his chest. "Tell me about Doug Weston, Kayla."

THIS COULDN'T BE happening.

Pain welled inside her. The kind that could drop a person to her knees. It shot from inside her stomach and flowed through her, covering and destroying everything else.

Her mind bounced from him to Kevin to her friends. All that blood. The questions. The accusations. She'd buried it all so deep and then . . . he was forcing her to think about things she wanted to forget.

She ached for him. If he thought she'd hate him or push him away that wasn't going to happen, but she couldn't let her truth come out. Couldn't join him in any sort of catharsis. She deserved the darkness and all the loneliness. That was a choice she'd made long ago.

She jerked her hand from his. Tried to pull away but the bed slammed into the back of her knees.

She couldn't breathe. She gasped, trying to bring air into her lungs, but her body refused to work. The walls closed in. She could swear she physically saw them move.

"No." She held up a hand, tried to ward him off.

"There's no judgment here."

He said that he'd been in that place and did what he had to do. She could picture it, knew how it felt to have suffocating desperation clawing at her insides. But their actions weren't the same. She wanted to pretend she was protecting someone else, but she'd been too late to do that. In her mind she toyed with the idea that she did it to avenge her friends. But she really killed him because no one else would.

"You will hate me." She forced the words out through gasps.

"Never. I'm the one person who understands."

She tried to go around him but he didn't move. He was right there, looming over her and talking to her in that smooth consoling voice. "I don't deserve redemption."

"I can't give it to you, but I can share the burden. You need to let the poison out while you let someone in. I want that person to be me." The color had left his face and exhaustion pulled around his eyes.

He had told her the worst. Let her see inside him to the thing he hid. She loved that he trusted her. Loved him. God, there it was. She did love him. She hadn't loved anything or anyone for so long, but with him those barriers fell away.

That made it even more important that she lock this in.

She shook her head, determined to hold it all back just as she'd been doing for years. Refusing to think about Doug and the horrors of that day. About the weeks after as the truth set in and no one would listen to her. As she shouldered the blame while she tried to grieve.

"He . . . he killed them." The words tumbled out before she could stop them. "All of them. Because of me."

Matthias reached out for her again, but she pulled away.

"No, don't touch me. I can't . . ." She scooted around him and broke into the open space of the room. She inhaled, tried to cool her mind and figure out a way to call it all back. To bury it again.

"He's dead."

Matthias said the words that she couldn't. Her gaze traveled over his face. He should run now. Should call the police. Do something.

"You said you can't disappear in the water, but he did." She made sure no one would find Doug. Took the gun courses, learned to shoot. Went to Internet cafés and researched the other things she needed to know, like how to make a body disappear. It had all been planned out, and that's the part she couldn't run away from.

"Right after the murders he taunted me, threatened to tell the police it was me. I took it and tried to ignore him, but then the police stopped looking at him. They had those cigarettes. That was the evidence." She remembered the day she found out about the discarded butts under the tree. She knew then and confronted Doug. He hadn't even tried to deny it. He said she pushed him to it. Shifted the blame to her.

"But you knew." Matthias's voice was coaxing now.

It worked because she remembered every second. It all unspooled in her mind and she walked through it as if she were living it again. "I knew and I watched him move on. Heard he was dating another girl. He would try to take over her life, scare her. Because that's what he did."

"So, you did what the police and the courts couldn't."

She acted as his jury and found him guilty. "I found him after the press died down. Went to him. Said we needed to talk about what happened. That time when he came after me with his threats, I had a gun."

The gunshot rang in her ears. Her shoulders jerk at the sound only she could hear.

"I always thought he was a guy no one would mourn, but I did. The throwing up, the crying. I did it all." Tears ran down her cheeks even now. She couldn't stop them. Couldn't beat back the guilt. She looked up at Matthias then. Finally faced him again. "I deserve the stalker."

"No, baby. You don't."

This time when he touched her arm she didn't flinch or pull away. She let him wrap his arm around her and buried her face in his chest. "You should hate me."

He lowered his head to look her in the eye. "Do you hate me?"

"No. God, no." She was back at the bed and she didn't know how it happened. Lost in thought and desperate to lean on him, she sat down on the edge.

Without a word he sat down next to her and pulled her close to his side. The simple gesture, the ready understanding and acceptance, broke her. The sob she'd trapped in her chest let loose. Tears ran down her cheeks and dripped off her chin. Her whole body shuddered.

He pulled her in even closer. Rocked their bodies back and forth on that mattress. He didn't stop her or try to calm her down. It was as if he knew she needed this moment.

Sitting there, his warmth wrapped her in a protective cocoon. The sound of her crying cut through the silence of the room. Her chest ached and her fingers dug into his leg. She thought the worst had passed, but the shame kept crashing over her.

"Can we just sit here?" She whispered the question.

"Yes." He placed a kiss in her hair. "For as long as you need."

The worst was out. Her sin. The choice she made that changed everything. That turned her into someone else. She expected to feel a weight lift but it didn't. The guilt was still there but she did have a weird sense of relief.

She understood him. They understood each other. They shared this horrible past.

She swiped at the tears. She never cried and now she couldn't seem to stop. "You should run."

He continued to hold her. Brushed his lips over her forehead. "We're both done running."

CHAPTER 27

Kayla still hadn't recovered by the next morning. She wasn't sure she ever would. Secrets were secrets for a reason. Once you told them, once they were out there, they touched everything. He might say it didn't matter to him and that he understood—words he repeated all night as he held her and soothed her—and she knew he meant them, but she expected things to change.

She saw him in a different way. Not a negative way. Not at all. Imagining Matthias as a little boy, trapped and afraid, gave her insight into who he was now. She understood the way he compartmentalized. How his rough exterior hid the decency and pain underneath.

"Kayla?"

She didn't realize she'd been daydreaming until she heard Elliot's voice. She shook her head and brought her mind back to the present. Standing behind the counter holding the coffeepot while she stared into space must have made a heck of an impression. "Sorry."

The concerned expression matched the sound of his voice. "I heard about Paul."

Matthias confirmed this morning what she already

knew—Paul broke into her place but he wasn't behind the shooting. Too many people had seen the chase to pretend it didn't happen. They played it off in public as the end to a stupid prank by a lovesick kid. She refused to press charges and Matthias somehow kept the police out of all of it.

Some of the marina shop owners were grateful she took pity on the guy they knew as Paul. Others thought she should have him thrown in jail for the break-in. Lauren was in a state of shock. She'd barely said anything when Matthias delivered the news and told her how he'd sent the kid to Wren for a wake-up call and hopefully some help.

Kayla knew she'd started all of this and couldn't really end it. It wasn't as if Paul could know the truth. He needed closure, but how did she tell him Doug was gone without implicating herself? She actually toyed with the idea of ending all of this and coming clean. Matthias talked her out of that, too. He believed deep down Paul knew the truth and would find a way to go back to being Ben.

She wasn't convinced. But she did add another victim to her list of people she'd destroyed with that one fateful act years ago.

"He'll get some help and be fine." She repeated the words to Elliot that Matthias told Lauren. She just wished she believed them.

"Maybe you should take a few days. Get the apartment back together and relax."

Not going to happen. "Maybe."

Elliot smiled. "Hey, come out with us on the boat today."

Her stomach flipped over. "No way."

"Lauren's teaching me. You can join in."

It was a sweet suggestion but she was pretty sure the throwing up would ruin his good time. So would her mood. She couldn't find the strength to celebrate anything. "I get seasick."

"Can't you take medicine?"

"I'd rather stay on dry land." She could barely walk along the dock to the end of the boat slips. She wasn't afraid of drowning, but the idea of bobbing up and down out there made her want to walk around wearing a permanent life preserver.

"So, you don't know anything about the water?"

She refilled his coffee. "Enough to stay out of it."

He held up a hand and laughed. "Fair enough."

She spent the next few minutes delivering food and chatting with patrons. None of her regulars asked about Paul and she didn't open the door to the topic. A blur of movement outside the front door grabbed her attention.

Matthias. She could always spot him. He towered above everyone else and looked more in control, suit or not.

He stood there talking with Garrett. Figuring out she was in love with him at the same time she shredded every personal vow she'd ever made and told him the truth about her past had her dizzy. It all scared the hell out of her. So did he. Not his size or his strength. It was the fact that with him she couldn't hide. He dragged things out of her that she'd never intended to share.

As she watched him now, nodding his head while Garrett talked and walking his usual confident walk, all tall and sure, her heart melted. When he pushed the door open and that bell chimed, she held her breath. She had no idea why but the minute Matthias looked at her and winked, everything inside her calmed.

"Coffees and pie," Garrett said as they walked up to her.

Yeah, he needed more sugar. "It's ten in the morning."

He shrugged. "Pie has eggs in it."

"Who can argue with logic like that?" Matthias rolled his eyes. Before she could say anything or even put the pot down, he leaned over and kissed her. Right on the mouth and in front of the entire café. "Good morning."

More than a few people watched them now. She had no idea what to do. The public affection thing was new to him and totally foreign to her. But she liked it. Would have liked for it to last a bit longer. "Hi."

Garrett smiled. "Well, now."

"That's what boyfriends do," Matthias said before he turned back to her. "And he thinks I'm the personality impaired one."

Garrett snorted. "You are."

The conversation was a stark reminder of their cover story. They slept together, made love, talked. He'd even suggested they go for a walk later. But this was pretend to him. A job.

Not for her. She'd fallen. Truth blended with fiction.

The excitement at seeing him turned to something else. Nagging doubt. When the shooter was caught, and she believed Matthias would track the person down and get answers, then what? It was one more unsettled question in her life, and she was getting tired of those.

She forced a smile. "I like you just the way you are."

"Romantic." Garrett pointed at the uncut desserts lined up behind her. "Now the pie?"

"Don't make me kick you out."

"Listen to the woman." Matthias touched his hand to hers then pulled away again to point at the table in the corner. "We'll be over here. No rush."

"KISSING IN PUBLIC?" Garrett asked as he sat down.

Matthias was impressed Garrett waited until they sat down to say something. "I'd tell you to shut up but you never listen."

"No." Garrett's eyes narrowed. "You look like shit, by the way."

He knew that was true so he didn't argue. "Thanks, man."

He felt like the inside of a dirty ashtray. Last night sucked. Telling her so much about his life left him feeling hollow. She needed to know and a part of him needed to say it, maybe as a warning so she'd know who she was dating. But the truth brought pain and when she wept it nearly killed him.

Watching her break down had hit him harder than the shock of reliving his past. She wept and all he wanted to do was make it better. His guard crashed down.

He'd spent the entire night just holding her. He thought it was the right thing to do, but it wiped them both out. He saw the exhaustion on her face and knew it mirrored his. Now they had to find a way through it all.

Garrett lined up his silverware on his napkin. "The light was off on your side when I got in last night."

"It was a long-ass day." And that didn't even begin to cover how awful it had been. Matthias ached for her, wanted to help Paul turn back into Ben and sensed a showdown was coming with Mary.

That's why he was talking to Garrett today. He'd found something and Matthias almost hated to ask what.

"You're weirder than usual this morning. You sure you're okay?"

Since Garrett sounded sincere, Matthias answered him that way. "I've been better."

"Are we going to talk about that?"

"Nope." He didn't want to relive one second of yesterday. The conversation with Kayla was off-limits as was his history. So, time to move on.

"Well, this conversation isn't going to help your sunny disposition."

"Just spit it out." It couldn't be worse than anything else he'd heard lately.

"Mary came into some money a few months ago. Big money. Tens of thousands, which is odd since she's been a waitress at a hotel most of her life."

Matthias relaxed. This was not a big deal because he had the answer. "Ninety thousand? We're good. It's from me."

"What?"

"She had a mortgage on her one bedroom and was about to default. I paid it off." He didn't regret that. He had the money and there was no need for her to suffer. He hadn't expected her to hand over credit card bills and her car payment, but she did. He took care of those, too.

With her debt-free he thought she could start over. Rebuild and try to find a life outside of Nick.

It was a good theory. He wasn't so sure it worked in practice.

"You gave the money directly to her?"

That struck him as a weird question but he answered it anyway. "By wire transfer. I got the payoff amount and sent it to her."

She insisted she pay. Said something about needing to feel as if the house was her responsibility and she'd handled it. He didn't get it and thought about refusing but gave in when she started crying. Crying women were not his thing.

"I can stop trying to trace that wire."

"Please do." He liked to keep his financial information private and had used a specific account for that transfer.

"You should know that she didn't use the cash as intended."

Anger spun through him. Matthias felt it build and he tried to punch it down, but it flared right back up. "What are you talking about?"

Garrett opened the file in front of him and turned it around to face Matthias. "She still has the mortgage."

Matthias paged through the documents. Bank records and credit card statements. It looked like she'd run up a few of her bills again. Then he saw the paperwork from her checking account. Cash withdrawals. Three of them totaling fifteen thousand dollars. "What the fuck?"

He said it loud enough to have people look at him. He almost didn't notice through the haze clouding his vision. What was she paying for?

"I don't see any gun purchases or anything like that." Garrett closed the file and took it back. "But it's suspicious."

"Hell, yeah." She'd promised and he believed her. That would teach him, but he hadn't really had any reason to doubt she'd used the money for the mortgage. Well, no reason except his instincts, which told him her story had holes.

"Do you think it's related to Kayla?"

"Isn't everything Mary does?" The two women in his life seemed to be tied together and he couldn't unknot them.

They had the money issue and Mary's talks with Paul. So many problems.

Matthias had been trying to forget Mary sat up in a hotel room just an hour away. Looked like he didn't have that luxury. He needed to talk with her. Ask her the hard questions.

Kayla showed up at the side of the table. "Here's your pie."

Garrett watched her put the plates down. "Thanks."

Her smile faded as she glanced at Matthias. "What's wrong?"

She knew. Of course she knew. She could read him as easily as he could read her. "Mary Patterson."

She made a strangled sound. "That can't be good."

"Never is." Ever. Matthias was starting to learn that. "Are you handling it?"

Not the response he expected. "You don't want to know what it is?"

"Not yet." She sighed. "Let me get through this day. I can deal with her tomorrow."

That sounded like a good plan. Matthias wished he could do the same, but ignoring Mary hadn't worked out for him so far. They needed to have a rough family chat. "Fair enough."

Kayla threw him a sad smile then walked away. Matthias did what he always did—enjoyed her walk. He blocked out the rest and for a second focused on her. He was starting to wonder if he was ever going to be able to focus on anything else.

"Bullet dodged," Garrett said as he scooped up some pie.

"No kidding." But only temporarily. Matthias was smart enough to know that.

"Now what?"

He shoved the plate away from him. He wasn't hungry now. "Apparently I need to go talk with Mary."

"Good luck."

"I'll probably need it."

CHAPTER 28

Matthias was starting to hate the drive back and forth to DC. As an avowed workaholic he normally got antsy whenever he was away from his office for too long. Turning his bodyguard duties over to Garrett and his men proved to be even worse. He wanted to be the one watching after Kayla. Leaving her in favor of a showdown about money just was not a choice he ever wanted to make.

It didn't help that Mary was in full dramatic mode today. She had her bag packed and sitting in the middle of her unmade hotel room bed. "You can't keep me prisoner here."

As if that was even happening. "You're in a hotel room and can go outside anytime."

"But I can't go to Annapolis." She plunked down on the mattress right beside the bag.

Wren's men watched her but so long as she didn't try to get to Annapolis and Kayla, everything was fine. Unfortunately, she'd proved completely capable of getting into trouble without moving one inch. Her bank records, the unexplained calls. That's why he'd come here today.

"What good would it do to leave here?" As far as Matthias could tell, she'd go straight to Annapolis and cause more trouble. He just wasn't sure why. She'd had years to exact her revenge. She'd used Paul back when he was still Ben. Who knew what else she'd done. So, why now?

"I have a right to see her."

He could not figure out what that would accomplish. A public showdown would send Kayla running, a thought he despised, but Mary wouldn't be one inch closer to avenging Nick. It was a sick cycle and it needed to stop because it didn't go anywhere and only made both Mary and Kayla miserable.

"I can show you a photo." Not that he planned to do that.

"This woman killed my son—"

"No." Again with this. He had no idea how Kayla lived with this bullshit. "There's no evidence to support that."

"You know better." Mary got up and went to the minibar. She opened the refrigerator door and the little bottles clanked and jingled. She took one out but didn't open it. She just stood there, holding it.

"Really? Enlighten me."

She turned and reached for a glass. "Don't talk to me like that. I am still your mother."

Matthias watched her reflection in the mirror. Tried to imagine what went on in her head when she said shit like that, totally ignoring the fact she'd abandoned him. The rage simmered under the surface, but not far under. She practically vibrated with it. He couldn't tell if it stemmed from her hatred of the situation or her disappointment in him as a son.

He couldn't get a handle on her agenda. Good thing he had one of his own. This, the real reason for his visit, was Kayla and not his continued frustration and disappointment over the reality of his mother-son reunion. He could work that out another time or do what he'd done for this entire life—bury it.

"The police don't think she did it. The prosecutor wouldn't bring charges." That was just the start.

Mary turned around holding a glass. Her fingers turned white from the force of her grip on it. "That's about them wanting to save their jobs. They have to be reelected, which means they can't bring cases where some pathetic creature on a jury might fall for the defendant's lies. The way she looks, some stupid idiot would."

She had this all worked out in her warped mind. She wouldn't listen to reason and facts, but he tried anyway because he had no idea how else to get through to her and get to his questions. He couldn't tell her the truth. That was not his secret to tell, and he'd die before he divulged it. But he could try to bring Mary around. "There's a list of suspects and, honestly, other people are far more likely to have done it. You need to trust me on this."

"Do you know another one of her friends is missing? From back at college, I mean."

He bit back an exhale. "Yes."

"The theory is he was her accomplice and died in a hiking accident. Convenient, wouldn't you say?"

If he didn't know what he knew, maybe. If he were blinded by revenge he might make those connections. He hoped his mind would stay clear.

He chose his words carefully. "No one thinks she had anything to do with a hiking incident."

"Why can't you see it? There's a line of missing coeds that leads back to her." Mary held the empty glass, flung it around as she talked. "You were supposed to go after her and end this. You were the one."

"For what?" She'd never said anything like that before. She'd asked for help and pulled every string and brought out the guilt to send him looking for answers about Nick. He bought it because he was willing to be bought. Because he was curious and felt partially responsible for the younger brother he'd never met.

"You were supposed to do this work and figure it out."

"I'm not an investigator."

She slammed the glass down without ever filling it or taking a drink. "Then I should have hired one. A better one."

She pivoted around him and went back to the bed. Unzipped her bag and started shifting the contents around.

Since the conversation was already going nowhere, he jumped into the topic that was sure to blow things up even more. "Is that how you found Ben Weston?"

Her hands froze and she looked over at him. "What?"

Matthias hadn't moved outside of a two-foot square up until then, but now he did. He walked over to stand at the end of the bed. He wanted to be able to see her face, try to read her. "He came to you and you told him your theories."

"She killed his brother. He deserved to know the truth." Mary folded and refolded her shirt. Her hands were constant movement.

"You filled him with half-truths, got him riled up and aimed him directly at her." He reached over and took the shirt out of her hands, forcing her to look at him. "You basically weaponized a confused kid and sicced him on Kayla."

"That's not her name."

He threw the shirt on the bed. "The point is that you are too close to this. You've decided she's guilty and refuse to listen."

"She got to you." Mary shook her head. "The way she looks. All those lies."

"Stop." He refused to dissect his relationship with Kayla or discuss it with Mary.

"That's what happened to Nick. She lured him in and he thought he was safe."

She twisted every fact to fit her theory. "They were never together."

"You believe her."

"God, yes." He was on the verge of yelling it.

A crack of silence broke through the room. "You're a complete disappointment."

Her words sliced through him. They shouldn't because he shouldn't care. But as soon as they were out there he realized he hadn't just been on this quest for Nick. He'd been looking for some sort of connection with her. That didn't happen.

He kept his voice steady. "I'm sure I'm not who you hoped I'd be."

"I was right not to trust you with this."

He was so tired of her cryptic bullshit. "What does that mean?"

"Nothing."

"Mary." He picked up her shirt and threw it onto the top of her bag. "Tell me."

"Some people need to learn the hard way."

THE BRIGHT MORNING had given way to a cloudy afternoon. Thunderstorms rolled in the distance, a typical thing for the area at this time of year. The air took on a twinge of dampness and impending rain showed in the gray sky.

Good thing this would be a quick errand. A run to the boat shed and back. Then the skies could open up and the weather could do whatever it wanted so long as Matthias drove safely.

He'd stopped into the café for a quick visit and a take-out coffee earlier. She tried to ask where he was going between customers but settled for a kiss goodbye. He'd done that twice now. Two kisses in public. She had no idea what it meant. She knew what she *wanted* it to mean and how right it felt. But Matthias always struck her as a guy who'd have wheels on the bottom of his shoes and speed off as soon as she was out of danger.

The sex, holding her at night. The kisses. The sharing of information and promises of trust. All of it pointed to something bigger than a fake boyfriend. It felt very real to her. Her tie to him mattered.

She'd expected a text from him once he was on the road. That just seemed like a Matthias thing to do. So when it came, it filled her with a surge of happiness. The man did not disappoint. He told her he was on the road and would be back for a late dinner. Warmth flushed through her. She'd even caught herself humming.

But now the café was closed and she was one stop from going back to the inn. She turned to her bodyguard of the day, Garrett. "Where's Matthias?"

He looked at the couple coming toward them and out over the water. "He had to run a business errand."

The lack of eye contact gave him away. "Is that true?"

He glanced at her then. "Sort of?"

Kayla stopped at the end of the dock, right where the wood turned into loose rock and the trail went from clear to the type that only locals would follow. The chain-link fence and big KEEP OUT sign made an impression.

She studied Garrett's face, wondering how much he would tell her about Matthias's top secret errand. Not that she thought Matthias would hide the information. He seemed to have learned that lesson, but he didn't exactly cough up unpleasant news without some prodding.

Speaking of unpleasant, this appeared to be about her least favorite topic. "So, his mother."

Garrett winced. "He doesn't really call her that."

The title wasn't the problem. Putting Matthias in the middle was. "I hate that he's forced to make a choice between us."

"You're kidding, right?"

It wasn't exactly a secret. Not now that Paul admitted talking to Mary and hearing her spew so much hate. Matthias had loyalties to Nick. Then there was the part where Mary kept poking around in Kayla's life, which only highlighted her connection to Matthias and made things more stressful.

"She's telling him one thing. I'm telling him another. We're both tugging and pulling him." The whole thing was a mess. Still, she didn't want to lose him. Not before they got a chance to see what they were, or if they could even be a *they*.

"It's not even a contest." Garrett shot her one of those come-on stares. "He's here for you, not her. He trusts you. Wants to be with you."

"I still don't . . ." Kayla didn't hate the sound of any of that. "Did he tell you those things?"

"Right, because I want to say stuff that will make Matthias kick my ass. You do know he's six-four and jacked. Bandage or not, I'm going to pass on that fight."

Oh, she was well aware of Matthias's body and what he hid under those clothes. She could catalog every muscle and call up the view by heart. Sometimes she did that during the day and it left her breathless.

"How long have you been friends?" she asked, because she'd been dying to ask that.

They finished the last stretch of open area between the end of the shops and the beginning of the hardcore fisherman area. The usually locked fence was open and the door stood ajar. The place didn't look like the type kids and others would break in to, but it was. Rumor was teens thought this was the perfect makeout spot.

The fishermen were a bit more practical. This was the place where boats pulled in, still submerged in water, and mechanics could stand on planks and work from above, or dive and work from below. All of it happened under cover and away from the rest of the marina.

Lauren loved the shack with the peeling green paint and leaky roof. She called it a marina institution. Kayla had never been inside the fence. Until now.

"I'm not sure Matthias would call us friends. The relationship is pretty complicated, but I do think of him that way. And the answer is years."

That was it. No more information, which meant she'd have to pull it out of Matthias. "You're so specific."

Now that she'd stupidly and unexpectedly fallen in love with him, the need to know more tugged at her. She understood his childhood and didn't want to force him to mentally venture there. But she had so many questions about Quint and the group of men Matthias had trained with and been shaped by . . . and where Garrett fit in, because that seemed to be a mystery.

"I would never admit this to him, but your boyfriend scares me," Garrett said.

That made two of them. But that wasn't the part of the comment she focused on. "He's not that."

"The boyfriend thing? Are you trying to convince me or you?"

"Neither."

"I'll come back to that." They stood just outside the set of double doors leading inside the shed. "How did we end up here?"

"Lauren texted that she got stuck doing some work in the boat shed. I said I'd bring food by."

"You know this place is on water, right?"

Kayla's stomach heaved at the mere mention of that fact. "It floats on top, which is a ridiculous architecture choice, but I'm aware."

He looked over the marina and out into the sound, which dumped into the bay. "I see all kinds of water out here. You going to be able to do this without passing out?"

The chances were not great, but she didn't want to admit that. "I'm tough."

"No kidding."

She motioned for him to open the door. They stepped just inside and she stopped. It took all she had not to slam her back into the wall and refuse to move. She held the brown bag filled with food in a death grip. It was tempting to hurl it at Lauren and race out of there. When the shocking smell of dead fish hit her, Kayla seriously considered the plan.

She turned to say something to Garrett in time to see him finish a text and pocket his cell in the jeans he wore today. "You're attached to that thing."

He shrugged. "It's work."

"Now you sound like Matthias." She was pretty sure they'd both work round the clock if they could manage it and not fall over from lack of sleep.

"Take that back." Garrett stepped away from her. "Wait here."

"Yeah, no problem." It was bad enough she could see water, smell it. The slip under the shed was empty.

Without a boat docked there, the inside of the shed consisted of a walkway that wound around the open water and a wall full of tools on the opposite side. Off to her right were stacks of crates and a few tarps. Garrett studied them before looking back at the water again.

Everything was there except Lauren.

Garrett walked right up to the edge and peeked over into the water. "You sure she said here?"

"Let me look at her text." Kayla would rather stare at her phone than watch him hang so close to the edge.

She scrolled through the messages. Yeah, here. It wasn't like Lauren to get things wrong or mess with Kayla. Not where water was concerned.

She was about to point that out when she heard a crack and glanced up. Garrett's head jerked forward and his eyes rolled back. In another second, his body slipped boneless to the ground.

Her mind went blank for a second, then she spun into action. Dropping her phone, she went down on her knees beside him. "Garrett! What happened?"

She saw blood on the back of his head. Then she heard footsteps and shoes appeared in front of her. When her gaze traveled up, she saw Elliot looming over her. Preppy, relatively charming Elliot, holding what looked like a pipe.

She stared, not understanding what was happening or what to say. Finally she spit out his name. "Elliot?"

"I really wish you wouldn't have brought him." Elliot shook his head. "I've only been paid for one."

"What are you talking about?"

"It's time for you to take a swim."

MATTHIAS SKIPPED THE shirt and the bag. He reached for Mary's arm and forced her to turn and look at him. "What happened to the mortgage money?"

She looked at his hand and frowned. "So, instead of spying on her, you've been spying on me?"

His head caught fire. It took all his control not to explode. He wanted to rush her words and get the answers—now. "I've been investigating, as you asked me to do."

"Then you know." Her voice had turned singsongy. All traces of fury had been replaced with an odd sense of peace.

Whatever she planned was already in motion. It could already be done. And that scared the shit out of him. Panic raced through him. He hadn't felt so help- less since he was a kid.

He wanted to shake her. "Tell me about the money."

She had the nerve to shrug at him. "What about it?"

"I am not in the mood for games." He forced his fingers to let go. It was either that or risk squeezing her arm. She had him on the edge of reason. "Your mort- gage. You still have one and shouldn't."

"Paying for this was more important."

"Where did the money go?" Possibilities bombarded his brain, each worse than the one before it. Without re- sources she'd wreaked havoc on Kayla's life. He hated to think what she could do with the power money provided.

"Let this happen." She patted his arm.

The condescending garbage had his nerves firing. His instincts switched to high alert. "What are you talking about?"

She'd morphed into a different person, calm and almost grandmotherly. "Nick would want this."

"Nick is dead."

Anger flared in her eyes, but only for a second. She visibly swallowed before starting to talk again. "Because of her."

"What did you do?" The cell in his pocket buzzed but he ignored it. Whatever *this* was, whatever Mary had done, trumped everything.

She lifted her chin and did not blink. "I used the money you gave me. My plan was to come check then leave the area before it happened, but it looks like that friend of yours will not allow that to happen."

"What exactly did you use the money for?" He'd keep asking until he got a real answer. His heart hammered hard enough to block out any other sound. His sole focus was on the woman in front of him. "Tell me."

"I couldn't do anything on my own, but with your money I could."

Dread nearly drowned him. He swam through a thick soup of it as he struggled to imagine what she'd bought. Even as he mentally catalogued the options, he discounted the worse. There was no way. "What are you saying?"

"I hired the gun, but you paid for it."

The world crashed down on him. A killer stalking

Kayla. Someone with skills and weapons. Someone who would shoot through an apartment window.

He looked at the woman who had given birth to him and felt nothing but revulsion. "You're fucking sick."

"Resourceful."

"You set Kayla up." He'd never thrown up on a job in his life but he almost did right there.

"Actually, Matthias"—Mary smiled then—"you did."

CHAPTER 29

Kayla silently begged Garrett to move. His body was so still. Blood oozed from a wound at the back of his head and his hands lay against the dirty floor. Not even a muscle twitched.

She reached over and checked his neck for a pulse. A harsh breath punched out of her when she felt the steady thump under her fingertips. She hoped his luck held.

"Move away from him." Elliot lifted his leg. "Now."

She couldn't let this happen. Her instinct jump-started and she threw her body across Garrett's. Closed her eyes, waiting for the incoming kick. Any attack would nail her first, but she didn't care.

The sound of crunching glass broke the silence. She peeked up to see Elliot repeatedly slam his heel down on Garrett's cell. For the first time she noticed the prep school clothes and sunny smile were gone. His all-black outfit was out of place here. It wouldn't help him fit in or slide behind the scenes.

Good. She concentrated on that possibility. This could be a matter of timing. Hold Elliot off until reinforcements broke in.

Elliot swept the broken pieces of phone into the

water with the side of his shoe. "I have to give you credit. You are a smart one."

"I don't understand any of this." He'd shown up days ago, right around the time Matthias did, to take boating lessons. He didn't lurk around or ask her probing questions. There was nothing suspicious about his behavior. She didn't even see him some days. So, what was happening now?

"This thing generally happens at a distance. No contact. But you, well, there's something about you." He reached down, grabbed her arm and yanked.

Pain shot through her from neck to wrist. She swallowed a scream. She would never let him know the manhandling hurt. She refused to make a sound when he dug his fingernails into the fleshy part of her arm.

"With the big bodyguard hanging around, I had to rethink my plan."

She tried to jerk out of his grasp but he held on. With every shift he just tightened his grip. She stopped moving and tried to think. Stall him. Find something to slam into him. He still held the pole and there was no way she could wrestle that away from him. But the shed had tools and she could run.

She forced her body to relax. It proved almost impossible with the adrenaline shooting through her. "Who are you?"

"My name doesn't matter." He shoved her away from him. "You kill three people, maybe four, and go on the run. You have locals helping you. No one turns you in. It's amazing, really. Not the way I do it, but it's interesting to see your way."

The shove had her off balance. Her feet tangled but she managed to stay up. She could hear the water lapping near her. One peek over her shoulder and she realized she stood just a foot from the edge of the water.

She tried to inch forward but he moved in front of her and shook his head. Because he knew. She'd told him about her thoughts on the water. Disclosed her greatest fear.

Inhaling, she tried to slow her heartbeat. It thundered in her ears, making it almost impossible to concentrate. "I didn't kill anyone."

"If that's true it's a real shame, because that's why I'm being paid to take care of you."

Money? This was about money . . . but why? "By who? That doesn't make any sense."

The revving up of a lawn mower sounded in the distance. She listened for other sounds, tried to pick up on noises or the sound of people talking. The shed sat away from the rest of the dock and over by the gas tanks. She could hear the clanking of boats as they bobbed in the marina. That didn't answer the question about how fast he could shoot compared to how fast she could run or duck.

But it wasn't just her. She wouldn't leave Garrett behind, which meant handling this on her own. Finding the right makeshift weapon and hoping Matthias was either close enough to help or far enough away to be safe.

"The reasons behind this kind of thing normally don't matter to me. I collect the cash and do the job.

The emotions don't mean shit." He threw the pole onto the stack of crates and far out of reaching distance. "Lucky for you, my benefactor wanted you to have the information right before you died. She wanted to know what your reaction was to finally being caught."

She. There was only one dangerous she trying to track her down. "Mary Patterson."

"Not just her." Elliot made a show of checking his gun. "You've been sleeping with the enemy. Her big-money partner."

Kayla had been so focused on his hands and the gun that she almost missed the comment. Her head shot up. "What?"

"Your fake boyfriend."

Fake boyfriend. Those were the words Matthias used. Doubt spun through her. But it couldn't be. He would never . . . *she would know*. "You're wrong."

"He's with her right now." Elliot laughed and his voice changed. Gone was the easygoing draw and soft-sell charm. He was all business and violence now. "Hell, he's up there having a mother-son chat about what's happening to you right now."

Her brain cells misfired. Memories bombarded her—how he'd acted that first day they met, how he held her at night. She tried to merge the two and her mind rebelled.

Not Matthias. He was the one she could trust. Bigger than that, she thought he was *the* one. "No, he's—"

"He's got her stashed in a hotel in DC."

The trips to DC. Not secret. He admitted *talking*

with her. He never said she was nearby or Kayla might have run. "This is coming from Mary and she's out of her mind with grief."

"You can blame her, but think about it. Who do you think really funded my trip here?" Elliot shrugged. "Hey, it was a surprise to me at first. I thought your guy and I were on opposite sides, but no."

She couldn't breathe. She wanted to double over and scream. Needed to get away from here. From everywhere and every person. "I don't even know who you are. Why would you do this?"

"I'm the one who makes problems disappear."

"And I'm a problem?"

"I tried to make it easy with that shot through the window, but Matthias moved. I figured he was trying to draw it out, sleep with you a few more times first." Elliot smiled. "Hey, there's your proof. Don't you think I would have taken both of you out right then if he wasn't in on it?"

She beat back the awful words. "Stop talking. I don't believe any of this."

"You don't need to, but it's happening." With his gun still aimed at her, Elliot squatted down. He patted his free hand over Garrett without ever breaking eye contact with her. "Let's get started."

He moved with lightning speed then. Stood up, put his foot on Garrett's thigh and pushed. Shoved him into the water with a loud splash.

Panic suffocated her. "No!"

She dropped to her knees again and plunged her arms into the murky water. A wave lapped over the side and soaked her shirt. Water got in her mouth. She gasped at the splash and the sharp smell. A voice in her head screamed for her to get her hands out of there but she had to grab Garrett before his body sank.

Frantic now, she looked around for something to help her drag him out. Bile churned in her stomach, threatening to overtake her. She choked it back. She could not freeze or get sick. She had to keep moving and turn him over, give him a chance to wake up and breathe.

"Here's what's going to happen." Elliot droned on as if he hadn't just sent a man to a drowning death. "In this scenario, your friend here dies because he figured out who you really were and that you were a killer. Then you disappear out on the water, because that whole fear-of-water thing has been an elaborate setup by you as part of an escape plan."

"That's the worst way to disappear." The words stumbled out of her as she snagged Garrett's arm and tried to drag him in closer to the side without going over.

"Whatever the fuck that means. I'm guessing your bodyguard will lay the groundwork for that part because that's now how Mary wants it done. Even paid extra for the drama of it."

Fear buzzed in her brain. She didn't have room for his accusations. They weren't true. He was trying to throw her off. "Don't do this."

"I'm going to make sure no one finds your body. The shooting would have been faster but this does have a bit of flare to it. I don't usually do flare." Elliot nodded toward the now calm water. "You can stop. He's gone. Consider him collateral damage."

No more. She would not let that be true.

She struggled to turn Garrett faceup with one hand and couldn't get enough of a grip on him to do it. Didn't have enough traction. "You'll never get away with this."

"Apparently murders related to you are never solved, so I think I will." Elliot typed something into his cell phone then dropped it on the floor and smashed that one to pieces, too. "Besides, no one knows who Elliot is. He'll slip away in the commotion."

"You've thought this through."

The double doors burst open. Matthias came barreling through on a roar. He dove, hitting Elliot with his good shoulder and sending them both flying back. Elliot's gun thudded on the wood floor near her but she didn't reach for it. Not now. She couldn't spend one second thinking her next move through because Garrett would die.

While Matthias and Elliot traded punches and slammed each other into the floor, she turned around and let her feet hover over the water. Terror froze her muscles. She couldn't manage to lower her legs. Couldn't slide into the same water that filled her with such horror.

Thuds and crashes sounded all around her. She could hear men shouting. Matthias had come and he'd brought his team.

Relief swept through her until she looked down into the water again. No movement. No sign of Garrett.

Forcing back the tears and the nausea, she tried to

shout but her voice didn't rise over the noise. She had no choice. She dropped in. Sank and kept sinking.

Water rushed up around her and stung her eyes. She couldn't see a thing. She moved her arms, reaching out for anything and came up sputtering. One hand grabbed into the shed floor above her and the other touched something slick. She pulled her hand back as she started to gag.

No, it had to be Garrett. Without giving her body a chance to react, she dunked her head again. Right there. An arm. Clothes. She didn't waste time. With her elbow locked around his neck, she pulled him up. The lift was probably dangerous and wrong but at least he turned over. His face bobbed in the water as he floated on his back.

The fight waged on above her. Elliot got the advantage when he bent back Matthias's injured arm. She could see his eyes widen as his knees hit the floor. But he didn't give up. He shot forward and nailed Elliot right above the knees and sent them both sprawling.

She saw the flash of a gun and heard the pounding of feet as people came closer to the shed. She tried to drag her body up to safer ground and away from the water, but Garrett's weight had her sinking back down and accidentally shoving him back under.

Matthias landed a punch and Elliot fell sideways. A scream of pain followed the loud thump. With wild eyes Elliot looked at her then to the gun that lay a few inches away. She tried to push up again and slapped for it. He was a second faster. As his fingers touched it, a shot rang out.

For a second Elliot froze. His body stayed upright and his mouth moved. Then she saw the blood. The dark stain spreading across his black shirt. He moved his hand and she feared he'd somehow get the weapon. With one last kick, she lifted her body up high enough to grab it and whip it into the water behind her.

The door burst open and Matthias's people filled the room right as Elliot fell face-first onto the floor. For a second she didn't move. She heard heavy breathing and saw Matthias sitting on the floor, holding his arm and the gun. His shoulder rested at a strange angle compared to the rest of his body, as if he'd popped it out of the socket. There was blood all over him and a new wave of fear hit her.

"Matthias?"

He seemed to give himself a shake. One of his men tried to help him up, but he crawled over to her. "Are you okay?"

She reacted to the worry in his voice. "Help me with Garrett."

Matthias looked past her. "Damn it."

Everyone filed in now. People from the marina spread across the floor. Strong arms reached in and plucked her out of the water, but her legs wouldn't hold her. The second her feet hit the wood she fell again.

Matthias sat next to her, catching her and bringing her body back to rest against his chest. He moved her to his side as two men dragged Garrett out of the water and started CPR. Lauren hovered by the door to make room for the ambulance crew running in with a gurney. Kayla didn't remember hearing the sirens.

Matthias's face was a mask of fury as he watched them work on Garrett. She silently sent all of her energy to him, willing him to open his eyes and breathe again.

She grabbed a fistful of Matthias's dry shirt. "How did you find us?"

"Garrett texted and I put a tracker on you and could find you with my phone."

He didn't look at her. He just rocked her back and forth. A man on his team squatted in front of them, studying them. "We need to get you both to the hospital."

"I'm fine," Matthias snapped out. "Deal with Garrett."

"You're bleeding," she said, remembering the tell-tale red.

His dazed expressions cleared as he looked down at her. "Did he touch you?"

"No."

He frowned at her. "You really got in the water?"

At the mention of it her stomach turned over. That turkey sandwich rushed up on her. "I'm going to be sick."

Garrett started coughing up water. The men rolled him to the side as Matthias called out orders. He wanted Garrett in the hospital and now. He said she needed to go, too. As usual, he was taking care of everyone but himself.

The relief at hearing Garrett battled with her confusion. "Matthias."

With the help of the men clearing the room and taking photos, Matthias stood up, taking her with him. He tucked her close into his side. The move should have put her at ease, but her brain cells kept jumping. She had so many questions.

He needed his shoulder checked and the fresh blood cleaned. He might need more than a sling this time. He had a cut by the corner of his mouth and blood trickled down the side of his head by his hairline.

This was the wrong time and wrong place. There were people all around and a dead man on the floor. Garrett had been strapped to a gurney with an oxygen mask covering his mouth and nose.

"He said you paid for this." The words slipped out as a whisper.

Matthias must have heard because he looked at her. "Yes."

"What does that mean?"

He stood so tall and sure, but his expression was unreadable. "It was my money. It was Mary's plan."

Kayla felt a stabbing pain in her stomach as her brain switched off. She fought to find the right words, ask the right questions, but nothing came to her. "You did this to me?"

"It's not what you think."

Pain surged through her as the dizziness hit. "You've been seeing her."

"Kayla."

"Yes or no?"

"Twice. Yes."

She moved away from him. As far as the crowded space would allow. "You're working with her."

"No." He didn't even try to touch her. "It's not like that."

But it was too late. She couldn't hold it back. An acid mix rushed up from her stomach. She doubled over just in time. Threw up on the floor and on Matthias's feet.

He put a hand on her back. "Hey, are you—"

"No." She shrank away from his touch. From the memories. From all of it. "Let go of me."

"Listen to me."

"Not now." The soothing voice and look of concern wouldn't work this time.

She'd fallen for him and he betrayed her. When it was time to pick a side, he didn't choose her.

Her brain couldn't process it and her heart felt battered and bruised. It took all her strength to lift her head. "Get away from me."

CHAPTER 30

Matthias sat at his office desk and tried to figure out how he was going to drag his body through another afternoon without Kayla. He'd made it less than three full days and already he was miserable and barking at staff and not able to concentrate on new contracts and the workload.

His was a job where his head needed to be one hundred percent in the game or people could get hurt. But right now he could barely think. Having Wren sit in the chair across from him, staring and not doing much else, was not helping.

After ten minutes of silence except for the ticking of the wall clock and clicking of the computer keys, Wren finally piped up. "Why are you here?"

That made absolutely no sense. "I work here. This is my office. I own everything, including the staplers."

"It's cute when you answer a question I'm not really asking."

That got Matthias to lift his hands from the keyboard and listen. "Clearly you want to say something."

Wren shook his head. "So many things."

That sounded bad. "How did you even get in here?"

"You basically let me in. Gave me a badge and told your people I can come and go. You probably don't remember because you're useless right now."

Matthias couldn't remember but he wasn't about to make that admission. "This is a fantastic pep talk."

"Is that what you need? I can cheer you on, call you a dick, tell you to get your head out of your ass. Tell me which one of those will stop this pathetic display."

That was the most annoying sentence Matthias had ever heard Wren utter. "Stop what?"

"The moping." Wren groaned. "So painful."

"You can leave."

"Or you could listen to me and stop pretending to work." Wren scoffed. "You're not even good at it. I can tell you're typing random words. Hell, do you even know how to type? You strike me as a dictation guy. Very old-school."

Matthias wasn't sure when he'd become Wren's target, but it could stop anytime. He pointed at the file next to his computer. "I'm trying to read this and take notes."

"It's upside down."

"Shit." Matthias glanced at the pages. "Wait, no it's not."

"And you would have known that had you actually been reading it." Wren leaned forward with his elbows on the far edge of Matthias's desk. "Look, I get that the last few days sucked—"

"Stop."

"You're trying to use the threatening tone on me? That's never going to work. We share too much history."

Matthias normally appreciated Wren's tenacity. Not so much today. "You're more annoying than Garrett this morning."

"The same guy you're checking on hourly. You, who pretend not to care about other people."

It was the absolute least he could do. Matthias knew that. "He almost died."

"He's fine. He's asked for a raise and a promotion and doesn't seem to care that the only job left in the building above his is mine." Wren let out a loud exhale. "Hell, I might have to make him a partner after this assignment."

"He could come work for me."

"Not happening." The amusement left Wren's voice. "But let's talk about Kayla and what's really happening here. You feel guilty."

"Mary tried to have Kayla killed and used my money to do it. There's not really a gray area." A member of his family tried to destroy her. Not metaphorically. Literally. Mary lied and schemed and used people, including him. It was a hell of a family legacy to carry around.

"Admittedly, those facts don't sound great for you."

That sentence was so typically Wren that Matthias almost smiled. "I'm supposed to be able to ferret that out. I get paid to do this sort of thing."

"Bullshit."

Not the answer he expected. "Excuse me?"

"You get paid to prepare your teams to go in and resolve no-win situations. Nothing can prepare you for having your life split apart by a woman you've known for ten seconds blowing into town to seek revenge." Wren sat back in his chair. "And then there's the fact she's your mother and you wanted her to be better than she is. You wanted her to give a shit about you. You deserved that and she couldn't deliver."

Matthias's automatic reaction was to deny the need. Jump back into his I'm-an-island mode and move on. But he didn't have the will or the energy. "I didn't think I cared. I'm still shocked that I do."

"Of course you did. You're human."

For a guy who wasn't known for being a good talker, Matthias thought Wren was doing pretty well. Made him think he should share more often . . . or, you know, at all. "You've never accused me of that before."

"For the record, that's why I hate her. She had a chance to turn this around, get to know you, and she blew it. She's knocked you off balance."

Wren wasn't the type to talk in flowery language or search for the right word to be as tactful as possible. He was a straight shooter, so when he said those words they meant even more.

"I'll be fine." Matthias didn't know when because right now all he felt was a dragging sense of loss and blindsided by the emptiness swallowing him.

"Of course you will. You fight dictators for a living. You know this is her loss. You've got a woman problem, but it's not her." Wren shook his head. "And we need to fix it before you end up curled in a ball in the corner."

"Let's not do this part." Matthias couldn't do this part.

"You're stupid in love with Kayla, but I'm hoping you're smart enough to know that. I'd love to shortcut the refusals and the part where you annoy me, and get to the next stage. The one where we clean up your mess."

Hearing her name sent a shot of pain through his chest. It hurt just to talk. "It's too soon."

"Love doesn't work that way. You don't get to pick the time line. Trust me, I know."

The word didn't even make any sense in Matthias's head. He was not the love type. He didn't get stupid over women. He didn't put them above his job. He didn't build his life around them. Well, he hadn't ever thought about doing that until her.

He shook his head. "I can't be in love."

"Too late."

Wren would pick now to be all pro-love after years of making fun of the guys he knew who fell hard. Matthias needed the old version of his friend, the hardened one. "You should tell me to get over her."

"I like you too much for that."

He made it seem simple, but Matthias knew better. "I'm not you. I can't just flip my life around."

"You keep telling yourself that. I'd say you have about fifty minutes." Wren stood up and reached across the desk. He snatched Matthias's car keys and pointed toward the door. "Ready?"

This was weird even for Wren. "What are you doing?"

"Driving you to Annapolis. I figure you can come to your senses on the way. If you don't, I'll drop you out on the side of the road and go have lunch."

"I'm not—"

"If she leaves tomorrow, slips under the surface and into a new name and a new life, would you be able to breathe?" Wren balanced his fists on the side of the desk and stared Matthias down.

He didn't even have to guess at that answer. "No."

"How do you survive losing her? How do you survive never seeing her again?"

Matthias felt all of the blood drain from his head. The room spun and he doubted if his legs would hold him if he tried to stand. "I can't."

"Then drop the ego, get your fucking coat and let's go."

KAYLA STOOD BEHIND the counter, just as she did every other Tuesday. Cecelia was on her way back to town. Between the shooting and near drowning, she wanted to check on things. Kayla feared that meant she was about to be fired. She seemed to bring trouble wherever she went, so she couldn't exactly blame her boss.

With Wren and Matthias handling the press and the police, the entire thing had barely made a ripple in the news. There was talk of a stalker. Most of the people working at and around the marina were supportive and sympathized with her for all she'd been through. Almost everyone told her they now understood why she kept to herself.

They got that she'd been in hiding. They just didn't understand the real reason. Whatever it took to get back to some form of normal was fine with her. She just knew that this time she wouldn't be moving on or taking a new name. So long as this cover held and no one uncovered her past, she'd settle in here and try to start over. No more running, and that meant trusting the friend who sat right in front of her picking at a piece of banana cream pie.

"I still can't believe it," Lauren said as she poked at the crust with her fork.

"The part where I got in the water or the rest of it?" Kayla could still taste it no matter how many cups of black coffee she downed.

She'd tried to block out the pieces and the words. Mostly, she wanted to call back the things she said to Matthias. Her coldness. She blamed the shock, but the pain that flashed in his eyes had been all too real. So was the fact he left town as soon as it was all over . . . just as she feared.

Her emotions rode a wild roller-coaster ride. Her relief at knowing Garrett was okay got trampled when Matthias got in his car and left. The anger and loss swept over her. So did the reality that he didn't want to stay and fight for them. To talk it out.

She could rebuild, go to school, find another place to live. Those were all on her list. But not seeing him, not being able to hold his hand and talk her confusion through ripped her apart. A choking despair settled over her. She didn't want to eat and couldn't sleep.

She'd spent most of the night on Lauren's sofa bed just staring at the ceiling. Now she dragged through the day, knowing the cycle would keep repeating if she didn't track him down and deal with this.

She'd told him to leave and maybe she meant it in that moment, but not really. Without him her insides shredded and every minute dulled. And the fact she looked up, hoping he'd walk through the door, every time that stupid bell dinged made her want to tear it down.

She had no idea how she was going to get through this day, let alone this week. After a lifetime of being alone and trying to be fine with that, she hated her own company. She missed him, ached to see him. Wanted to punch him for not sticking around and fighting for them.

"Your life, that idiot Elliot, the water. The fact Matthias left without saying goodbye." Lauren shook her head. "You've had a shit time of it."

"I threw up on him." Between the water and the shock of losing him so fast it was amazing she'd stopped throwing up.

"On Matthias? Oh, please. He's tougher than that."

"I also had a momentary lapse where I questioned the truth of the story about the money and him being in on it." She'd relived that conversation a million times and wished she could call it all back.

"That was a mistake."

"Yeah, thanks."

Lauren threw down her fork. "Jesus, Kayla. You're human. We do dumb things and then fix them. It's part of the DNA."

Sure, that sounded reasonable, but nothing about what happened fit into a nice little box like that. But her already shaky life careened out of control in those minutes in the boat shed. The gun and the look on Matthias's face. It was like she'd slapped him.

The way the men battled and her frantic search under the water for Garrett. It all raced back at her. Every word and all that fear.

Her hands shook and her heartbeat thumped in her ears. She turned around and pretended to fiddle with the coffeepot handle. Anything to hide the panic crushing her as she remembered how close Matthias came to getting shot again.

"I can imagine that conversation. 'Gee, I'm sorry I believed you hired someone to kill me.' I bet that would go over well." She tried to make a joke but the café behind her had gone silent. She'd somehow managed to nearly shout the sentence into a room that didn't know the specifics.

This day sucked.

"You could just tell me you don't believe it." Matthias's voice carried from one end of the dining room to the other.

She spun around and there he was. Tall and dangerous in his dark DC suit. He no longer wore the sling, but he held his arm bent at an odd angle, almost cradling it.

She took it all in. The confidence and the . . . weariness. He looked tired. She could see the exhaustion around his eyes and flat mouth. He still stole her breath. She looked at him and a part of her danced with excitement.

The door . . . she hadn't heard the bell. Hadn't been prepared for the full force of seeing him again. "Matthias."

Wren stepped around Matthias and gave the crowd

a little wave. Everyone was watching. No one even pretended to eat.

"Good morning, all. Hello, ladies." Wren looked at his watch. "Maybe we've slipped into afternoon. Either way, I'm going to go over here."

He pointed to a table just a few feet away. One of the few that wasn't taken. The café had a steady crowd today. Lauren told Kayla it was a show of community support. People nearby wanted her to know they believed in her. They did it by coming in and getting pie. Kayla loved that about this town.

Lauren picked up her plate and joined Wren. "I'll sit with you."

People moved around and some whispered. She saw more than one older woman smile at another. Everyone seemed mesmerized by the man standing in the middle of the café looking about as out of place as any person ever had.

"Why are you here?" Her words came out as a whisper.

He answered in his usual booming voice, not even trying to hide their conversation. "To apologize."

Longing hit her. That was the only way she could describe it. She wanted to jump over the counter and rush to him. She wasn't the big-romantic-gesture type. She was barely the dating type. But she saw him and wanted it all.

"You saved me." In so many ways. This went past the boat shed and handling Paul and Mary. Matthias had brought her out of the shadows and made her feel again. Made her want things and no longer be satisfied just to survive.

"But I still shouldn't have left without explaining."

"That was a crappy thing to do." She heard some laughter and ignored it. Blocked everyone out but him.

"I was messed up from the Mary stuff. The whole thing had me turned around and doubting my judgment." He blew out a long, haggard breath. "When I realized what she'd done I broke every law to get to you in time."

"I knew you would come." Kayla did. Through all the lies and confusion, she'd believed he would storm in.

He gave a quick look around and hesitated before he just started talking. "I didn't know about the money. I gave it to her for something else and she used it for . . . well, you know."

"I do." She put down the coffeepot and started to slip around the edge of the counter. "That's not who you are. You didn't know."

"I should have."

She knew he was going to say that but she hadn't expected to hear such pain in his voice. "You're human, Matthias. You get to make mistakes. We both do."

"You don't hate me?"

"God, no." Anything but that. The opposite of that.

"Then why are we living in two different cities?" His voice broke on the words. "I don't understand why I'm sleeping alone."

She went to him then. Stepped in front of him and took his hands in hers. "I think I was giving us both time. I needed to think and you needed space. Maybe I wanted you to miss me. I don't know."

She didn't need a grand gesture, but she'd wanted him to come back and he had. She had needed to know that she wasn't an assignment he could walk away from, that she meant something to him. And now she knew. She could see the devastation in every line of his body and hear it in the sadness in his voice.

"I miss you every fucking hour." He winced as he did a quick look around the café. "Sorry."

"Wow, he's got it bad," Wren said.

Lauren smiled. "It's cute."

Matthias didn't spare them a glance. "Shut up."

Wren just laughed. "But we need to work on his people skills."

Through all the chatter and laughter in the café, Kayla only saw Matthias. People mumbled and a few said something. She missed it all as she looked into those intense dark eyes and for the first in a long time felt hope.

He gave her fingers a gentle squeeze. "I love you."

She almost fell over. "Whoa."

"Okay, wait." His words rushed and ran together as he talked. "That's not what I intended to say. Look, I—"

No, she would not let him backtrack now. She stepped right up against him and put her hands on his chest. "But do you mean it?"

"Yes." His arms came around her in a crushing hold. "It's new and confusing and I'm not sure what to do about it, but it's not going away. So, I can wait for you to catch up. Try to win you over . . . maybe there's a how-to guide I can read."

Light flooded through her, wiping out the panic and doubts. He wasn't saying flowery nonsense. He was being honest. He loved her and she could see it stunned him. She wasn't offended because she felt exactly the same way. "Good."

"I don't understand how or when. I just know losing you was like being plunged into darkness." He put a hand over hers and opened his mouth as if he was going to say more. Then he closed it again. "Did you say *good*?"

"I love you, too." Nothing had ever felt so right or so freeing.

He made a face. "God, why?"

The whole café laughed that time.

"Because you're everything I could want. You make me feel beautiful and protected. With you, I matter." That was it. In so many ways, he'd brought her back to life. "I don't want to hide anymore. I want to live and enjoy and not look over my shoulder every two minutes."

He shot her a big sexy grin. "You're more important to me than work."

Happiness bubbled up inside her. That was his ultimate statement of commitment, and she knew it. "That's big."

"You have no idea."

"We'll figure it out. Take our time."

He leaned in a little closer. "We're still going to have sex, right?"

Yeah, he was predictable. "Not right here, but yes."

"Okay." He nodded. "I can live with that."

"How's the arm?" She brushed her hand over it, careful not to press too hard.

He slipped his hand behind her neck and brought her in closer, until their mouths almost touched. "Want to come to check in to the inn and take a look at it?"

He kissed her then. It was demanded and all-consuming. He had her brain scrambled and her knees going weak.

The clapping registered first. Then came the cheers. She lifted her head and glanced around the café. Ignored the heat rising in her cheeks as she looked at him. "I want it all."

"You got it."

CHAPTER 31

Kayla really might kill him this time.

His breath left his chest and excitement welled deep inside him. Matthias threw his good arm behind him and grabbed the headboard for balance. He needed to hold on while her body lifted over his. While his body cried out for more.

He watched her skin flush and her mouth drop open. She was so sexy and alive.

They'd been back together for three days and still had barely ventured from the inn. Her boss came into town, and she got some time off. He ignored work, which never happened except when she was involved. He wanted to go back home and take her with him, but he wanted this more.

The intimacy. The connection. The mind-blowing sex.

She dug her fingernails into his shoulders as her breasts skimmed across his bare chest. From the tightening of her thighs against his hips to the way her body shuddered over him, he knew she was close to finding release. She would move around until she found it. The way she knew her body and what she needed was the hottest thing ever.

She was not alone in being ready. He was a second from takeoff. His body begged for release, but he held back. He wanted her with him. Satisfied and panting.

She lifted her body again, almost separating from him. He flexed his hips and brought her in closer. Made sure they stayed joined. When she plunged down again, he slipped his finger against her, against the spot guaranteed to drive her wild. Touched her, caressed her, until she moaned.

Her head fell back and her breath punched out in hard gasps. She clenched around his length, pushing his body right to the edge. And he didn't fight it. His hips pushed forward and he started to come. Without any command from his brain, his body bucked and his chest ached from holding back. But now he let go.

One more swipe of his finger against her clit and she came with him. Heat filled the room and the smell of sex wound around them. Her body started to pulse and her shoulders fell forward as she came. She moved up and down and her shoulders shifted and her legs clamped down harder against his sides.

The orgasm drew out for what felt like minutes. Then her elbows gave out and she fell against him. They were both spent and exhausted and neither of them moved.

He let his arm fall back down and wrapped it around her. He could hear her breathing and feel it blow across his chest.

Their bodies were wrapped together and entangled, just the way he liked it. She fit against him in a way that made every cell in his body jump to attention.

He loved to touch her, smell her, kiss her.

He just plain loved her.

"Who needs two good arms?" He lifted his sore shoulder, ignoring the pang. It would heal eventually, but not quite yet. But that didn't mean he planned to hold her one-handed for the next four weeks. Hell, no. He vowed to have both hands all over her, all the time.

"I admit I wasn't really thinking about your arms just then." She mumbled the words into his chest.

He was humbled and grateful that she thought of him at all. This amazing woman, so sexy and smart. A resourceful survivor. Fearless in so many ways and so perfectly human in others. "That's what I like to hear."

"I do love you, you know." She lifted her head and stared at him with wide eyes, clear of any haunted pain from the past. "It hit me when I wasn't expecting it and it keeps getting bigger and stronger as I find out more about you."

He felt the same way and it stunned him. He'd never been about relationships or bought into the idea of having one person to spend time with to the exclusion of everyone else. He worked, he had sex when he got the urge and he relied on a few people now and then. That summed up his entire life before her. Now everything felt bigger. More complete.

"Not seeing you for days made me grumpy as hell." He'd been stomping around and ready to rip down his office walls with his bare hands. "I actually pitied the people who work for me."

"Speaking of which, how's Garrett?"

He didn't bother to deny the work relationship. Garrett might work for Wren, but Matthias was happy to claim him. "Demanding a raise, so he's fine."

Kayla traced a finger over Matthias's mouth. "And Mary?"

He caught her hand and placed a long, lingering kiss on her palm. "I don't want to talk about her."

"We'll have to." She cuddled in closer. "Eventually."

"I know." He hated that she was right, but she was. But today was not the day. Wren was working on her case. The attorney Matthias paid for had stepped in. There was talk of her getting a psychological assessment. Through it all, Kayla said she'd refuse to testify if that provided Mary with an incentive to get the help she needed.

"Then know that you're not her." Kayla put both her hands on his cheeks and forced him to look straight at her. "What she did? That's her sin, not yours."

She'd said that numerous times. Wren said it. Garrett said it. Even Lauren said it. He heard the words but he wasn't prepared to believe them yet. "I'd be lying if I said I bought that line completely."

"I know it will take time." She gave him a quick sweet kiss. "Just understand that I'm here for you no matter what."

"I like hearing that." Because she understood. She knew what it was like to stare into the abyss. He didn't have to talk about how hating Mary made him hate a piece of himself. How he blamed himself for so much, even the things he had no power over like not being there to save Nick.

Through it all—the pain and confusion—Kayla supported and loved him. For a guy who hadn't known a lot of luck and very little love in the first twenty years of life, he embraced it now.

She was everything to him.

"Okay." She winced. "There's one more thing."

That unsure tone spelled trouble. "I'm going to hate this."

"Oh, yeah."

Then it was better to get it out and over with. He was done hiding and shading the truth, or avoiding it all together. No more. "Go ahead."

"I need to talk with Paul. Or Ben." She waved a hand in front of her face. "Whatever name he goes by these days."

The sudden emptiness in his stomach scared him. "About what?"

"He needs to know the truth."

God, she couldn't possibly mean . . . "About the murders only, right?"

She eased back just a little on Matthias's lap. Her hands rested on his chest and her eyes filled with the confidence he loved so much. "I can't be responsible for him spending his entire life searching for Doug. That's a hollowness I wouldn't wish on anyone."

He could try to fix that somehow. Nothing came to him but he could get Wren involved. Anything to keep her out of the press and out of jail. She deserved privacy and to be happy, and her proposal threatened both. "If you tell him, he'll go to the police."

"If he does I'll face it. I'm not a frightened guilt-ridden twenty-year-old anymore."

She acted like this wasn't the biggest decision in her life next to killing Doug in the first place. There was nothing light or unimportant about this.

He put his hands on either side of her waist. "Jesus, Kayla. You don't want that much heat."

"Maybe I won't be able to go through with it when the time comes but don't you see that I have to try?"

She really was determined to kill him. "I want us to be together."

The thought of losing her, of watching her go through a trial, shredded him. He couldn't think and the arguments refused to come to him. "That requires neither of us to be in jail. Talk about putting pressure on a new relationship."

She smiled at him. "Do you trust me?"

Loved her and was desperate to protect her from the horrible disaster she was about to invite into their lives. "More than anyone."

"And I trust you." She leaned in and kissed him again. There was nothing short or sweet about this kiss. It blinded and disarmed. When she pulled back her lips were red and full. "We can figure this out."

"Kayla." God, he would give her anything. But this? "Please."

Her determination overwhelmed him. He could feel his life splintering apart. The only way he knew to repair that was to try to control it. "You know I'm going to want a strategy and to have Wren on board. He's a fixer. We might need him to step in and handle the fallout, and he'll have to be ready."

She wrapped her arms around his neck. "I love you."

His heart flipped over. "Then don't leave me."

"Never."

CHAPTER 32

Kayla dreaded dealing with this, being there today, the conversation—everything. This was about closure. For her and for Paul. She'd insisted she had no choice and still believed in that, but facing her past now nearly dropped her to her knees.

She probably would have fallen right there in the middle of Matthias's room at the inn, but he'd never let that happen. He'd stood beside her, letting her lean against him. Ready to catch her because that's what he did.

He'd argued against her divulging her secret, now, after all these years. He wanted her safe and free. She understood the extreme risk here, and that she likely would be dragged into another police station and interrogated. She'd explain about Doug and what he did and his threats and how he lunged at her that day . . . just as a part of her hoped he would.

There were excuses and explanations, but the bottom line was the same—she had killed him and gone to see him knowing that might happen. Now she had to figure out a way to live with herself. That was the only chance she had of a future with Matthias. And she desperately wanted one of those.

Paul walked to the far side of the room and turned around to face her. Getting him to meet her here hadn't been hard, not after Matthias worked his magic and made sure the kid wouldn't spend a minute in jail. But looking into those eyes so filled with wariness, she wasn't sure what to say. She'd practiced a speech but the words fell away when confronted with a person instead of a bathroom mirror.

Paul erased the opening-line jitters by talking. "I heard about what happened on the boat."

She still couldn't deal with the memory of those harrowing minutes without breaking into a full-body sweat. Hopefully someday, but not yet. Her past had put Lauren in danger. Matthias risked his life to step in. There'd been so much destruction, all because Mary wanted vengeance on the wrong person.

Rather than explaining any of that, Kayla told the simple truth. "It wasn't a great night."

Paul's eyes narrowed. "You're okay?"

"Yes, but a few days ago you might have considered that bad news."

"I get why you think that." Paul leaned back against the wall with his hands behind him. "But I was never going to hurt you."

"Then what was the plan?" Matthias slipped his arm around her and balanced a hand on her lower back.

"Scare her. Get information . . . I dunno."

Matthias shifted again, this time to angle his body in front of hers. Not fully but he'd morphed into protector mode. "Terrifying her made her more likely to run than answer any questions."

Kayla glanced at him, hoping to send a silent message. She hadn't asked for the meeting as a way to scare or warn Paul. They needed to step carefully here.

"I'd been told . . ." Paul shook his head. "Forget it. Doesn't matter."

"It kind of does." After all, they were talking about her life. Every move had been dissected and analyzed over the years. She'd been tracked and threatened. Every ounce of stability had been robbed from her. She accepted a huge portion of the responsibility for how her life had spun out, but there was a lot of information she didn't know. So, if he had insight, she wanted him to speak.

"I thought I might find something in your apartment. Some sign of Doug. Some information about his whereabouts or confirmation that you guys were in contact." Paul looked everywhere but at her as he said the words.

Matthias sighed, as if he'd run out of his last drop of patience. "That wouldn't be a very wise move for a scheming killer, would it?"

"I didn't know what she was. I knew what I'd heard."

Kayla could guess from where but Matthias didn't need her to belabor this topic. He'd been sifting through all of her choices and threats for days now. He'd handled enough.

On this one issue, she'd tried to take the lead. "From Mary Patterson. Enough said on that. Look, Paul—"

"It's Ben." He threw her a half smile. "Please use my real name. I actually miss being me."

"Right." For a second she'd forgotten. Seeing him one way for weeks then trying to merge him into another person in her mind turned out to be harder than she expected. "Sorry."

Paul, now Ben again, pushed off from the wall and came to stand in front of them. "Just tell me."

The time had come. A swell of indecision hit her. It hugged her chest in a vise. She wanted to push his comment away and keep talking about easy things like names. "I don't know what you're—"

"He did it, didn't he?"

Her throat closed and a banging headache echoed in her brain. He'd made it so easy. All she had to do was agree, but for some reason she couldn't open her mouth. Panic flowed through, overwhelming everything else.

She looked up at Matthias, looking for guidance. He nodded and the hand on her back began to move. It brushed over her, calming her. It was a subtle reminder that he was there for her.

The strategy shouldn't work, but it did. The fierce tightness in her neck eased enough for her to swallow. "Yes, Ben. He killed all three of them."

She'd said that sentence so many times in the beginning. She told her dad and the investigator. She repeated it until people turned it on her and tagged Doug as her accomplice. After that, she stopped talking at all.

Now reality crushed her. The truth sat right there. Doug, in a fit of anger or just to prove he could or to punish her—any or all of those—killed three of her friends. Swept in and destroyed them before they could fight back. She still wasn't sure how. They all would have fought back, which suggested to her that Doug launched a sneak attack. That fit with the coward she knew.

As she ran through it all in her mind, Ben stood there. Silence thumped around them. No one moved and she could not think of a single helpful word to say, so she didn't even try.

After a few seconds, Ben shifted his weight. His gaze searched her face then he glanced at Matthias. By the time he looked back at her again, Ben's face didn't show any emotion. "Did you know he was going to do it?"

"I don't even think he knew. That's how his personality worked. He would be fine one minute then rage the next." It was more than a bad temper, which was the excuse everyone used to explain his anger away. It wasn't a minor thing. He lost control over nothing. A violent energy swirled around him whenever anyone questioned him in any way. Nick and Steve had hated Doug.

"But something happened that day."

If only the answer were that clear. "I'm honestly not sure what set him off that day compared to any other day. Not exactly."

"Something about you?"

Matthias started to answer, but she put the back of her hand against his chest and he stopped. Ben wanted to understand. She got it because so did she. "Probably. See, I didn't actually put it all together at first. I was too stunned to think about who killed them while I was still reeling from what I'd seen. Then I heard about the cigarettes, talked with Doug about the deaths and got a strange vibe from his reaction. It didn't take long for me to know with absolute certainty that he did it."

"The police said the cigarettes could have been there for a long time."

She'd heard the story, and maybe that's how forensics worked, but the timing explanation wasn't true. A defense attorney might depend on it to create reasonable doubt. God knew the second the excuse came out it became gospel. "When we broke up I went into this weird sort of frenzy. I went all over the house removing any sign of him. Nick and Steve helped, and we searched outside and . . ."

Matthias nodded, supporting her and holding her just as she needed him to do. "Go ahead."

"Doug always smoked under that tree. After we broke up, I saw him standing out there, watching my window." Sometimes right after dinner. Other times she'd wake up with this odd sense of discomfort and find him there.

His presence proved to be a silent vow that he owned her. Only he could decide if they were over. It was abusive and suffocating and she'd blocked so much of that part that when it rushed back on her now it plowed right into her chest. He'd warned her and she'd assumed his goal was fear. He'd certainly achieved that but even she hadn't been prepared for the killing rage.

"So this was all about you dumping him?" Ben shook his head as if the explanation didn't make sense.

She understood the confusion, too. Ben acted and thought like a rational person. He knew people broke up in college, got upset and moved on. But there was nothing about the way Doug reacted to what he viewed as bad news that could ever be considered usual or healthy. "There were two sides to your brother. He liked sports and parties and could skip classes but still pick up everything. He could be charming and funny. I know because that was part of what attracted me to him."

Matthias's thumb kept running over her back, keeping her panic from spiking. "And the other side?"

"When someone embarrassed him or questioned him, something happened." She didn't even know how to explain the way fear would paralyze her when Doug's mood shifted. "He couldn't stand being challenged or wrong. This anger would sweep over him. It was as if this evil took hold of him and he'd get mean and wild. Throw things, grab me."

Ben wiped a hand over his face and continued to shake his head. Whatever was happening inside him, he clearly had trouble taking in all he heard. "That's shitty but it's not murder."

"He escalated. I should have called the police, but I thought I could handle him." She tried to breathe but the air wouldn't fill her lungs. "I cleaned the cigarettes the day before the murders. They were there right after. I guess he'd been watching us again."

"You didn't know that side of Doug?" Matthias asked Ben.

"The temper, sure. He could be mean." Ben stopped there. For a few seconds he didn't say anything else. When he finally started talking, the blank look had disappeared. His face pulled taut with stress and his voice shook. "My parents sent him to boarding school. My mom had trouble controlling him and my father traveled a lot."

She had to say it. The last thing that would lead to her ultimate sin. "He told me he left me alive to teach me a lesson."

"You're telling me that because he's dead." Ben delivered the comment without any question in his voice.

She hadn't said the words. Hearing them from Ben had her reaching over and touching Matthias's side. A second later he slipped his hand from around her back and slid his fingers through hers. "I don't—"

"I'm not asking." Ben held up a hand even as he stared at the floor. "The use of the past tense. We got a message that he was going hiking, which he often did, but no calls or status checks. He disappeared. Combine all that and it seems obvious now."

"I'm so—"

"Don't say anything else." His head came up and he looked at her then. "I'm thinking I know what I need to know."

That quick she was thrown back to the moment. She could see Doug standing in front of her and remember the weight of the gun. She could pretend she didn't mean to kill him, but she'd taken the weapon with her and that fact would always condemn her. "Are you going to go to the police?"

The wait for Ben's response seemed to tick on for an eternity. Kayla felt her insides shrivel. Every part of her deflated as she waited for the final blow to land.

"Maybe we've all had enough?" Ben almost whispered the response.

For a second she thought her brain had filled in the answer she wanted, the one that left her off the hook and stopped her from having to defend herself. Then she shook her head, sure she'd misheard. But Matthias's shoulders fell as some of the tension choking the room eased. She swore she could hear the breath whoosh right out of him.

"That's a big statement," Matthias said.

"I can blow this up and drag us all through it, but for what end? I can remember him as I saw him, as his twelve-year-old baby brother. He was smart, detached, fun at times and difficult at others."

The words bounced off her. She could hear them but the shield she'd erected, the one to protect her from when Ben inevitably unloaded, kept her from processing the words. It was as if her brain clicked in a minute or two behind the actual conversation.

"He was also violent as fuck," Matthias said.

Ben exhaled. "If I don't dig, I don't have to deal with that."

This couldn't be happening; she never got lucky. Not ever. This time she didn't deserve the fortune. But just because Ben might be ready to move didn't mean anyone else in his family would. "What about your parents?"

"It's over for them. After the allegations came to light they shut down. Then Doug disappeared and it was like they just accepted it in silence. As if it was easier than dealing with the potential monster they'd created." Ben let out a harsh laugh. "No wonder they never wanted to talk about him."

Matthias squeezed her fingers but kept his focus on Ben. "So, now what?"

"My parents think I'm at Georgetown, so I should get there." Ben reached in his pocket and took out his keys.

Before he could leave, she stepped in front of him. She should say something, apologize. They'd basically silently agreed to not discuss Doug's death. Ben was letting her walk away without taking any legal responsibility. The thought humbled her. It was a gift she'd never be able to repay.

She reached out but dropped her hand before she actually touched him. "Tell me what else I can do for you."

"You've done it." His voice cracked as he talked.

"Closure." The word broke something inside her. The heaviness that had dragged her every step for seven years started to lift. A ray of light shone underneath. "You're letting me live my life."

"It sounds like you've earned it."

An hour later Kayla still sat on the couch in the room Matthias never intended to stay in. Ben had said a few more words and they'd exchanged contact information. Little did the kid know Matthias already had it thanks to the investigation. But after all the goodbyes and the stunning end to the horrible tragedy, she sat there, not moving and not talking.

He wanted to give her time to let it all sink in. Hell, he needed a few minutes. Listening to it all, watching Ben listen while she struggled. All Matthias had wanted to do was rush in and resolve this. To take her out of there. But in the end she didn't need to be rescued. She made the hard call and followed through. He respected the hell out of her for that.

She had more guts than most of his men in the field. Even more than he did.

He walked over to where she sat and squatted down in front of her with his elbows balanced on his knees. "Do you feel any relief?"

"Not really." She sighed and her hands went to her lap then she rubbed them together. "It's more like I'm happy Ben might be able to move on."

"I'd put my money on him being okay." Matthias would make sure that happened. He'd already talked to Wren about helping the kid. Between the two of them, they should be able to point Ben in the right direction and help him find a new and much healthier obsession. One not fed by Mary.

"And now you have the answer about Nick. Your mom . . ." Kayla's words stumbled. "Mary . . . likely won't believe it, but she has bigger problems now."

Hiring a paid assassin out of the back of a magazine had not been a smart move. Elliot, or whatever his name really was, was dead, which made the proof harder, but every move she made looked suspect. She'd done a horrible, destructive thing and didn't see it. When he told her Kayla was alive and the attacker hadn't been successful, Mary broke. She cried and begged him to try again. Didn't even seem to notice when the police took her away for questioning.

"I still don't think she realizes how huge her choice was." He doubted Mary was in a place to hear the truth or ever believe it.

"She's lost, Matthias." Kayla reached out and grabbed his hand. Pulled him up on the couch beside her. "She's been buried in hate. She has guilt about Nick and you—"

Not likely. "You're half right."

Kayla moved closer. She almost sat on his lap. "Is it possible that she won't let herself get close to you because getting close means she might lose another son and be broken all over again?"

"That's a pretty nice spin on her behavior."

He understood what Kayla was doing. She ached to make this better for him. After all she'd been through, so much uncertainty and fear, she put his mind and his heart first.

Damn, he loved her.

"I want to see what we can do to keep her out of jail." Kayla dropped her little bombshell then stared at him.

"No fucking way." That wasn't even a hard call. He had the money, but that wasn't the point. She'd made Kayla's life hell. Hired a killer . . . who the hell did that? He would not give her a free pass.

"She needs help, not jail." Kayla's fingers tangled with his. "I think you know that. Why else would you have hired a super lawyer and paid her fees?"

When Kayla pleaded, his control floundered. "Because you told me to."

"No, you did it because it was the right thing to do and you're a decent, loving man."

She was playing him, but he kissed the back of her hand anyway. "I assure you that you're the only one who sees me that way."

"I'm the only one that matters."

"True."

"And in keeping with that, I want us to move forward." She slid a hand over his thigh. "We've each done things we're not proud of. Things that were right in the moment and maybe even right in general, but still unspeakable things. From here on we'll try to make amends and make different choices."

The heat of her hand made him want to scoop her up and hold her even closer. So, he did. He tugged her out of her seat and put her on his lap. Wrapped his arm around her.

He also wanted to move on to another topic, and he'd been looking for a way to broach this one. "You mean that we'll move on together."

"Definitely, but don't stall." She placed a quick kiss on his mouth then pulled back. "About your mother—"

"She's not really that." But the anger that flooded his gut at the thought of Mary and her games didn't burn as hot this time.

That's how it worked with Kayla. She smoothed out his rough edges. She made him give a shit about something other than work. She made him better on every level.

She sent him an I'm-going-to-win-this look. "Having you hate the woman who gave birth to you doesn't feel like moving on or starting with a fresh slate."

"She doesn't deserve forgiveness from you." A fact that seemed obvious to him.

Kayla snuggled in closer. "Oh, I'm not there yet. I probably never will be, so don't go thinking we'll have a family Thanksgiving."

"Never, at least not with her." He'd rather leave the country than go through that.

"The other families, all the friends and people at the university—all those caught up in this as collateral damage—won't get peace, but we can try to give it to Mary. It's up to her to decide whether she takes it."

It sounded logical and decent and sweet. He was one of those and needed Kayla for the others.

He smoothed a hand over her cheek. "I love you."

"And I love you." Her eyes were soft. "So, please. Let's put this behind us so we have a real chance to start over."

She won before she resorted to begging, but he didn't tell her that. She would have him wrapped up and following her around on his knees if he wasn't careful. But he was pretty sure she knew that.

"Fine." He tried to sound dramatic but, really, he'd give her anything.

"Really?"

"Yes, so now let's talk about the other thing."

"What?" A new wave of wariness moved into her voice.

"Any chance I can convince you to go to school in DC somewhere and live with me, or maybe move between DC and Annapolis?" They could move across the country for all he cared. He'd set up a satellite office for Quint or work remotely. He'd make it work if he had her with him. "Anywhere but the inn."

The corner of her mouth lifted in an inviting smile. "You want to live together?"

That was only the start of what he wanted. They'd talked about going slow and building something. They'd do that, but he knew where this ended for him. In forever. She was the one he hadn't even known he needed. "Give me time and I'll prove I'm a good investment."

"I already know you are." She shifted on his lap. "But I would warn you it sounds like you're making a commitment."

Much more of that and they'd be celebrating by getting her naked. "I'm old enough, if that's your concern."

"Well, technically, I don't have anywhere to live. My apartment seems to be a perpetual crime scene, so it would be a help to me."

He loved her like this. Fun, charming and so sexy. "A very practical response."

"And then there's the part where I don't want to sleep without you." Some of the amusement had left her voice. "Not ever."

"We're going to make this work." He'd never made a promise like that to a woman before, but he made one now. And he would devote all his energy to making her happy.

She kept shifting until she straddled him. Leaned in and put her face close to his. "Then let's get started."

Hell, yes. "I knew we'd be perfect together."

Acknowledgments

If you got this far, you're likely a reader. Please know I am so grateful when you pick up my books and give them a chance. I love this series and hope you do, too.

A huge thank you to my fabulous editor, May Chen, and everyone on Team Avon. You guys manage to pretty-up these books and make them shine. Think you're all amazing (and very pretty).

Thank you for my agent, Laura Bradford. I appreciate your guidance every single day.

And to my husband—big love, always.

Don't miss the first book in HelenKay Dimon's scintillating Games People Play series,

THE FIXER

He's known only as Wren. A wealthy, dangerously secretive man, he specializes in making problems disappear. A professional fixer, Wren hides a dark past, but his privacy is shattered when Emery Finn seeks him out—and what she wants from him is very personal.

Some people disappear against their will. Emery's job is to find them and bring closure. Wren is the only person who can help solve Emery's own personal mystery: the long-ago disappearance of her cousin. Just tracking down the sexy, brooding Wren is difficult enough. Resisting her body's response to him will prove completely impossible.

Anonymity is essential to Wren's success, yet drawn by Emery's loyalty and sensuality, he's pulled out of the shadows. But her digging is getting noticed by the wrong people. And as the clues start to point to someone terrifyingly close, Wren will have to put his haunted past aside to protect the woman he loves.

CHAPTER 1

Emery's mind kept wandering no matter how hard she tried to concentrate on her skim vanilla latte. She tapped the coffee stirrer against the side of her cup and stared out the large window to the busy Washington, DC, street outside. The sun beat down as the late August humidity trapped passersby in a frizzy-hair, clothing-sticking haze of discomfort.

She enjoyed the air-conditioning of The Beanery. An unfortunate name for the perfect spot. The shop sat right on the edge of Foggy Bottom. Businessmen and students filed in and out, past the wall of bags filled with exotic beans and decorated mugs. The proximity to her house just down the street made the place a convenient stop for quick visits before heading into the office.

At ten o'clock on a Monday she usually sat at her desk. Today she needed room, space to think about the best way to track down the one man she needed to see and couldn't find. Endless computer searches had failed. She'd looked through property records and tried different search engines. Next she'd call in every favor and ask a work contact to check driver's license records. She was *that* desperate.

She didn't hear footsteps or see a shadow until the legs of the chair on the other side of the café table screeched against the tile floor and a man sat down across from her. Strike that, not just a man. Not part of the usual striped-tie, navy-suit business crowd she waded through each day. This one had a lethal look to him. Dark hair with an even darker sense of danger wrapping around him.

He didn't smile or frown while his gaze searched her face. Broad shoulders filled out every inch of the jacket of his expensive black suit. Those bright green eyes matched his tie and provided a shock of color to the whole Tall, Dark and Deadly look he had going on.

He managed to telegraph power without saying a word as a hum of energy pulsed around him. She fought off a shiver and reached for her spoon. Hardly a weapon, but something about this guy made her insides bounce and the blood leave her head, and she had no idea why.

"Excuse me?" She used a tone that let him know just sitting down without asking was not okay. Some women might like the commanding, takeover type of guy who assumed his presence was welcome everywhere. Not her.

"We need to come to an understanding."

The voice, deep and husky with an edge of gravelly heat, skidded across her senses. She felt it as much as she heard it. The tone struck her, held her mesmerized, before the meaning behind the words hit her. "Uh-huh, well, maybe *we* should understand that seat is already taken," she said.

"By?"

"Literally anyone else who wants it." She looked down, making a show of taking the lid off her cup and stirring the few inches of coffee left inside. That struck her as the universal not-interested signal.

She waited for him to grumble or call her a name and scamper off. She had issued a dismissal after all. But his presence loomed and she glanced up again.

"Emery Finn." Her name rolled off his tongue.

That shiver moving through her turned into a full body shake. "Wait, do we know each other?"

"You've been making inquiries."

It was the way he said it as much as what he said. How he sat there without moving. Perfect posture and laser-like focus that stayed on her face, never wavering even as a pretty woman openly gawked at him as she passed by.

The surreal scene had Emery grabbing on to her cup with both hands. "It sounds like you're reading from a really bad screenplay."

"This isn't fiction."

"Uh-huh. You know what it also isn't? Interesting." She waved him off. "Go away."

"You need to stop searching for information." He finally blinked. "No more questions. No more inquiries through back channels at government agencies."

In her line of work she sometimes angered people. Never on purpose, because ticked-off people tended not to open up and share. "I research for a living. If I've somehow upset you or—"

"This is personal, not business."

That sounded . . . not good. Like, time-to-call-the-police not good. "Who are you?"

He continued to stare. He didn't move or threaten her, not directly, but his presence filled the space in front of her. The noise of the café faded into the background. A loud male voice a few tables away flattened to a mumble and the people shuffling by blurred.

"Someone who is trying to help you."

That sounded like something a serial killer might say right before he lured some poor woman into his white van. *Yeah, no thanks.*

She curled her fingers around the spoon just in case. "Maybe you're unclear about the meaning of 'go away,' but I can start screaming and I'm sure someone will explain it to you. Maybe a police officer."

"You're skeptical. Good." He nodded, seemingly not even slightly concerned that she was six seconds from reaching for pepper spray. "But you need to understand the ramifications of all these questions."

She'd heard phrases like that every day in her work life as a researcher for the Jane Doe Network. She searched for the right piece of information to match missing persons to unidentified victims. To bring closure to cold cases and family pain. "I've found that people who say that sort of thing to me have no intention of actually helping me."

"I'm the exception." The corner of his mouth twitched in what seemed to be his version of a smile. "You're being careful right now. That's smart. My only point is that you should continue to do so and heed my advice."

Every word sounded as if it were chosen for maximum impact. No wasted syllables, not even an extra breath. He sat there, stiff and sure with a brooding affect that acted like a warning shot even as something about him reeled her in, had her leaning forward, waiting to hear what he'd say next.

She forced her body to stay still. No fidgeting or spinning her cup. "Tell me what you think I've done that's wrong or dangerous."

"You have been asking questions and taking photographs."

She'd taken exactly two photographs lately. Not for work, for her side project. The one that had haunted her for years and begged for closure. "Both activities, which, if they happened, are legal."

"Wren." He said the word and stopped talking.

Not that he needed to spell it out. The name echoed in her head. It was all she could do not to launch across the table and shake this guy. "Are you him?"

"I'm someone who knows you're searching for Wren."

Because that wasn't an odd answer or anything. If Wren sent someone to find her, stop her, this had turned very personal. She'd been hunting in relative secret. She basically knew the name Wren from a scribble on a piece of paper.

So much for thinking she'd been discreet. She'd called in favors and asked friends to dig quietly. She'd made it clear no one should leave a trail or take unnecessary risks. Either someone had messed up or . . . she didn't even want to think about the "or" part.

She forced her brain to focus. Pushed out the fear and confusion as her mind clicked into gear. This guy had information about Tiffany's disappearance. Emery didn't know what, but something.

The chair creaked as the man sat back. "The point is, you need to stop."

"Yeah, you said a version of that already." Not that she could forget that voice.

His head tilted to the side as if he were examining her and for a second that harsh façade slipped. "What do you hope to accomplish here?"

She held up her cup and shook it. "I'm drinking coffee."

"When you search for a recluse who may or may not exist—"

"He does."

The guy nodded. "Possibly."

"Okay, fine. We can play that game." But she knew the truth. People in power shook their heads and whispered the name Wren. She'd seen it when she talked with the senator who once promised a favor for matching her friend's missing child to a John Doe case four states away. Even the senator backed away at the mention of the guy.

"Do you think if you ask the right question someone is going to hand over Wren's home address?" His hands stayed folded on his lap as he asked the question.

As much as the conversation had her nerves zapping, she needed to keep him talking. Get him to slip up or at least touch the table or something so she could get her resources to check for fingerprints. A desperate hope, but then she dealt daily with desperate hope. "Do you have it? If so, give it to me. This conversation will go a lot faster and you can get back to doing whatever it is you do, which I somehow doubt is legal or particularly nice."

His mouth twitched for the second time. "Why do you want to see Wren?"

Apparently they'd entered the never-ending-questions portion of the conversation. As the minutes passed, she became less interested in participating in his game and more in playing her own. "Tell me your name."

"I'd rather you listen to me." He leaned forward. "You are wading into danger here. There are some people who prefer anonymity. Denying them that brings trouble."

The words shot into her, had her back slamming into her chair. "Are you threatening me?"

"I'm trying to keep you from being hurt." He cleared his throat. "You might awaken a beast you cannot possibly control."

The conversation, this meeting, it all spun in her head. "What does that even mean?"

"I think you know." Without warning, the guy stood up.

"You drop that kind of overly dramatic comment, don't bother telling me who you are or how you know Wren and then storm out?"

"Yes."

She sputtered, trying to think of something brilliant to say after that, but only babble filled her brain.

"And for the record." He actually smiled this time. "I do not storm."

"My word choice offended you?" This guy sure had the whole mysterious thing down. The suit, the stubble . . . that face. But this was a good place to talk. In public with plenty of people *right there* in case she needed to hit him with a chair. "At least get a coffee and sit back down so we can discuss this."

"I already have one." In a few steps he went to the counter and grabbed a to-go cup with the name *Brian* on it that had been sitting there since she picked up her drink more than a half hour ago. Then he was back by her side at the table. "Think about what I said."

She doubted she'd be able to think about anything else. "I don't take orders well."

"Take this one." With a nod he headed for the door.

She scrambled to her feet, grabbing for her purse and swearing when it caught around the back of the chair. She hit the sidewalk a few seconds later, looking up and down, past the groups of people walking and talking. Frustration screamed in her brain as a siren wailed in the distance. Still, nothing. No sign of black-suit guy. He'd disappeared.